THE WHOLE TRUTH

That night Susannah waited for Dan's call. She was in bed, the light out—and wide awake. When the phone rang she forgot she'd decided not to answer it on the first ring. The moment it jingled, she lifted the receiver. "Hullo," she said, her voice unexpectedly sultry.

"I must have dialed the wrong number. This sounds more like Marilyn Monroe than Judge Susannah Ross."

Dan's voice came teasingly across the wire, and Susannah found herself suddenly tongue-tied with frustration. She wanted to tell him what a great job he'd done in court today, but any mention of the trial was taboo. She wanted to ask about the missing witness, but she couldn't.

"Da-a-an!" She rolled his name out in a helpless sigh. "I've a million things to say to you, and every one of them is against the rules."

Jenny Loring lives in California with her lawyer husband who was more than willing to act as her legal adviser for *The Whole Truth*.

This book is lovingly dedicated to
my in-house lawyer,
with special thanks to Judge James F. Roach,
the Superior Court of Yolo County, California.

THE WHOLE TRUTH

BY

JENNY LORING

W★RLDWIDE BOOKS

LONDON • SYDNEY • TORONTO

Anatomy of a Fisherman by Robert Traver. Copyright 1978 by Gibbs M. Smith, Inc./Peregrine Smith Books, Salt Lake City, Utah. Copyright 1964 by Robert Traver and Robert W. Kelley.

First published in Great Britain in 1989 by Worldwide Books, Eton House, 18–24 Paradise Road, Richmond, Surrey TW9 1SR

© Jenny Loring 1987

Australian copyright 1987
Philippine copyright 1987

ISBN 0 373 57535 1
11-8906

Made and printed in Great Britain

CHAPTER ONE

JUDGE SUSANNAH ROSS. He never thought of the name without a spurt of adrenaline.

A bee flew through the open window that warm mid-April morning, its strident drone breaking the pretrial stillness of the hundred-year-old River County courtroom.

At one of the counsel tables, waiting for the judge to appear, Plaintiff's Attorney Dan Sullivan was oblivious to the sound, hearing only that name ringing in his head. Leafing at random through the open file before him, he was hardly aware of his client beside him or of Robert Corwin, the insurance company lawyer at the adjoining table, here from Los Angeles for the defense.

Susannah Ross. Sullivan tried to block out the name from his mind, as he'd done for most of the past ten years. In all that time he hadn't said it aloud. Now, in maddening counterpoint to the sounds around him, it came back to haunt him with poignant reminders of a lost euphoria and to stir the shades of an old resentment. With it came a dull, half-forgotten pain and the firm conviction he'd felt that Dan Sullivan had better stay the hell out of this River County courtroom with its recently appointed judge.

It was a piece of wisdom he'd had every intention of following—*had*, in fact, followed before the case ran afoul of Murphy's Law: "If anything can go wrong, it will."

Still unnoticed by Sullivan, the bee made a quick circuit of the empty high-backed chair on the judge's dais and moved on down to hover momentarily over the space where the two counsel tables came together in an L shape. The defense attorney watched nervously, visibly relieved when the bee zoomed off in the other direction and zeroed in on his adversary.

"Hey, Sullivan," Corwin hissed *sotto voce* across to the other table, "the little bastard must like your after-shave. Swat it, man! You're going to get stung."

Sullivan raised his head and looked around blankly, taking a second or two to focus on the bee as it bore down on him. Considering all things, he was of half a mind to let the damn thing sting him. If it packed enough poison to put him out of commission until his partner was in shape to take over the trial again, he wouldn't mind giving it a try. But there wasn't a chance. The way his luck was running, he'd wind up with a grotesque lump on his nose and still have the case to try. Facing today's judge—*any* judge, for that matter—with his twice-broken nose looking like the red ball nose on a clown was something he could do without.

Alarmed now at the danger inherent in his situation, Sullivan froze. The slim scar marking one lean cheek, put there by a high-school football cleat, deepened in a hint of a smile. *Minerva Farms* v. *Ag Dusters* was only one of the many things Corwin was dead wrong about, he thought wickedly. The big-city attorney obviously didn't know much about bees. The only way to deal with something buzzing your head was to hang tight—a piece of wisdom known by any kid raised on a farm.

The bee zoomed in on him in a final pass that grazed his cheek harmlessly, then sailed back across the room and out the window.

Sullivan let his muscles go loose and settled back in his chair. The morning air from outside seemed to close in upon him, cloying and oppressive. Already the day had turned too warm for midspring and was heavy with moisture from the flooded rice checks and the irrigated fields that surrounded the county-seat town of Cacheton, California. His hands were sticky with perspiration. Even after a janitor closed the open window and the air conditioner kicked on, his palms felt damp when he flexed his hands.

It was an old anxiety symptom that hadn't surfaced since his first days as a trial lawyer twelve years ago—not to be blamed on either the heat or the humidity. The only difference was that this time it wasn't caused by pretrial jitters. What gave Sullivan sweaty palms was the thought of the judge who was to hear the case he'd come two hundred miles to try.

Susannah Ross. She of little faith! Gemini. Two women in one. A mountain stream . . . deep, iridescent pools and laughing shallows; flower and flame; fire opal and tiger's eye.

One thing they'd never taught Sullivan in law school was how to comport himself in the presence of a judge with whom he'd once shared an apartment . . . and life and laughter and a consuming love that, in spite of its bitter ending, still whispered through his mind sometimes like the rustle of dry leaves in the wind.

BEYOND THE DAIS in the judge's chambers, surrounded by floor-to-ceiling shelves of law books, Judge Susannah Ross sat reading a book that had nothing to do with the law. In the five months since she'd been appointed judge, she'd found it the best way to clear her mind of distractions—such as disquieting thoughts of the upcoming election that might well unseat her—before she turned to the serious matters of the court.

As a woman, a stranger to River County, and, at 33, one of the youngest superior court judges in the state, she'd gone into court that first week feeling it was she who was on trial. Knowing she must prove herself, she'd devoted the last minutes before court each day to reading law and indulging her anxieties. After a while, when she began to see that all she was doing was tying herself in knots, she'd put aside law books in favor of light reading that brought with it quick escape.

Her tastes were eclectic—romance, mystery, poetry, classics, suspense; often favorite books she reread from her own overflowing shelves at home; sometimes titles that caught her eye among the paperbacks on the retail shelves. She'd traveled the roads of others' imaginations long enough to recognize which books were most likely to counteract the tensions that built inside her every day during that last half hour before she put on her judge's robe—tensions that grew ever more pressing as the June elections came rushing toward her like an oncoming train, with the reminder she had too little time and not enough money for the kind of aggressive campaign she must wage to win.

Today's book was a dog-eared copy of *Anatomy of a Fisherman* by a former Michigan State supreme court justice, John Voelker, who wrote under the pen name Robert Traver. It was a book that seemed to speak to her, particularly now, when her career was fraught with uncertainty. Its sentences evoked soothing memories of a singularly happy time ten years earlier when she'd often gone into the high Sierra on weekends with the man who'd given her the book, the man who'd taught her the intricacies of casting a fly.

She'd taken easily to the graceful, precise art of flicking out a silken line with a modified gray hackle fly tied to it and laying the fly on a given spot without a ripple of the dappled water. Though she had a natural knack for the sport, her greatest satisfaction came simply from being where it took her. Each time she made her way along the banks of a cascading stream where the air was spiced with conifers and the sound of the water fell like music on her ears, she felt rejuvenated. The frenetic demands of the city would recede into some unobtrusive waiting place, not to return until she left the mountains, her senses newly alive, her spirit ready again to cope. They used to call it her "Sierra high."

When the judicial appointment brought her to live near this part of the Sierra, which she'd never explored, she'd promised herself she would find a stream and look again for that lost high. But where was the time? Now as the pressures of her new work and the coming election mounted, the pull of nostalgia grew ever more tantalizing. She'd been away too long.

With a sigh she returned to her open book.

"The truth is that fishing for trout is as crazy and self-indulgent as inhaling opium," she read, and raised her eyes at the sound of a knock on the heavy oak door to the adjoining room. It would be Jill Fitzgerald, the secretary she'd inherited with the judgeship. Susannah was in no hurry to have her come in.

She still didn't know what to make of this secretary who'd been trained on the job by the late Judge Randall. She looked like a teenager—an uncommonly serious, freckle-faced teenager with a turned-up nose. Jill was only twenty-three, but she was formidably competent and knew the last word on judicial procedures and protocol.

Jill disapproved of her, resented her, she sensed, but she wasn't sure why. It was as if she felt Susannah had no business sitting in the place of the highly revered old judge. In her early insecurity, Susannah had taken no exception to the thought, since she'd often felt that way about herself, but enough was enough!

In the twenty-odd weeks since the governor had appointed her to fill the vacancy left by the old judge's death, she'd seen Jill Fitzgerald unbend with others, but never with her. Jill's ready humor surfaced in easy give-and-take with acquaintances among the lawyers and courthouse people who came in, but with Susannah she was courteous, helpful almost to a fault, and unfailingly reserved. Susannah had the disturbing sense she'd already been measured against the late, great Judge Randall and fallen short.

If she happened to leave one of her paperbacks out on her desk, Susannah could be sure she'd find it hidden discreetly under legal papers when she returned; Jill's way, she soon concluded, amused but nonetheless annoyed, of telling her that you'd never have caught the *old* judge indulging in frivolous reading before court.

Susannah marked her place in the book with her forefinger and called out somewhat reluctantly, "Yes, Jill. Come in."

Physically they were opposites. Susannah was a bit on the tall side with a subtle hint of well-sculpted bones beneath the flesh. At five feet three, Jill was five inches shorter and a study in compact curves that effectively hid the substructure that held her body together.

In coloring they were opposites, too. Susannah's dark brown hair, falling loosely to within an inch or two of her shoulders, provided a soft frame for the slender face with eyebrows like two black wings arching above dark brown, slightly elliptical eyes. Jill's round, resolute face, liberally spiced with freckles, was encircled by a feathering of short, crisply styled sandy hair. Her eyes were as blue and impersonal as the sky.

"Here's the brief on that well-drilling case, your honor," Jill said formally. "Mr. Clothier's secretary just brought it in."

"Thanks. I've been waiting for it. Put it on the work cart, and I'll get at it when court lets out this afternoon."

Without further talk, the secretary moved to the three-tiered dolly at the end of the desk and set about arranging the files and papers piled there according to some meticulous order of her own.

What goes on beneath this facade of efficiency? Susannah wondered. Were the two of them as different in their ways of thinking as they were in the way they looked?

She'd thought surely by now the shell of reserve would have fallen away, but as each day passed the secretary seemed no more comfortable with Susannah than she'd been in the beginning. Susannah, missing the easy, informal relationships she'd enjoyed with previous secretaries, became all the more uncomfortable with Jill. Between them they carried out the business of the judge's office, each according to her own role, with a formality Susannah found increasingly frustrating.

The words of a veteran judge at her swearing-in rose in Susannah's mind: "May I warn you, my dear, that you are starting a career often associated with loneliness."

She'd laughed and said, "But the challenge is worth it, isn't it? I'm sure I'll always find friends."

She'd been right about the challenge but wrong about the other. It was easy to *say* she'd find friends, but not so easy to find them—not when she happened to be the new judge in a county that in the last election had voted solidly against the governor who'd given her the judgeship. Not when the people had expected River County's most exalted office to go to one of its own.

Susannah stared down at the bright melon pink of her linen dress, and something like panic geysered up inside her. Was the lofty isolation of the judgeship squeezing the color and warmth out of her life?

A wintery grayness settled upon her. She felt a sudden compulsion to detain her secretary, who'd finished her chore and was on her way to the door.

"Wait a minute, Jill," she said, not knowing as the other turned back what she was going to say next. Her eyes fell on the title of the book in her hand. "Do you know anything about fishing?"

For the first time Susannah saw a revealing glimpse of genuine expression in the blue eyes. Surprise first, then, before the veil of reserve slipped back in place, she detected a shadow of some secret vulnerability. Could shyness be hidden beneath all that competence? she wondered suddenly.

Once again within the safety of her Miss Efficiency front, the secretary replied with her customary formality, "Cacheton is just a short drive from some of the finest fishing streams in the Sierra, your honor."

On a wave of nostalgia, Susannah said impulsively, "I used to be a pretty good fly caster," and was surprised at the sound of wistfulness she heard in her own voice.

"Oh?" Jill responded politely. "I've never tried it myself, but I have...well, a...friend...who used to. Still does, I suppose."

Puzzled by the unhappiness she saw in the other's eyes, Susannah hesitated, then, having at last caught the attention of the inner Jill, she seized the moment and dared go on.

"Here's a former Michigan State Supreme Court judge who makes me really want to get out on one of those Sierra streams you mentioned," she said, turning the book over to show the title. "He says fishing is older than love or chess. Listen to this: 'Fishing is...an endless source of delight.'" Not venturing to look up, she read on. "'A small rebellion...not terribly important, but many other concerns of men are equally unimportant...and not nearly so much fun.... Someday I may catch a mermaid.'"

She glanced up from the book to find her secretary staring at her in bewilderment and at once doubted the wisdom of her overture. From beside the desk, Jill Fitzgerald watched her uncertainly. Now you've *really* convinced the woman her new judge is a flake, thought Susannah in disgust.

There was an awkward moment before Jill consulted her watch and instantly fell back into her role.

"The bailiff will be seating the jury in a few minutes, your honor," she reminded formally. "Are you ready to put on your robe?"

"Yes, I'm ready," Susannah said, disappointed that the moment had borne so little fruit. Reluctantly she put aside her book and watched her secretary cross to the closet to take out the black judicial robe. In spite of what had just happened with Jill, the thrust of excitement she'd come to expect immediately before she walked into the courtroom hit her. She gave a small nervous shiver, then composed herself and began reviewing what she knew of the trial that was about to begin.

From her file, she could see it was to be the most complex case to come into court in the five months she'd been on the bench, and the longest. The question to be decided had to do with alleged damages to a field of tomatoes by a commercial crop-dusting plane spraying an herbicide on a neighboring safflower field.

It appeared that Hubert Bancroft, the local vice president and manager of Minerva Farms, the man who'd filed the suit, hadn't considered any of the seven Cacheton attorneys equal to handling the case. He'd gone all the way to the much larger town of Fresno in the San Joaquin Valley to hire a specialist in agricultural law. Jerome Curtis was here from the law firm of Curtis & Sullivan to try the case. He and the defense attorney had finished selecting the jury the week before in time for the Friday adjournment. The actual trial was ready to begin today.

Susannah hadn't seen Curtis's partner, nor did she expect to, but she couldn't get the name "Sullivan" out of her mind. It was a disconcerting reminder of that other Sullivan she hadn't seen since their stormy parting in San Francisco ten years earlier. The last she'd heard, he was working in the field of law back in Washington, D.C. Unexpectedly, try as she would to ward them off, held-back memories of that other time came crowding into her mind.

Dan Sullivan—as Irish as his name. She saw him in detail as if it were today—tall and brawny with a thatch of tawny brown hair that tended to go its own way. He had green eyes, wicked with humor and a hint of fire. They were shot with intelligence, their color splashed with bronze like the trefoil of the real Irish shamrock. He might almost have been handsome but for an oddly aligned nose.

Damn it, Sullivan, get out of my life! something inside her cried out angrily. Just when she thought she was rid of him, some small thing would bring him back. She'd learned to live without him, but she could not forget—any more than she could forget the slow, relentless deterioration of their relationship. It had reached the point that even when they made love, there had been a bitter after-taste. The ugly words they'd flung at each other that last night had had a finality about them. They'd been a long time coming and, once said, were irrevocable.

Involuntarily she raised her hand, as if by a physical act she could wrench him from her mind, and suddenly became aware that Jill had returned with the robe, still on its quilted satin hanger, and was waiting for her to put it on.

She gave the secretary a sheepish grin and rose hastily to her feet.

"Sorry...off in another world," she said vaguely, turning to slip into the robe Jill held open for her. There was no way to explain, she thought, and resolutely turned her mind to the empty chair on the dais that awaited her on the other side of the wall. As she slid her arms into the long, flowing sleeves, everything else settled into the background. A shiver of anticipation rippled across her shoulders.

"Are you all right, your honor?" Jill asked.

"Stage fright," Susannah admitted.

There was no mistaking the surprise or the clear note of skepticism in her secretary's voice as she repeated, "Stage fright?"

"No. It isn't exactly that. More like plain old garden-variety scared."

In the act of smoothing the robe across Susannah's shoulders, Jill paused. After a moment she laughed uneasily. "For a minute I thought...you meant it."

"But I *do* mean it," Susannah said. "It's an awesome responsibility, being a judge. Every time I go out there I go out thinking, 'My God, suppose I make a bad decision. I could mess up some innocent person's life.'"

The secretary ran her hand across the back yoke of the robe in a final adjustment and moved around to face her. Susannah saw a new empathy in the eyes that met hers—eyes unveiled for the first time in their association.

"Look, your honor...uh..." Jill began hesitantly. The pause lengthened, and then, as if throwing aside all caution, she said matter-of-factly, "Let me tell you something. You won't be the first judge to call one wrong. Judge Randall used to say, all you can do is keep reminding yourself you're human not God and that no one expects you to be."

Susannah was surprised to feel tears well up in her eyes.

"Thanks, Jill," she said, only the slight break in her voice giving away the fact she was touched by the unexpected support. She managed to grin again. "If you'll forgive the cliché, I needed that."

Under the dusting of freckles the secretary's color rose. Her eyes moved away uneasily. As if to cover her embarrassment, she self-consciously raised the hanger she still held in her hand and sniffed the perfumed sachet in the padding.

"Mmm . . . this is the way a robe should smell," she said, her voice flustered. A brief spark of humor lighted her eyes. "Judge Randall's robe...well, Judge Randall smoked the most horrendous cigars."

In the next second the secretary within came to the rescue of the young woman's shy alter ego, erasing all trace of emotion from her face.

"It's about time for you to go into court, your honor," she reminded Susannah in the formal tone she had come to expect.

We must do this again sometime, thought Susannah dryly. At least it was a start.

Like the robing ritual—learned under the tutelage of Judge Randall, Susannah guessed—it was the secretary's practice to open the door to the courtroom for the judge's entry. As Jill went ahead, Susannah followed, fastening the front closings on the black robe and making sure the bright dress beneath was discreetly hidden. In an irrelevant flash of insight, she knew what had sent her to her shelves for the well-worn Traver's book, which she hadn't browsed through in a long time. It was the law firm name, Curtis & Sullivan, on the complaint—a subliminal reminder of that other Sullivan, who, in another time she'd come to think of as the year of wine and roses, had convinced her there were mystical wonders to fishing far beyond a fish and a worm and a hook.

The siren song of Traver's words came back to her: "A small rebellion...crazy and self-indulgent..."

Suddenly, searingly she saw herself for what she was: sober, conscientious; a workaholic who'd forgotten—probably never really knew until Šullivan came into her life—how to play. How long since she had done anything crazy and self-indulgent? If she didn't do something soon, she would forget how. So what was she waiting for?

With a small shiver of fear, she saw that the choice was up to her.

IN THE COURTROOM beyond the chambers wall, Dan Sullivan struggled with a compulsion to fasten his eyes on the door through which Susannah would soon come. At the same time he made a valiant effort to pay attention to the raspy *non seqs* his client kept muttering in his ear. The bailiff ushered the jurors into the courtroom, and Sullivan blocked out both distractions to concentrate on the jury box.

In all his years of trial work, it was the first time he'd had to go before a jury made up of faces he'd never seen before. The fact that he hadn't been here to help pick its members, but the opposing attorney had, put him at a disadvantage and added to his edginess.

Experience had taught him one learned much that would be useful later in a trial during the *voir dire*, that process of questioning, weighing, choosing and dismissing that goes into the selection of a jury.

There was a gut feeling about it. A feeling after the jury was sworn in that, right or wrong, it was *your* jury. Today's situation was hopelessly frustrating. He should have been here to pick this jury. Nobody, not even his partner, Jerry, could do it for him.

To make up in part for the handicap, he'd spent most of the past forty-eight hours memorizing both Jerry's notes on the jurors selected the week before and his comments, issued later from his bed of pain. But it wasn't the same. In the few minutes before the trial began he knew it was up to him to make some kind of match that would serve him in the trial ahead between those memorized names and descriptions and the people seated now in the jury box.

Though it was not a new thought, he wished to God he'd said a flat-out no when Jerry first suggested the firm take the *Minerva* case. His own father and two brothers still farmed the family land he grew up on in the San Joaquin Valley, and the thought of fighting a court battle for a huge "meg-ag" corporation of the kind that was gradually swallowing up family farms like the Sullivans' in California had turned his stomach.

But Jerry had argued it was pretty damned self-indulgent to refuse one of the best cases ever to walk in their door. Even his dad said they'd be crazy to turn it down. Minerva Farms had been damaged and was entitled to recovery. Also, as a lawyer, Sullivan was obliged to concede that even Bancroft was entitled to be represented by the law firm of his choice—unless there was an acceptable reason for the partnership to turn the case down, which there wasn't.

Still, his every instinct had been against it, and Dan knew that if he had actually balked, Jerry would have given in to him. The success of the partnership was based in part on an understanding that since Sullivan did all the trial work, he should have the final say on what cases they'd try.

Too bad he hadn't known then what he later found out. He would have *listened* to the voice that kept telling him, "Back off, Sullivan!"

It wasn't enough that they'd drawn Hubert Bancroft for a client—Hubert Bancroft, vice president of Minerva Farms, the world's worst bore no matter which of the three ways you spelled the word and the greatest living authority on all things, not excluding how to try his own damned lawsuit. There was also the matter of the missing witness.

But all these dissatisfactions paled to nothing the morning he read in the paper that the governor had appointed Susannah Ross as the new River County judge. Only then had he realized how bad it was possible for a case to get.

Uncomfortably he remembered the look of betrayal on Jerry's face when he had said flatly that he wasn't going to try *Minerva* v. *Dusters*. It meant that Jerry, who hated trial work, would have to take it to court himself or hire an outside lawyer, which he wasn't about to do.

It had threatened to put such a strain on the partnership that Sullivan had felt obliged to tell Jerry that he and Judge Susannah Ross had once been lovers, at which point Jerry reluctantly agreed to take the case to trial.

The voice of the bailiff broke the silence of the courtroom and brought Sullivan back to the jury with a start. Not one to let his mind wander from business at hand, he swore silently at himself for allowing valuable minutes to slip away with little more than a glance at the jury. Now he would have to wing it. Court was about to begin.

"The Superior Court of River County, California, is now in session, the Honorable Judge Susannah Ross presiding. Please stand," the bailiff sang out.

The hard muscles of Sullivan's abdomen tightened. For the umpteenth time he wished Jerry hadn't elected to rescue a neighbor's cat from his roof over the weekend or at least had taken more care not to fall off. He rose with the others in the courtroom in traditional deference to the judge. His gaze came to rest on her, and it was as if someone had hit him across the chest with a lead pipe. For a moment he couldn't get his breath.

It occurred to him then, seeing her robed in black, that in his mind he'd never pictured her as a judge. He'd seen her as she'd been when they were together—a young city lawyer who wore bright uncluttered garments set off with eye-catching contemporary jewelry. The jewelry and the jaunty colors had given him his first hint that beneath the solemnly determined front there was a playful spirit daring him to set it free.

Now as he watched her move across to the dais with composure, as if born to the job, he remembered the first time he'd seen her on her maiden venture in court. Sizing her up, he'd decided she was intelligent and lovely, stubbornly serious, intriguingly complex. She'd worn a ruby-red dress and was plainly scared to death.

As he observed her now—her face like a magnolia petal above the solemn, judicial black, the dark eyes opaque and soberly aware of the dignity of her office—all his old forgotten feelings came flooding back. It was something he hadn't expected and didn't want. What he'd felt for Susannah had been so muddied during the last torturous half year they'd been together, he couldn't think clearly about her even today. For the sake of his peace of mind, he preferred not to think of her at all.

THE DOOR TO HER CHAMBERS closed behind Susannah. She stepped out into the courtroom, the Honorable Judge Ross now, personal considerations left behind, mind in disciplined focus on the case she was about to hear. Seating herself in the high-backed, ornately carved great chair that had accommodated the posteriors of male judges through all the years since the court was established—but never a woman's, till hers—she waited for the bailiff to give the order for everyone else to be seated.

While the courtroom settled down, she let her eyes travel over the jurors and move on to the attorneys' table. Expecting to see the short, solidly built man who'd been in court for the plaintiff the week before, she noted his absence but did not at once grasp the fact of the tall man in Attorney Curtis's place.

"Mr. Curtis is not..." she began. Her mind did a classic double take, which she caught before it could reflect in her face.

Dan! Oh, God! It couldn't be. Not here in her court. Dan Sullivan was in Washington, D.C.

All at once everything was unreal. She felt light-headed. The courtroom scene seemed for an instant to fade away and come back.

The room was still and waiting. The unfinished sentence hung in the air like an obscene word, but she had no voice to complete it. She shuffled blindly through the papers before her in a bid for time. Time to erase from her voice the emotions that threatened to undo her. Time to bring in control the slight give-away tremor of her hands. As her composure gradually returned, she forced herself to look up from the papers and then down at the ghost from her past.

CHAPTER TWO

SURELY THIS couldn't be the wonderful homely-beautiful face she'd never expected to see again, she thought dazedly, looking for differences that would tell her it wasn't so. But though there were differences to be found, they simply confirmed the truth. The man before her was Dan. The maturity that muted the youthful joie de vivre and lent new strength to the face, the feathering of silver in the thick golden brown hair and the fine lines at the corners of his eyes were all no more than stunning reminders of the lost years that lay between them. The dreadful confrontation that had torn them apart flashed vividly across her mind. She caught her breath at the sudden stab of pain it brought to her heart.

The savagery of the emotion warned her she dare not turn her thoughts back to that bitter night. Striking around for escape, she took refuge in noting the changes in Sullivan's outward appearance.

The Dan Sullivan she'd known would never have thought of coordinating a shirt and a tie. His entire supply of neckwear in those days had consisted of six ties in six different colors—all with the same trout-fly design.

Steadying herself, she observed that while his clothes now appeared custom-made, he still wore them with the same indifferent grace he'd worn the motley collection of loose, wrinkle-prone sales-rack suits he used to put on for court—not to impress, but because the faded blue jeans that were his usual dress, even in the office, were not allowed within the court's tradition-bound walls.

Like a cold hand on her heart came the thought that the green silk tie accenting his eyes looked suspiciously like the choice of a woman. Did he have a wife?

She was aware of the silence in the courtroom and realized it was becoming oppressive. She really didn't care who picked his clothes or if he *did* have a wife, she told herself, frantically collecting her wildly straying thoughts. When she could trust herself to speak, her voice was controlled and cool.

"According to my papers, the attorney of record for the plaintiff in this case is Mr. Curtis," she began, as if her lapse had been to reaffirm the fact. "Mr. Curtis is not in the courtroom this morning?"

Sullivan unfolded himself from his chair at the attorneys' table and got to his feet. Irrelevantly she noted that the long, loose-jointed body she had once known well was still as lean and sinewy as it had been at twenty-six.

"Your Honor, my partner, Jerome Curtis, met with an accident over the weekend and is in the hospital. I am here in his place. My name is Dan Sullivan of the firm of Curtis & Sullivan."

"I am sorry about Mr. Curtis. If you wish to ask for a postponement until he recovers...?" With the implication that she would grant such request, she awaited his answer and found herself holding her breath again.

"No, Your Honor, my partner's injuries, while not critical, require him to remain in traction and a body cast for an indefinite period of time in order to ensure complete recovery," Sullivan replied in the stilted courtroom language of attorneys. "Our client is strongly opposed to the lengthy postponement which this conceivably might entail. Inasmuch as Mr. Curtis and I have worked together throughout the preparation for trial, with Your Honor's permission, I will carry on."

Damn you, Dan, don't do this to me! the inner voice cried out again. In light of their final six months together, fraught with hostile innuendoes and barely concealed resentments, what made him think their past relationship wouldn't impair her judgment?

She would have to disqualify herself, of course. She would step down and tell them to bring in a judge from some other county to hear the case.

But even as she seized on this route of escape, she knew it wasn't something to be done lightly or for a trivial cause if she wanted her career as judge to continue beyond the coming election day. To disqualify herself would mean a lengthy delay and additional costs to the county. Having to pay another judge to do work they were paying her a salary for would not set well with the taxpaying voters.

Again she was aware that the courtroom was waiting for her to speak. She would not let herself be rushed.

Her whole spirit rebelled against sitting as judge in a case where Dan Sullivan was an attorney. And yet— *Oh God!*—had she any right, in honesty, to withdraw? Her every instinct told her she could perform her judicial duties without prejudice, one way or another, in spite of their shared past. But was she certain of it beyond a doubt? If she was, she had no choice but to serve.

Could the memory of the sweet, hot taste of his mouth setting fire to her senses sway her judgment *his* way in court? On the other hand, might she be tempted to use the power of the bench to get back at him for old hurts?

These were questions that deserved long and serious consideration, not ones to be tossed off the top of her head in the next thirty seconds. A maelstrom was beginning to churn in her head. What made Sullivan think she wouldn't hold their past against him? Why hadn't he asked for another judge? And what about Corwin? Didn't the defense attorney have a right to know and have a voice in whatever was to be done?

Still the courtroom waited. She could feel the silence closing in on her, the growing impatience in the air.

Bracing herself, she looked down at the attorneys' table.

"This court will be adjourned until two o'clock," she said. "May I see Mr. Corwin and Mr. Sullivan in chambers, please."

There was a stir throughout the courtroom as Susannah gathered her robe around her and rose from her chair with a silent prayer that her knees, which had turned to putty, would not give way and send her sprawling. Chin high, she managed to sweep across the floor without incident and disappear into the haven of the chambers from which she had emerged with blithe confidence not six minutes earlier.

IN THE COURTROOM the bailiff left his place by the door and walked to the entrance of the jury box, motioning the jurors to file out.

"Well, that's a woman for you!" Sullivan's client, Bancroft, muttered in the lawyer's ear.

From the defense corner Corwin asked across the table, "What's going on?"

"Beats me," Sullivan said, not entirely candidly. He knew damn well what was going on, but he couldn't begin to guess what Susannah had in mind to do about it. Did she still hold enough anger against him to fear it would affect her judgment in this case? If that's what this unexpected recess was about, he knew her better than she knew herself. Had he thought it possible for Susannah Ross to let her emotions corrupt her principles, he would have asked for—no, *demanded* another judge. He was still so sure of what Susannah *was* that the thought had never occurred to him—not even as an excuse to get out of having to appear in her court.

"Looks like we're going to have to put up with female foibles through the whole goddamn trial," Bancroft said in an irascible stage whisper that carried halfway across the rapidly emptying courtroom.

Sullivan cringed. The remark wouldn't endear his client to the female members of the jury, several of whom were still within earshot on their way out.

"Even male judges are obliged to call an unscheduled recess on occasion, Hubert. Sex has nothing to do with it," he said in a normal voice he hoped would reach the departing jurors and perhaps in some small way neutralize whatever damage Bancroft's gratuitous slur had done.

The color in the florid face beside him deepened, spreading up over the forehead, staining the bald scalp red. Knowing how much his client hated to be told he was wrong, Sullivan still made no pretense at placating him. He'd signed on to win Hubert Bancroft's blasted lawsuit for him, not to coddle his overblown ego. He had every intention of winning the suit, but not at the expense of truckling to the man.

"I"m not talking about *sex*, Sullivan, I'm talking about gender," Bancroft retorted with ill-disguised petulance. "I'm saying a person of the female gender has got no business presiding over a court of law." He pushed his way past Sullivan and stepped out into the corridor, spewing angry words back over his shoulder. "I'm a busy man. I'll be at my office. When I come into court at two that woman better get things rolling or I'll damn well know the reason why!"

IN THE JUDGE'S CHAMBERS, Susannah shut the door behind her and let her body slump against the protective barrier of solid oak. She laid her cheek on the cool waxed surface of the wood and closed her eyes as if to gather strength from the solid feel of it, momentarily grateful for her escape, even as she recognized it for what it was—no more than a small reprieve.

Her whole future seemed to hang in balance. *Where do I go from here?* she asked herself from the very edge of desperation.

She straightened and moved to the desk, where she buzzed for Jill Fitzgerald. The communicating door to the reception room opened almost at once, and Jill came in. The mask of efficiency was again in place, hiding any curiosity the secretary might have felt at the change in agenda.

"Are Mr. Sullivan and Mr. Corwin out there yet?" Susannah asked.

"No one has come in, Your Honor."

"Good. I asked them to see me in chambers. They will be here in a minute." She only had until they walked through the door to make up her mind what she was going to do, she told herself with a sense of panic. Oh God, what *was* she going to do? She raised her eyes in helplessness and met those of her secretary.

"Your Honor, are you all right?"

The look of concern on the other woman's face, the troubled note in her voice were like a hand stretched out in friendship to Susannah. It made her poignantly aware of how alone she was. For a moment she felt lost. What had become of the person who used to be known as Susannah?

"Your Honor..." The voice now was hesitant, the blue eyes worried.

Emotions close to the surface, Susannah felt a sudden testiness quite foreign to her.

"Damn it, Jill, I swear if you call me 'Your Honor' one more time, I think I'm going to throw my gavel at you," she blurted out crossly.

"But, Your Honor..."

Susannah stopped her. "Would you believe it... in the five months since I came to Cacheton, not one River County man, woman or child has called me Susannah?" She was helpless against a lump that had risen in her throat to block her words. She turned her eyes away from the young woman and fixed them on the papers before her, riffling through them blindly.

"Wait a minute, Your Hon—*I'm sorry*," Jill stopped short in apology. Recovering, she asked, "Do you mean you . . . want *me* to call *you* . . . ?"

The secretary's voice sounded shocked and faintly disapproving. Looking up, Susannah realized that to urge the small informality would be a mistake. Clearly it violated principles of judicial etiquette ingrained in Jill Fitzgerald by a judge from a more mannered past.

"Never mind," she said with a sigh. "I know. In the courtroom 'Your Honor' is a traditional mark of respect. But respect for the *bench*, you understand . . . not necessarily respect for the person who occupies it. Here in chambers we're both simply employees of the court. I'm still a fumbling greenhorn at my job, and you're about as good as a person can get at yours, so by rights I should be calling *you* 'Your Honor.'" She saw a brief, reluctant spark of appreciation in the other woman's eyes.

"Call me Judge Ross, if you must, but please, Jill, no more 'Your Honor.'"

Judge Ross. Quite right, she told herself wryly. *Never mind Susannah!* She could survive without hearing the sound of her name.

She'd called the secretary in to ask her to stall the two attorneys in the reception room until she had time to . . .

Time to do what? *Think* about her situation? What in the world was there to think about? She'd known what must be done from the first, but her innate need for privacy had rebelled against the thought of it.

Her face masked the conflicts that played within her as she said to her secretary, "When Mr. Sullivan and Mr. Corwin come, please send them in."

She had only a moment more to compose herself before the two opposing attorneys entered her chambers from the reception room. As if to take courage from the air around her, she drew a deep breath, held it a long moment and slowly let it out as they took their seats.

"Gentlemen," she began in her best courtroom manner once they were seated, "I have asked you here in the light of an unexpected situation which has arisen. I feel it imperative that Mr. Corwin be advised before the trial goes any further that Mr. Sullivan and I are not strangers to each other."

Corwin leaned forward in his chair, face questioning, his pupils distended, giving his eyes a goiterish look. Sullivan sat loose, curious but wary.

"You are entitled to know, Mr. Corwin, that Mr. Sullivan and I—"

Sullivan was on his feet, cutting her sentence short. "Wait, Susannah, are you sure—"

Susannah stopped him, her voice cool and forbidding. "Mr. Sullivan, you forget yourself. May I remind you, in chambers you are to address me as Judge Ross or 'Your Honor,' just as you do in court. Please sit down."

With a shrug of resignation, Sullivan lowered himself back down in his seat. Corwin turned his head slightly to glance from one to the other with open curiosity.

"Mr. Sullivan and I were . . . friends," Susannah continued. "We've been out of touch for a number of years. I assure you, Mr. Sullivan's presence in court this morning has taken me by surprise." She stopped suddenly, unable to go on. It had been a closed chapter in her life for a long time, so personal, so private, so beautiful and yet so painful at the end that she had opened it to nobody until now. How could she speak of it to a stranger, and in the presence of Dan? What should she say? How much was enough?

Aware that Corwin was watching her shrewdly, she would not let herself flinch under his gaze. She kept her attention on him, grateful that he sat far enough away from Dan for her to be able to avoid Sullivan's eyes as she talked.

"Friends, you say? Forgive me, but I must ask your honor how . . . close your friendship was?"

"Mr. Sullivan and I lived together in San Francisco ten years ago for a little more than a year and a half," she said, her voice level. Though his mouth was closed, Susannah had the distinct feeling Corwin was staring at her agape. Dan's eyes were hooded, and he flexed his hands.

"My own immediate feeling is that the past will not interfere with my judgment in the case before us, but if either of you disagrees, you have the right to disqualify me and ask for a new judge."

Corwin's lip twitched in a slight, cynical smile, and she knew something more must be said.

"Mr. Sullivan and I parted on exceedingly unfriendly terms, Mr. Corwin, and have had no further contact with each other since that time."

There was silence in the chambers, broken only by the hum of the air conditioner. A crop-dusting plane passed over the courthouse on its way to the open fields, rattling the ancient window with its labored, bulldozer drone, drowning all other sounds.

When the noise had died away Susannah said evenly, "So, Mr. Corwin, there is no need to smile. Mr. Sullivan, too, may feel he has reason to distrust my ability to judge this case fairly. I believe I can, but we all need time to think about it." She rose to her feet to indicate the end of the conference.

"We have three hours till court reconvenes. If any one of us, at the end of that time, feels the case should be heard by another judge, I will declare myself disqualified."

Sullivan stood and turned to leave. His bearing cried out his frustration, but his face was closed and unreadable. Corwin reached for his briefcase and pushed back his chair.

"By the way," he asked, about to leave, "if we should go that route, how long would it take to bring in another judge?"

"Court calendars are crowded all over the state," Susannah told him. "It could take weeks, even months, I suppose."

"In that case I'm inclined to go along with your confidence in your own fair-mindedness, Judge Ross, and let things stand as they are," the lawyer said. "My client would not be happy with a delay."

"That may be, Mr. Corwin, but let's not be precipitous about it. I'm sure both of you will agree that the matter warrants serious consideration by all sides and should be fully understood by your clients before you arrive at any conclusions."

Sullivan hesitated for a moment as if to turn back, then moved on toward the outer door. Corwin followed.

"We'll meet here again in chambers at one forty-five," Susannah said. "By then we should know whether we are to go on with the trial or look for a new judge."

Under normal circumstances, Sullivan would have turned back and made an effort at polite small talk with Corwin, who followed close behind him into the corridor. It was his nature to leave hostilities of a lawsuit in the courtroom and keep on friendly terms with opposing counsel when the two of them were on the outside. Now as he left the judge's chambers his teeth were clenched, and he did not bother to unclench them or turn to speak to the other attorney. He was in no mood for talk. Eyes ahead, he quickened his step and walked out of the courthouse, relieved when he lost Corwin somewhere along the way.

Not that he could blame Corwin for what had gone on inside, he admitted as he made his way down the courthouse steps, seeing nothing on either side. If their positions had been reversed, he supposed he would have done the same, in fairness to his client's interests.

And, damn it, Susannah had asked for it. She didn't have to drag this all out in the open. It had been ten years! Who would have known up here in the backwaters of River County? Even the few who'd known in the city had forgotten long ago. Why hadn't she just kept still about it? But he knew why.

The answer was, because she was Susannah. It was her relentless passion for fair play. She couldn't have done otherwise.

At the foot of the steps he came to a halt and considered what he should do for the remainder of the recess. One thing he *didn't* have to do was decide whether to let Susannah stay on as judge. He had no desire to disqualify her, much less any grounds.

Except for Bancroft! he thought suddenly. *Did he have to tell Bancroft?* He could see no way out of it. Bancroft had to be told.

Retracing his steps, he went back into the courthouse, where he found a phone booth in the basement and dialed his client's farm headquarters office. Bancroft hadn't yet had time to get back to Minerva Farms, but it didn't matter. He'd be there by the time Sullivan arrived. He didn't like the idea of having to talk to Bancroft about it in the first place, but since he had to he did not intend to do it by phone.

"This is Dan Sullivan," he said to the voice that answered his call. "When Mr. Bancroft comes in, please tell him I'm on my way out to talk to him." He hung up and headed for one of the ground-floor doors to the parking lot.

IN THE IMMEDIATE RELEASE from tension after the door had closed behind the two attorneys, Susannah realized she was trembling inside. Resting her elbows on the desk, she pressed the heels of both hands against her forehead and relived the scene that had just been acted out, seeing it almost more clearly in retrospect.

Suddenly she knew that the very idea her relationship with Sullivan might color her judgment in the trial ahead was untenable. If, after ten years, she couldn't be objective where Dan Sullivan was concerned, she had no business calling herself a judge. She had a duty to go on with the trial unless one of the litigants took it upon himself to disqualify her.

In those first moments after she'd seen Dan in the courtroom, she'd been ready to snatch at anything that offered escape. Now she saw that disqualification wasn't something she could so readily accept. The implications of incompetence, bias and bad faith that came with being asked to step down from a case would be black marks against her, especially in the eyes of those who said she was appointed to the bench only because of the governor's well-known political friendship with her father.

She had to keep reminding herself that she'd been named River County judge because of legal work she'd done for the state. It had benefited the farm counties and gained her a respectable level of acclaim in the press. She sought comfort in believing she'd gotten the appointment on merit in spite of—not *because* of—her politics or her relationship to her father.

At the same time, she had no illusions about her appointment. The governor had forgiven the fact she was not of his and her father's political persuasion for two reasons: he needed a qualified "token woman" to please the female voters of the state, and he hoped her record on behalf of agriculture would woo back some of the farmers, who had voted solidly against him in the last election.

Forget the governor. *She* could show the people of River County she was the kind of judge they needed. But Susannah was a realist. She didn't need anyone to tell her that if the voting took place tomorrow, she would lose the judgeship. She needed time. How could she possibly get the message across to the voters before the early June election day?

In spite of the steady hum of the air conditioner, the room seemed stifling. The black robe weighed oppressively on her shoulders, and she left her chair to peel off the heavy garment, putting it on the padded hanger in the closet. She crossed to the window and stared, unseeing, down on the courthouse grounds below, feeling unnaturally depressed. After a moment her eyes came into focus on a tall figure standing two stories below on the courthouse steps. Her pulse leaped wildly.

"Dan...Dan..." His name slipped softly over her lips. There was something so *right* about Dan Sullivan. A wistful regret for that rose-tinted other time drove immediate worries from her mind.

She watched him turn and look back up the stairs down which he'd come, his eyes squinting against the sun. His face was deeply tanned and almost the color of his hair, both glossed with gold in the morning light. Never mind that he had a crooked nose and wore size twelve-and-a-half shoes so narrow only three shoe stores in northern California had ever been able to fit him. Standing there in the sun, a wing of hair falling carelessly across his forehead, he looked...like the kind of man any woman would be crazy to let slip out of her life.

Only he hadn't exactly *slipped* out. *Thrown* out was a more apt term for what she had done.

"There's no room in my life for people like you, Dan Sullivan. Take your stuff and get out!" Her own voice, shrill with anger and hurt, came back to her, as ugly and clear as if the words had just left her lips. They had sprung unbidden out of the resentment that had been building in her over the months since Dan had taken the job at Bradley and Hammer, and the man she loved turned into someone she no longer knew. Nevertheless, as the words rolled out, she'd been horrified at what she'd said.

She'd realized, as the first shock in court this morning wore off, that she'd been waiting a long time to tell him she hadn't meant them, any more than he had meant it when he accused her of using feminine wiles to beat him in court. The ugly accusation he'd flung at her was not the real Dan Sullivan speaking, she knew, but a kind of last hurrah from some adolescent, not-quite-outgrown inner pride. She'd wondered if the years had endowed them with enough maturity to talk things over without one or the other of them going up in smoke.

But there could be no talk between them now, she remembered. Not if she was kept as judge on this case.

Her eyes still on the man below, she saw Sullivan seem to come to a decision and reverse his course. In a dozen long, easy strides he was up the steps and out of sight as he entered the courthouse again. It was as if he'd read her thoughts. Her heart took off like a greyhound.

Oh God, he's coming up here to talk to me, she thought. But he couldn't! Until he or Corwin removed her, she was still the judge in the case. She and Dan were both bound by the proprieties of the court. Dan knew what the California Commission on Judicial Performance would have to say about such a meeting. But when had Dan Sullivan ever let propriety stand in the way of doing something he'd set his mind to do? Remembering, she found herself smiling faintly.

As she waited expectantly for the moment he would come striding through the door to her chambers, the lost, wonderful excitement his presence had once invoked came thrilling through her. She counted the time it would take him to get to the room by elevator.

When he didn't come, she counted the time it would
take him by stairs. Then she quit counting.

What had she expected him to do? she asked herself, deflated. Ask her to step down from the case so
they could have a few minutes of private talk without
violating the integrity of the court?

Her pulse slowed. Reason returned and she reminded herself again that even if he had been on his
way to her, she couldn't have let him come in. As long
as she was judge on the case there could be nothing
private between them. She would have had to tell Jill
not to let him into her chambers. That wouldn't have
set well with the Dan Sullivan she'd known, she
thought wryly, and was ashamed of the moment of
perverse satisfaction the thought gave her.

She wondered, then, what would happen if Corwin
or Dan disqualified her this afternoon. Would Dan go
back to his home base and out of her life again while
they waited for another judge? Would he come to see
her first? And what was to stop *her* from making a
move, once she was off the case? But the very thought
of it was crazy. Hadn't she spent the better part of ten
years learning to forget Dan Sullivan? Did they really
have anything to say to each other? It had all happened so long ago.

Before she could explore the possibilities, there was
a rap at the door. Her heart took off to the races, but
it was only Jill to say she was leaving for lunch.

"Could I bring you a sandwich, Your..." Jill began, then broke off uncomfortably in the midst of the
forbidden title.

"It's all right," Susannah said wearily, sorry she'd
made an issue of such a small thing. Her stomach re-

belled at the thought of food. "Never mind the sandwich. I don't feel much like eating."

"Is something the matter?" asked Jill with concern.

Susannah hesitated, then her deep need for a sympathetic ear to pour her problems into outweighed discretion.

With a weak grin, she said, "I think I'm about to get fired from the job."

Jill gazed at her in surprise. "They want to *disqualify* you?" Stepping into the room, she closed the door she was holding open. "Why would they want to do that?"

Encouraged by the flash of indignation she saw in the other's eyes, Susannah said, "It has to do with the fact Plaintiff's Attorney Dan Sullivan and I . . . well, we . . ." Why couldn't she just come straight out and say it? She began again, "We're not exactly strangers."

"You and that beautiful hunk of man are an item?" Jill exclaimed, her voice suddenly young and excited. "Now that's really neat!" Her face fell. "Somebody found out."

"I thought it had to be brought out in the open."

"*You* told them?" There was no mistaking the new note of respectful awe in her secretary's voice. "You *knew* Mr. Sullivan would have kept still about it, and yet you . . . you *told* them! Even knowing you didn't *have* to."

"Of course I had to. Take a chair, Jill. You may as well sit down and hear the whole story."

Once seated, the young woman leaned forward, reserve lost in a fluster of youthful eagerness. The flax-blue eyes fixed on Susannah's face, scarcely blinking as she listened, unquestioning, to the candid account of Susannah's past relationship with Dan Sullivan and how it led into the events of the morning.

When Susannah was finished, Jill closed her eyes with a small sigh of satisfaction. She raised long-fringed eyelids and gazed at Susannah in bemusement, a wistful smile turning up the corners of the pretty, bowed mouth.

"Are you ever lucky!" she said softly, hurriedly, talking in small snatches. "Here you've got this fantastic man...and ten years later... Most people screw up, and that's it! But you...you're getting a second chance. Makes you almost believe in fate."

At the risk of turning Cinderella back into the scullery maid, Susannah said wryly, "I hate to spoil your romantic dream, Jill, but whatever fate's got in mind, I don't think that's it. What makes you think I even *want* a second chance?"

"We-ll...but in case you *do*, it'd be crazy to let an opportunity like this slip away from you," Jill replied, her voice practical again.

"Aren't you forgetting something? He's an attorney, and I'm a judge. And he's trying a case in my court."

The round, piquant face with its dusting of freckles looked stricken. Wide-eyed, she gazed dolefully at Susannah for a long moment.

"Oh my gosh, I completely forgot," she murmured. "It wouldn't be right for you to see him alone, would it...or even talk to him on the phone."

Susannah felt suddenly as if she were looking at her younger self instead of the intimidating secretary who ruled her office with such efficiency.

Touched, she said gently, "Don't let it worry you. I don't. I've no desire to get involved with him again. For all I know, he may be married by now."

"No, he's not. I heard Mr. Corwin asking him on the way up in the elevator this morning if his wife was here with him from Fresno, and Mr. Sullivan said he didn't have a wife," Jill told her in a satisfied voice, and Susannah realized then that the question had been lurking in the back of her mind since the first moment she'd seen him. She refused to acknowledge the feeling of relief that came with Jill's answer.

"Judge Randall used to say you should never sit around and wait for fate to get something done for you," Jill volunteered. "If it were me, I'd find a way to see him."

"Well, we can always look at it on the bright side. I may be disqualified," Susannah said acidly.

In the chair next to her desk, Jill's face blossomed into a grin that turned her into a gamin more nearly sixteen than her actual twenty-three.

"Right! There's always *that*! Considering everything, you probably *will* be disqualified."

To Susannah, the word all at once sounded shameful.

"What would your fine old Judge Randall say to his successor if he knew she was about to be disqualified after only five months on the bench?" she said broodingly.

To her surprise, the round, freckled face broke again into a tentative grin. "Are you sure you want to hear? Judge Randall talked pretty profane."

"It couldn't be any worse than what I'm saying to myself."

Jill's voice took on a querulous tone as she mimicked the old judge. "Now, see here, young lady, don't let the bastards get you down!"

Susannah stared across the desk at her secretary in astonishment, her face gradually breaking into a smile. Then, as if some invisible barrier had collapsed between them, together the two women began to laugh.

CHAPTER THREE

BEHIND THE WHEEL of the heavy four-wheel drive Jeep sports wagon that suited his way of life better than a conventional car, Sullivan speeded along the country road that would take him to Minerva Farms. A fringe of his mind heard and disregarded the rat-a-tat of gravel sprayed up from the tires against the vehicle's underside. His foot pressed hard on the throttle, and his thoughts were far away from his body's mechanical responses to the machine.

Old half-forgotten longings welled up in him like sap rising in the trees in spring, filling him with new regret for that single, childish, sore-headed sentence spoken long ago that had spoiled what had been the only real love affair of his life. He suddenly realized that every other involvement—even his misbegotten marriage, which ended when he went back to Fresno from Washington, D.C., had failed because with each new woman, he'd been looking for Susannah.

He realized, too, that it wasn't his stinging charge that last night or her enraged reply that had sent their relationship up in flames. Sullen embers had smoldered between them for the better part of a year before those inflammatory words acted like bellows, setting latent resentments on fire.

What a fool's paradise they'd lived in, he thought sardonically. Theirs was a relationship based on two shaky premises: a conviction that their love was big enough to withstand all things, and that their law practice could flourish on the ideal that anyone with a problem was entitled to legal advice.

The memory of the erstwhile ma-and-pa grocery building they converted into law offices, with living quarters overhead, brought a wry grin to his face. They'd been so sure of their own rightness, doling out legal advice to decent people down on their luck, charging whatever the clients felt they could afford to pay. Soon they'd attracted a strange assortment of deadbeats who would wander in off the streets with causes of action that existed only in their heads.

It was a red-ink operation. Still, they were developing a solid core of responsible clients and learning to spot the phonies and send them on their way with a cup of coffee. Given time, the well-meaning arrangement might have paid off. But time ran out, thanks to a bad year for the Sullivans. There was a money pinch at home. His brother, Brian, always on the wild side, had gotten into a scrape that could have ruined his life—*would* have, if the job with Bradley & Hammer hadn't fallen into Sullivan's lap, so he could bail his brother out and get him back on the right track.

Thinking about it now, he realized he should have told Susannah about Brian, but it was a matter of family loyalty. Sullivans kept their disgraces to themselves. If he had told her he'd taken the job because of Brian, would their relationship have survived those last six months they'd stayed together?

Probably not, he thought broodingly. Nothing seemed to go right between them toward the end, though after the first big flap there were no more major confrontations. Not till that last night when he'd charged her unfairly with using feminine ploys to best him in court. That's when she'd called him a quitter and accused him of taking the job with B. & H. to escape the squalid law practice they'd shared. It was like a blow to the belly, but even then he couldn't bring himself to tell her about the mess Brian had been in.

A young cock pheasant rose out of the tall grass along the roadside and skimmed across the graveled road in front of him, shattering the memory. He swerved the vehicle sharply to miss the fledgling as it passed to safety almost under his wheels. When his mind turned once more to Susannah, he saw her as she'd faced up to him and Corwin in chambers some twenty minutes ago—clear-eyed, chin firm, her black-robed shoulders squared against the unwelcome task circumstances and her unflinching conscience had thrust upon her.

He gave a grunt of frustration. Damn it! She didn't have to do what she did. She should have kept still about their relationship. Nobody would have been the wiser. Nobody would have been hurt.

But that was Susannah. The same Susannah whose integrity—at a time when the two of them didn't know where their next month's office rent was coming from—had cost her a fee that would have paid the rent and then some for the next five years.

The case had looked like a sure winner, and then the client admitted to Susannah he'd lied under oath in pretrial depositions and had every intention of swearing again to the lie when he took the stand in court. She couldn't make the man see the folly of his acts, so what did she do? She asked and was granted permission to withdraw from the case.

He remembered, too, how she'd shrugged off without rancor the substantial fee lost to a lawyer who later took over the case and won it. "He's welcome to it," she'd said cheerfully, and he'd known she meant it. She wanted no part of a case that made a joke of the court with perjured testimony.

She was born to be a judge, he thought, and was struck by how singularly unfair it would be if her work was diminished by her removal from this trial simply because he was the one who was trying the case.

He berated himself for having sat helplessly by in her chambers this morning as he watched her put herself and her career in jeopardy because of their love affair years ago. Yet he knew that short of tearing the place apart and getting himself disbarred, there wasn't a damn thing he could have done to stop her. Now she would never be allowed to sit on the case.

Oh, Corwin might let her, if it were left up to him. Corwin knew he wasn't taking any chance when he had a judge who would embarrass herself just to make sure he got a fair shake. But he'd never sell her to his client—not when she'd admitted to an affair with the opposing attorney. And there was his own client. Bancroft was dying for an excuse to dump Susannah simply because she was a woman.

From a side road directly beyond, a tractor turned in ahead of him, pulling a large piece of farm machinery, and he noted absently that there was no room to pass. He fell in line behind the rattling metal behemoth, his mind full of Susannah as he'd seen her for the first time this morning in court.

She was honestly beautiful! Not beautiful by Madison Avenue standards, maybe, but the sight of no other woman had ever made his breath stop short in his throat as it had today. Lovely, yet utterly untouchable in the austere trappings of a judge. In spite of himself, his eyes had embraced the ripe curves of breasts that lifted the somber robe of her office, knowing they were not for him. He'd felt a stirring of longing and with it an unwilling sense of loss for the woman he had once known. This woman looked like a judge and talked like a judge, he'd thought hopelessly.

And then in her chambers later, he'd caught a glimpse of something pink under the black robe, like the pink of a valley sunset, and behind the judicial mask he'd seen the sudden familiar spark of humor. He'd known then that in spite of the awesome trappings, Judge Ross was still the Susannah he once had loved.

For a single blinding instant, he'd imagined her again in his arms, her round, full breasts pressed hard against his chest, their bodies flowing into each other, making them one. The memory of her sensuous fragrance stirred an indefinable something in his heart, and in his loins he felt a pulsing of desire.

He was lost in time, oblivious to Minerva farmland, which spread out on either side of him, the rich brown earth half hidden by recently planted tomato seedlings that had already put out small umbrellas of new leaves. Not until the tractor ahead of him hauled its road-blocking machinery off to the side ahead did he pull himself back to the present with an involuntary shudder. His foot went heavy on the gas pedal. He passed the sign that said Minerva Farms, Inc., and with a muttered expletive turned back.

A minute later he was at the headquarters compound, where an assortment of corrugated metal warehouselike buildings of various sizes and shapes formed a backdrop for a handsome fieldstone office building and manicured grounds.

As he walked into Hubert Bancroft's office, he rallied arguments in favor of keeping Susannah as judge with scant hope of driving a wedge in his client's closed mind. Considering the man's strong, outspoken bias against a woman in the judiciary, neither the argument of a long wait for another judge nor the additional cost to the county was likely to carry much weight.

Characteristically, once in the presence of his client, Sullivan drove straight to the point, keeping his disclosures minimal.

"I have something to say to you, Hubert. Something I haven't motioned before because I could see no need for it. Now it appears there is. Ten years ago Judge Ross and I were . . . very fond of each other for a time. Later, we went our separate ways. Until this morning in court we have not seen each other since."

"Go on," said his client expressionlessly when Sullivan came to a stop.

"That's about it."

Behind a massive carved walnut desk, surrounded by walls hung with lithographs of vintage farm machinery, Bancroft leaned forward in his thronelike chair and eyed Sullivan speculatively.

"That's it? Why ya telling me this now?"

"Because Judge Ross felt she had to tell the other side about it this morning. It's only right you should know, too."

"God damn!" blustered Bancroft. "She told Corwin? The fool woman. What the hell did she do that for?"

"Because that's the kind of person she is, the kind of judge she'll be on this case," Sullivan said. There was something lethal in the very quiet of his voice.

"Women! Never know when to talk and when to keep their traps shut."

It took all Sullivan's control to keep his voice level. "Look, Hubert, we've got a good case. The evidence is all on your side. If it weren't, we might do better with a less perceptive and high-principled judge. As it is, we'd better consider ourselves lucky and keep the one we've got."

Bancroft looked at Sullivan as if he'd lost his mind.

"I assume you want to disqualify her?" remarked Sullivan.

"Disqualify her? Hell, are you crazy, man?" Bancroft said impatiently. "But you can bet the other side will, now that she's tipped them off."

"Corwin says no."

"You're sure of that?" Bancroft's eyes were bright with guile. "Then hell, Sullivan, of course we'll keep her. Don't tell *me* a woman won't do all she can for a man she's had the hots for. For all you know, she may *still* have the hots for a stud like you."

Sullivan held his tongue. He'd won his point. Boiling inwardly he left Bancroft's office, taking some comfort in the certainty that his client would have turned inside out if he had mentioned that he and Susannah had parted in a state of open hostility. He supposed he should have, but then he lacked Susannah's fine-honed principles, he told himself without guilt; if anything, he felt rather pleased.

At least he wouldn't have to be the one to disqualify Susannah. If it was going to be done, let Corwin do it. And he had no doubt Corwin would. Bancroft's capitulation meant nothing. Corwin's client would never agree to let her sit on the case.

"GENTLEMEN, the matter is in your hands."

The time was some three hours later, and Corwin and Sullivan were once again seated in the judicial chambers. The moment of truth had arrived. Characteristically, Susannah went directly to the question that brought them there.

"I can assure you with complete confidence that I will preside over this case without prejudice," she said flatly and without preliminaries. "In good conscience, I can't find justification for withdrawal on my part. If either of you or the people you represent have a problem with this, now is the time to make it known. Mr. Corwin?" She braced herself for what she felt was inevitable.

"My client wants to get this thing over with and has left the decision up to me, your honor," replied Corwin. "As I've already said, I'm satisfied to have you stay on as judge."

In spite of the tumult of conflicting emotions within her, Susannah forced herself to turn her eyes to Dan, who met them with a strange expression of satisfaction on his face. Why, he *wants* to be the one to disqualify me! she thought.

"And you, Mr. Sullivan?" she asked crisply, hiding an unexpected feeling of hurt. "What about you and your client? Your client *has* been informed?"

"Yes, your honor. Neither Mr. Bancroft nor I see any reason to disqualify you."

It caught her unprepared. There was a moment before she could speak.

"I see," she said then, her voice reedy. "In that case, gentlemen, we may as well get on with the trial." She glanced at her watch. "Court will resume in ten minutes."

FOR A MOMENT after the two men left her to return to the courtroom Susannah was powerless to move. She watched blindly as the door closed behind them. The poignant, almost forgotten yearning for the man she'd known intimately welled up in her once more—insistent, suffocating. *This can't be happening,* she told herself. Her whole being cried out in fierce, silent protest against the emotional turmoil she saw looming ahead.

Under the circumstances, she'd never doubted one side or the other would move to unseat her. But neither of them had! How could she go out there and face Dan day after day under the rules of ethics that bound them both? How could she forget that he was not simply the plaintiff's attorney in another trial but the man she'd loved so extravagantly, even after he destroyed her illusions so long ago.

It crossed her mind then that it still wasn't too late to disqualify herself. For one relieved moment she even thought seriously of doing so, but the old burr that was her conscience gouged her. With a resigned sigh, she dismissed the possibility. The fact he was *Dan* wouldn't influence her in the job she was sworn to perform, and she knew it. There was no way she could make an escape hatch for herself by declaring herself out of the case.

Feeling trapped and resentful, she was at the same time troubled by the wave of relief she'd experienced when she'd remembered there was still time to remove herself from the trial.

Why, she actually *wanted* to be disqualified! she thought in stunned disbelief. For the first time, she realized that for all her surface concern about damage to her judicial career, the matter that had concerned her most was the unfinished business with Dan.

Now, unexpectedly, the time had come when the bitter words written on her memory in those last moments they'd been together could be erased. It waited only for her to be disqualified for them to be unsaid.

Would he come to her? Or should she send for him? Or would she listen to the voice of prudence reminding her that though her life with Dan had been a joyous ride on a carousel, in the end he had let her down. When the fun was over, there was nothing more. Nothing but memories. Memories too light and purposeless to outweigh the pain.

Still, whatever the outcome, the words must be unsaid—if only because they owed it to each other to acknowledge that those words were never meant.

So had run the strain of her thoughts, like background music to all that was going on.

And now the question of who would make the first move, who'd be the first to speak—let alone all the other questions—was moot. Her disappointment, like an uncured olive, left a bitter aftertaste.

Jill's familiar tap on the door to her chambers nudged Susannah out of her momentary trancelike state. Still half dazed, she met her secretary's inquiring eyes.

"You won't believe this—they're keeping me on as judge," she said dully, not quite believing it herself.

"They didn't *disqualify* you?" The sound of dismay in Jill's voice was so genuine it brought Susannah back to reality, her mouth curling in a slight, ironic smile.

"Well, I can see if I was looking for congratulations I came to the wrong place," she said dryly. "Need I remind you, dear Jill, that I'm coming up for election shortly. If they'd disqualified me, my opponents would make political hay of it."

The secretary sniffed. "Judges get disqualified all the time. It doesn't necessarily have anything to do with what kind of a judge you are."

"Tell that to my constituents!"

"But now you won't be able to see Mr. Sullivan, except in court, Your Ho..." Jill stumbled unhappily over the forbidden "Your Honor," her face rosy with embarrassment.

It would only add to the discomfort of them both to tell her that if she felt easier with it, "Your Honor" was all right, Susannah decided ruefully. She said instead, "I can't if I'm to stick to the principles of judicial ethics—which I most certainly intend to do."

"I suppose that's all you *can* do. But if *he* was to make a move? Couldn't you..."

In a rare flash of impatience, Susannah cut her off sharply. "Jill, you know as well as I do, the same canons apply to him." Almost too virtuously, considering something inside her *wanted* Dan to disregard the rules, she added, "But if he did, you *know* I couldn't go along with it, even if it meant holding him in contempt of court."

Still Jill wouldn't let go. "Suppose the two of you happened to run into each other purely by chance? What if you had a flat tire, for instance, and he hap-

pened to come along? You wouldn't be expected not
to talk to him then, would you?''

"Of course not. But we'd have to bend over backward to stay away from anything that might be con-
strued as having to do with the trial.''

"You don't really think if you and Mr. Sullivan
found yourselves alone together you wouldn't find
something better to talk about than this dumb trial?''
Jill asked archly. "I don't see how it could be unethi-
cal for you to talk to each other if you met by accident and what you said didn't have anything to do
with what's going on in court.''

Susannah gazed at her secretary in astonishment.
The conversation suddenly struck her as ludicrous,
and she swallowed a laugh, saying teasingly, "Why,
Jill Fitzgerald, under that no-nonsense front of yours,
I do believe you're a closet romantic! What on earth
are you getting at?''

"What I'm getting at is, you're not doing anything
wrong if you just talk," Jill persisted. "You know,
about...*other* things. If you should meet by accident.''

"Have it your way, Jill," Susannah said, all at once
weary of their discussion. "Just don't let me catch you
tampering with my tire valves!''

She must have been crazy to tell Jill about her past
with Dan, thought Susannah with an inward sigh. It
was high time she brought the fruitless exchange to a
halt. With a glance at her watch she stood up quickly.

"I've got exactly two minutes to put on that robe
and get into the courtroom," she announced briskly.

Jill walked to the closet and pulled out the robe.

"This darned black thing doesn't exactly turn a
woman into a sex symbol," she observed as she

slipped the offending robe over Susannah's shoulders. "Too bad he can't see you in that fabulous pink dress you're wearing. I bet if he did, he wouldn't waste any time finding some way to get you alone."

Susannah didn't see any need to remind Jill that Dan had seen her in the dress only a few minutes before. She wondered uneasily why she hadn't followed her usual practice of wearing the robe of office in chambers when receiving people on official business. *Sex symbol, indeed!*

"Good grief, Jill," she said a bit querulously, "what would your Judge Randall say...to all this?"

Jill's clear blue eyes gazed at her thoughtfully for a moment. When she spoke, her voice took on the tone of mimicry she used whenever she imparted the wisdom of the late judge. "'Where the heart's concerned, young lady, it's not always wise to pay attention to the head.'"

IN THE CORRIDOR outside the reception room Corwin pulled the door shut behind him and hurried his steps to catch up with Sullivan, who walked on ahead toward the door of the courtroom.

"God, what a gutsy lady," Corwin said in an admiring voice. "And a damned good-looking one, too. Who'd ever guess there was a sexy body under all that black."

Without breaking step, Sullivan turned his head and eyed the other man coldly.

"Hey..." Corwin said, looking uncomfortable. "I wasn't thinking. I'm sorry."

Sullivan, facing front again, his strong jaw grimly set, walked on in silence. The other lawyer kept pace.

They arrived at the courtroom door with no further words.

Corwin tried again. "Look, Sullivan, I was out of line. I *said* I was sorry. I have nothing but admiration for the judge. You were a damn fool to let her get away."

This time Sullivan did not deign to acknowledge his fellow attorney as he reached for the ancient brass doorknob.

Corwin let out a frustrated grunt. "Well, okay, damnit, if that's the way you want it," he said sourly. "But as long as this case is in her court, don't even *think* about rekindling old fires. I'll be watching, brother. Don't forget."

They walked on into the courtroom and took their seats beside their respective clients, Corwin's face flushed with annoyance, Sullivan feeling none too pleased with himself. He'd just violated his own rule about not tangling with the opposition outside the courtroom. Furthermore, he had overreacted. There wasn't any malice intended in what Corwin had said. He just had a big mouth.

It wasn't even what the other lawyer had *said* that ticked him off. It was that Susannah had given Corwin a glimpse into the intimate world that had once belonged to the two of them alone. He was surprised at how much the thought of it bothered him.

He took a moment to assure Bancroft that the trial was about to begin and that Judge Ross would continue to preside, and was rewarded with a noncommittal grunt. He was about to turn his attention once more to the strangers in the jury box, whom he hadn't even begun to sort out, when Susannah walked out of chambers and crossed over to take the dais, looking every inch the judge.

Seeing her in the somber, unfamiliar black again, Sullivan felt cheated. Still imprinted on his mind was the image he'd had of her when they left her a few minutes before. The dress she'd been wearing had made him remember the *woman* she was, before he could bring himself to remember she was a judge. It was some kind of pink—the dress—he thought; colorful, anyhow, like the things she'd chosen to wear when he'd known her before. If pink, an uncommonly provocative pink. The dress bared her arms and was cut in a sharp vee that invited his eyes to follow its lines from the delicate hollow of her throat to the seductive shadow between her breasts.

For a moment he'd thought his heart was going to pound its way out of his chest. He'd felt that old, heady urge to do something outrageous that would drive the reserved no-nonsense look from her face, as had been his way in the past. He wanted to make her laugh aloud—to call up one of those rare bursts of laughter that used to come bubbling up from some deep well of humor inside her. Long after they'd parted, he used to hear her laugh sometimes in the lilting music of water cascading over the rocks when he walked by a mountain stream, and it would fill him with a vague ache of loneliness and regret.

As he saw her there in her chambers, stripped for the first time of the sexless black robe, the memory of the mystical secrets of her body known so well to him in that other time had flooded through him, and for a moment he'd forgotten why he was there.

"The Superior Court of River County of the State of California is now in session," sang out the bailiff.

Sullivan shook his head to rid his mind of the pervasive images and conceded he'd better be glad the judicial armor hid from his senses the Susannah he remembered. If she walked into court every day wearing the pink dress or something like it, he'd never get the blasted case tried.

He made himself let go of the captivating picture and reminded himself that this was the woman who placed such high value on principle and integrity but had refused to give him credit for having a reasonable supply of it himself.

Uncomfortable with his mind's ambivalent meandering, he brought his attention around to the matter at hand, but still he kept his eyes on the austere black below the level of the judge's chin, out of range of the ruby seduction of her lips. It was the only way he could make himself forget that under the forbidding robe, Judge Ross was really Susannah.

Now speaking from the dais, Judge Ross brought him to full attention.

"Mr. Sullivan, are you prepared to make your opening statement at this time?"

He wasn't sure exactly what he'd been expecting from her on the bench. Foolishly he hadn't looked for her to sound so much like a judge, he supposed. Serious. Formal. Depressingly remote.

In his attorney's voice, he said aloud, "Yes, your honor. Thank you, I am."

Susannah was well aware that every muscle in her body was as tight as a fiddle string. She made a conscious effort to let them go loose before she began her routine introductory instruction to the jury.

"Ladies and gentlemen," she said, formally addressing the members of the jury, "before the plaintiff's attorney begins, I must ask you to keep in mind that in your deliberation it is your duty to consider nothing but the evidence. Evidence includes only what is sworn and will come to you mainly from the witness stand. You must at all times be aware and remember that nothing either of the attorneys says is evidence, including their opening statements, which are merely to help you understand the case when the evidence is actually heard. Before you begin your deliberations, I will instruct you on this again and will remind you of it from time to time throughout the trial."

"You may proceed, Mr. Sullivan."

As she watched Dan push back the big, old-fashioned oak courtroom chair and rise, she realized her hands were curled into two tight fists. Consciously she opened her fingers and reached for the pencil and clean yellow legal pad the clerk had placed on her desk, not to take notes on the opening statement but to give her tense hands something to do.

He's really quite wonderful looking, she thought, as he left the attorneys' table and moved toward the jury box with an easy, deliberate step—long, hard-muscled and to all appearances completely relaxed. She was surprised at the small thrill of pride that raced through her—an almost proprietary pride hardly justified under the circumstances.

She watched him come to a stop a few feet from the jury box and stand at ease, his face serious but pleasant, as if to give the jurors a moment to take his measure before he began.

"Ladies and gentleman of the jury," he said with an introductory smile as his eyes moved over the faces before him, "may I express my regret that I was not here last week to become acquainted with you as individuals through the *voir dire* procedure by which you were chosen. I've lost the opportunity to get to know you as well as you no doubt will get to know me during the course of the trial. I'm sorry about that."

His affability was rewarded with faint smiles of empathy on the faces of several jurors. Already he was sorting them out, thought Susannah, approving.

"However, my partner, Mr. Curtis . . . as you've already heard, Mr. Curtis met with an unfortunate accident and is in traction and considerable pain. . . . Yet he was still able to tell me a great deal about you. I almost feel we've met. My partner expressed great confidence in your ability as jurors to evaluate the evidence in this trial with intelligence and fairness and without prejudice. I feel sure his confidence has not been misplaced.

"I am not unmindful of the inconvenience and, too often, real personal sacrifice accepting the responsibility of being a juror costs. It is my hope you will find satisfaction in the experience that will repay you in some small way for any burden that may have been placed upon you."

As easily as a man welcoming new acquaintances into his home, he gave each juror a moment of friendly attention with his eyes as he played out his opening remarks. He paused and with perfect timing turned to include the judge as he began his case.

"Now, if it please the court, I should like to take you back with me two years ago to a morning late in the month of August when this matter, which today brings us all here to this courtroom, began."

Simply and directly, paying respect to the quality of his jurors by not talking down to them, Sullivan began. The entire focus of Susannah's attention turned involuntarily to the emerging case. The woman who but a moment before had been bemused by her physical awareness of the man was at once lost in the judicial persona. Without any conscious effort on her part, scarcely noting it had happened, she assumed the role that distanced her from the Dan Sullivan who had once been her lover. She saw him now only as another lawyer in another trial.

In his own role as plaintiff's attorney, Sullivan took the jurors through a quick summary of his case with particular emphasis on what a certain Minerva Farms field checker by the name of Martin would soon be telling them from the witness stand.

Martin's testimony would bear out the Minerva contention that a bumper crop of its prime tomatoes had been destroyed by a chemical used to dry up neighboring safflower plants, a procedure that made them easier to harvest.

On a routine check of the tomato field on that fateful August two years before, Martin would testify he looked up to see an Ag Dusters plane laying a path of fine mist from its spray boom across the length of the adjoining safflower field. He saw the nose lift to clear telephone wires that marked the dividing line between the two fields and was alarmed when, instead of shutting down over Minerva land, the boom continued to drizzle spray on the tomato plants below. He watched the plane climb steeply to its apex at the far end where it rolled over in a sharp turn and went back across the tomato crop for another pass at the safflower field. He would testify that he watched the procedure twice to verify his first observation before he called his superintendent, who notified Ag Dusters and was told there was nothing wrong with the boom, and in any case the job was finished.

The field checker's story was what his case was about, but even as he told it, Sullivan was hard-pressed to keep the sound of anxiety out of his voice.

The trouble was he hadn't found anyone else who had seen the leaking boom, and unless he did, the jury would discount Martin's testimony because he was a longtime employee of Minerva Farms, something Corwin would make sure they didn't forget.

The pilot of that crop-dusting plane was the man Sullivan had to find. The pilot had told another employee at Ag Dusters that he'd seen the boom leaking and told the owner, Ashton, about it, but Ashton had told him to keep his mouth shut. By the time the suit was filed, the pilot had vanished and Sullivan was left with nothing but hearsay, which wouldn't be allowed in court. With the pilot to back up the field checker's testimony he had an airtight case. Without him, Sullivan suspected glumly, the case was up for grabs.

CHAPTER FOUR

SULLIVAN TOOK ADVANTAGE of the recess that followed the opening arguments to talk to Hubert Bancroft one last time about what he would say on the witness stand when the recess was over. His client was the garrulous type who couldn't be shut up if given his head, and as his attorney, Sullivan had to make sure Bancroft didn't spout anything that couldn't be backed up.

"Remember, Hubert, as vice president and general manager of Minerva Farms, all you have to do when you get up there on the stand is set out the circumstances of the case," he said, fully aware that his client didn't take kindly to being *told*.

"I know what I'm doing, Sullivan," Bancroft asserted truculently, and Sullivan had to be satisfied with that.

"Do you swear to tell the truth, the whole truth and nothing but the truth...?" The oft-repeated words were reeled out a few minutes later in a rapid monotone by a court clerk who appeared on the verge of a yawn. Bancroft, Sullivan's first witness, took the stand.

It went better than Sullivan had hoped. True, there was the gratuitous tidbit about the unnamed "tomato expert" who had gone for sixty tons per acre in the company's harvest-yield pool. It brought a howl of

"irrelevant . . . immaterial" from Corwin and a reprimand from the judge. But it could have been worse.
At least Bancroft hadn't said anything the defense was
able to use to its advantage in cross-examination.

The second witness was Rex Horner, field repre-
sentative for one of the canneries. His job throughout the growing season was to evaluate fields his
company bought from to determine the potential of
the tomato supply. He was a self-styled "expert"
whom Sullivan had seen testify in agriculture cases
before and suspected was a professional witness—one
who hired out to give desirable testimony for pay.
Sullivan's gut instinct was not to use the man, but his
client was insistent, and when Horner agreed to keep
his testimony within limits set by Sullivan, the attorney
had given in.

With the intention of making short work of the
witness, Sullivan got the introduction over with and
asked the only question he expected to ask.

"Mr. Horner, how did this field compare with other
fields you were assigned to watch that summer?"

Horner, a handsome, even rather imposing looking
man, took a well-timed pause as if to give the question his most serious consideration.

"That field would have yielded sixty tons to the acre
at harvest time, Mr. Sullivan," he said portentously.

There was a rustle in the courtroom, and for a moment Sullivan was so angry he couldn't see. *Why, the
double-crossing . . . !* The bastard had agreed to an es-
timated yield of somewhere in the neighborhood of
fifty tons—the figure the bona fide experts would testify to later. It would be hard enough to make the jury
believe even that, since forty tons was normally con-

sidered a very good crop. You couldn't blame the jury if, in the end, they didn't believe any of the estimates.

"Your witness, Mr. Corwin," he said, half inclined to hope Corwin would rip Little Jack Horner to shreds.

SULLIVAN SLEPT BADLY that night. When he came into court next morning he still felt bruised from the day before. He had started off as if it was his first time in court. He was far too aware of Susannah. It was distracting him from the job he was here to do.

You'd better pull up your socks and start winning this case, Sullivan! he told himself derisively, grateful that his first witness of the day was Walter Short, head man for Minerva Farm's tomato-growing operations. Walter's testimony would take up the full day.

Sullivan took a last glance around to make sure all his props were in order—the charts, the screen, the projector, the slides—tools to add proof to Short's testimony. Knowing he had planned his attack thoroughly and was ready to go, he felt a sudden surge of new energy, like the fighter about to enter the ring. Energy tempered with caution.

Motioning Short to the stand, Sullivan placed himself where he could focus on his witness and still not turn his back on either the jury or the judge, then began his questioning. His man was knowledgeable in his field and answered with a laconic assurance that inspired confidence in what he said. Despite an occasional objection from Corwin with no apparent purpose except perhaps to get the witness out of step, the questioning went smoothly. The objections, predictably, were overruled.

And so the questioning moved on through the morning to be resumed in the early afternoon. Watching the black-robed Susannah covertly from the corner of his eye as, for the third time, she denied one of Corwin's gratuitous objections, Sullivan suddenly wondered how she would handle an objection against himself if he pulled something out of line. On impulse, he had to try it.

Blatantly leading the witness, he asked, "Isn't it true Mr. Short, that if that field hadn't been damaged, you were looking forward to the biggest crop of prime tomatoes you've ever harvested in the many years you've been growing tomatoes for Minerva Farms?"

A side glance to the dais caught the slight flush that rose to Susannah's cameo face. A flash of warning in the dark eyes telegraphed that the judge had read his mind and knew what he was up to. She didn't wait for Corwin to object.

"You are leading the witness, Mr. Sullivan, as I am sure you are quite aware," she said sharply. "If it was inadvertent, I caution you to exercise more care in phrasing your questions. If it was intended to lead the witness, I must warn you that it will not be tolerated in this court. Please don't let it become a habit or you may find yourself in contempt."

Her eyes, which normally reflected a warm spirit, had turned steely. Sullivan accepted the reprimand with a slight, respectful dip of his head and turned back to his witness. What had he expected? he asked himself. He'd always known he'd be granted no favors in Susannah's court, and he wanted none! But "Don't let it become a habit"? Damn it, she knew him better than that! And "You may find yourself in contempt"? On such trivial grounds? Where the hell was that sparkle of humor he could always bring rising to her eyes like a rainbow trout to a mayfly? Not in those two dark orbs that glowered down at him now.

Disgruntled, he went back to his witness, Short, taking particular care to frame the questions in proper form. Court recessed shortly for its customary mid-afternoon break, giving Sullivan a respite in which to regain his own sense of humor and his aplomb.

IN THE HAVEN of her chambers, Susannah headed for the cubicle that was her private washroom. She reached for the aspirin bottle behind the small mirrored door and popped two of the tablets into her mouth. The bottle had been there since the day she had taken over the bench, but this was the first time she'd had to resort to it.

She almost never had a headache; maybe she was coming down with something. But she didn't really believe that. She knew very well where the headache was coming from. Darn Sullivan, anyhow! It wasn't even as if he was trying to coach the witness. This witness knew the right answers without having them fed to him. After all, his business was keeping a check on that tomato field.

So what had Sullivan been up to? Whatever it was, it had so incensed her to think he was deliberately baiting her that she'd done what she'd sworn with her oath of office she would never do. She had let her emotions overrule her judgment. She'd even gone so far as to threaten him with contempt of court.

After all, what had he done? He'd asked a leading question. It wasn't as if she'd never heard one asked in her court before. Often a lawyer would try to slip one in to make sure the jurors heard an answer he

particularly wanted them to hear. It was hardly a
mortal sin. In Dan's case it even appeared he had little to gain by it, so it was quite innocuous, and she'd
overreacted! Her use of the powerful contempt-of-
court threat was nothing short of irresponsible.

It was a disturbing thought. Almost as disturbing as
the quick dip of Dan's head and the look he'd given
her from under that heavy fringe of bronze lashes after she'd lashed out at him. He must have remembered from the past how helpless she'd been in the face
of that ridiculous, self-mocking, bad-kid look he
could count on to make her break down and laugh.

To find that it could still turn her resolve to jelly had
unsettled her, and it had taken all her willpower to hide
her disarray from those discerning eyes until he had
turned back to his witness.

*Darn you, Dan Sullivan. Why won't you behave
yourself?* The reproach formed in her mind, and in
spite of herself a corner of her mouth turned up in a
forgiving smile. Aware of it, she gave a huff of annoyance and marched up to the work cart at the end
of her desk where she picked up the file folder on a
barn burning that Jill had put on top of the cart that
morning—a morning that now seemed a year ago. She
stared at its contents blindly. Even if she could make
her mind give the arson pleadings the attention they
deserved she had no time to do so now. The afternoon recess would soon be over.

Leaving the file on the cart, she crossed to the soft
leather sofa along the far wall of the room and gave
herself up to its silken embrace. Closing her eyes, she
tried to free her mind from the pervasive image of Dan
Sullivan.

"Oh Dan, Dan," she whispered softly. "What in the world are we going to do?"

BACK IN THE COURTROOM after the break, Sullivan concluded his questioning of Walter Short and turned him over to the defense for cross-examination. After a few cursory questions, Corwin dismissed the witness and court was adjourned to the following day. At the attorneys' table, under the guise of putting his papers into his briefcase, Sullivan watched Susannah step down from the dais. There was a certain self-indulgence in observing her walk away that was irresistible. He saw a kind of inborn dignity in her movements that owed nothing to the black mantle of her new office. It had been there even when she wore no more than a bikini...or less. He found it infinitely enjoyable to watch.

A picture rose to his mind and superimposed itself on the black-robed actuality about to disappear behind the chambers door. For a moment he imagined the stern, judicial garment falling away gently to expose not the sunset-hue of the dress he recalled under it, but the creamy slope of bare shoulders, the straight back that narrowed and curved into the erotic rise of delectable buttocks, pink from a long afternoon on the beach.

The last provocative swish of the somber robe as she disappeared into her chambers raised the short hairs on the back of his neck in an involuntary shiver. God, what a sight it had been in those days to watch the rhythm of that splendid naked body as she walked away from him. He felt a strong emotion rising in him as he pictured her in his mind. It took a conscious effort to snap himself back to the immediate scene.

Gathering his books and papers, he headed for the county law library down the corridor from the courtroom to look up a point of law he wished to explore.

Sometime later he glanced up from the collection of law books he had piled around him on the study desk and realized that the others in the library had left and he was alone. He unfolded his long frame and stretched, acutely aware that the muscles in the back of his neck were tied in knots. Walking to the open door he caught a glimpse of bright color moving down the corridor away from him toward the elevator, and for a moment his heart took off after it.

It was Susannah, the woman. She'd left the judge back there in her chambers. He felt an overriding urge to go loping after her.

He was halfway out the door when she disappeared around the corner that housed the elevator. He skidded to a stop. What the hell! Was he out of his mind? He'd been down that road once and he'd be damned if he'd go down it again. They hadn't been able to make it when they were peers. What chance had they now that she was a judge? And he with a law practice a couple of hundred miles away.

Stay away from her, Sullivan, he told himself. *Forget it.* And yet as he turned back into the library he knew that she was part of him and always would be. The only way he could forget was to take himself far away and stay there as he had for the past ten years.

She was the *judge,* damn it! He'd do well to bear it in mind. Judge Susannah Ross. *Keep your eyes on the black robe, Sullivan. You can forget the rest.*

IT WAS ALMOST DUSK when Susannah pressed the button that triggered the electronic door opener and drove her car into the garage attached to the house where she lived. It was a small house but aesthetically pleasing, located in one of Cacheton's better neighborhoods and equipped with every conceivable convenience. It had been built twenty years before as an in-town residence for a well-to-do farm couple who were active at the time in community affairs. Finding in their later years that they seldom came in from the country, they had put it up for lease.

Her arms loaded with law books and a briefcase full of papers that would occupy her for the evening, she pushed her way inside, dumped everything on the kitchen table and drew a long breath. She couldn't remember when she'd had such a ghastly day, and from all appearances things were going to get worse. After a moment she moved into the living room, where she plucked a stereo tape at random from a music collection as eclectic as her books. She slipped the tape into the stereo without bothering to see what it was and smiled as the first sprightly strains of a Mozart concerto reached her ear. She let the magic of the music wash over her for a moment, soaking it in.

Absently she made a mental inventory of her refrigerator's contents and was about to go to the kitchen to see what she could assemble for a quick meal before knuckling down to work when the telephone rang. For no good reason Dan Sullivan leaped to her mind. Her heart pumped wildly for an instant, then settled down. Dan was the last person in the world she could expect to call, she told herself.

But her hand was unsteady as she reached to turn down the volume on the stereo, and her step was quick as she crossed the room to pick up the phone.

"Susannah? What's going on? You sound out of breath."

At the sound of her father's voice, Susannah felt an unreasonable disappointment, at once replaced by guilt.

"It's good to hear your voice, Dad," she said contritely and with a feeling of genuine concern. He so seldom called! "Is everything all right?"

Her father brushed the question aside impatiently. "Of course, everything's fine," he said. "I just called to find out how the campaign's going."

Campaign? Going?

"I can't say it's 'going' at all. Honestly, Dad, I haven't had time to think about a campaign *or* the election, but I *will*." She spoke with more assurance than she felt, inasmuch as she didn't know the first thing about getting herself elected to office.

"That's about what I figured!" her father's voice exploded across the wire. "You'd *better* start thinking about it, or you'll wake up one morning and find yourself looking for a job."

Why did he always make her feel like an incompetent adolescent? thought Susannah uncomfortably. The minute after he started talking she'd find she was apologizing for something that didn't affect anybody but herself. Like now.

"I'm really sorry, Dad, but when there's a long trial going, it's almost like working three jobs. In a one-judge county the trial and other legal matters are set aside Wednesday mornings for juvenile court and Friday mornings for domestic court. You're always changing gears. I can't take on anything more—much less plan a campaign—till I'm through with this trial I'm in."

"Now you listen to me, daughter. I've been in politics longer than you've been around, and I can promise you one thing—the electorate doesn't give a damn how many jobs you have to juggle or how well you do them. If you don't get out there and sell yourself the voters'll turn you out at election time."

"Dad..." She hated the note of pleading she heard in her own voice. "Look. I'm right in the midst of...I promise, the moment it ends I'll..."

Unexpectedly her voice broke. As she struggled to regain her composure her father's voice came again, quieter now but gruff, uneasy, placating.

"Go on back to what you were doing and don't worry about it, Susie." He hadn't called her Susie since she was a little girl. Her heart warmed to it, only to have the moment spoiled. "I've got a few chits to call in. You can count on money to put out all the signs and flyers and newspapers ads and TV spots you need when the time comes. I'll round up a crew of first-class PR people and bring them up there to snowball River County the last three weeks before election. You leave it to me."

"Dad, you can't do that!" she said indignantly. "Those people don't have a vote in River County. I can't win this election with outside money."

"Which just shows how little you know about politics, my dear. I'll get back to you later." Then, almost as an afterthought, he said, "Get a good night's sleep." The line went dead. Outraged, she felt her hand tremble as she laid the phone back in its cradle.

Damn it! She had to stop him. One sure way to lose the election would be to offend the voters with outside money and a big-city political campaign. He was right about one thing, of course. She shouldn't have put her campaign off for so long. Now that he'd decided to take over, she'd never get him to back off, she thought unhappily.

Still, she wasn't so sure. Except for the time, right after law school, when she turned down the job he had lined up for her with a big law firm and went into practice on her own, and again when she and Sullivan became involved, when had she ever put her father to test? On those issues he'd given ultimatums, but he never followed through. Suddenly she understood for the first time that regardless of what she did, she'd always taken it for granted that her father was pleased and proud to have her as his child.

With her mother it had been different, she realized. Her mother had set goals. Susannah had learned at an early age that the sure way to win the approval she hungered for from her mother was to throw herself into attaining those goals.

Goal after goal after goal.

For that she had pushed to finish high school in three years, was chosen valedictorian of her class and had been accepted at sixteen by the college of her mother's choice. Then it was the Dean's List and Phi Beta Kappa and graduating *summa cum laude*, and then law school and "making" the Law Review. At twenty-two—the year her mother died of an aneurysm—she had passed the state bar examination that made her a lawyer.

As she looked back on the years of her growing up they seemed unbelievably depressing, though she couldn't remember minding back then. There had been no time for just being young, but she hadn't missed it. It wasn't until Dan came into her life that she'd realized there might have been more to those years than what she'd had. Dan Sullivan taught her to play.

The thought of Sullivan made her restive, and she turned to the kitchen to pour herself a glass of white wine and forage absently through the refrigerator, searching for leftovers to assemble into a meal. A feeling of melancholy for the teenager she'd never been hung over her. What was worse, she couldn't get Dan Sullivan out of her mind.

What about Dan? she wondered. Was it possible they could put the past behind them once the trial was over? Maybe even be friends? But she knew friendship would never be enough between the two of them, and there was no room in their lives for anything else.

The Mozart on the stereo, so soothing when she first put it on, seemed suddenly intrusive. Slipping her evening meal into the microwave oven, she went to make a change of tapes. A quick search rewarded her with a midthirties blend of jazz and blues featuring Linda Ronstadt with the late Nelson Riddle's orchestra. It was music more suited to her mood, and when it segued into the time-honored "What'll I do?" it seemed to Susannah that the rich earthy Ronstadt voice was singing directly to her.

WEDNESDAY MORNING was given over to juvenile court, but when the trial resumed in the afternoon, Sullivan brought three expert witnesses to the stand in orderly succession—a botanist, a plant pathologist and an agricultural chemist, all with University Ph.D.s, all experienced and knowledgeable in their respective fields.

After the break, Sullivan called the field checker, Martin, to the witness stand to tell the story he had primed the jury to hear in his opening statement. Martin was a good witness. He knew what he'd seen and stuck to his story throughout a hard-driving cross-examination by the defense attorney that might have rattled a man less secure in the absolute truth of what he had to say. Corwin used every known courtroom tactic, trying to get him to contradict himself, but Martin stolidly held his ground.

There were times when Sullivan could scarcely restrain himself from objecting to the lawyer's harassment of his witness, but the field checker appeared undismayed, and Sullivan could see that some members of the jury were not taking kindly to Corwin's attack on the stolid young farm worker, who had a great deal in common with most of them. It was Susannah who brought the questioning to a halt.

"It appears to me, Mr. Corwin, that you have exhausted both this line of questioning and Mr. Martin," she said firmly. "You come perilously close to badgering the witness, and that I will not permit. If you wish to ask further questions, you may do so as long as they are not along the line you've been taking."

"Sorry, Your Honor. That is all. The witness may step down."

Sullivan knew well enough that Susannah's rebuke to Corwin was not done as a favor to himself, but he gave her a silent cheer. She'd made it clear the day before that she didn't intend to let Sullivan play fast and loose with the court. Now she'd given a similar message to Corwin. And about time, Sullivan thought. Almost from the first, the defense attorney had been trying to manipulate the witness in cross-examination, attempting to throw the questioning off track with objections, continually interrupting for rulings from the bench.

"I object, Your Honor! Counsel is leading the witness."

"Objection! Testimony is incompetent, irrelevant and immaterial."

"Objection! A proper foundation has not been laid."

In a flash of insight, Sullivan wondered if Corwin were testing Susannah, too. Was he trying to determine if she really was as free from bias as she'd declared herself in chambers to be? On the other hand, maybe Corwin figured if he pressed her into making enough rulings, sooner or later he'd catch her in some mistake. The defense attorney knew he had a weak case. The evidence, as Sullivan had pointed out to his own client, greatly favored Minerva Farms. Could Corwin be gambling on provoking her into judicial errors, hoping he could take it to the appeals court and perhaps get the verdict overturned, should he lose?

But Susannah wasn't making mistakes and wasn't likely to, if he knew Susannah. She was handling the case like a veteran, Sullivan thought, and was surprised at the feeling of pride that came over him, as if this woman who disposed of Corwin's roadblocks with such equanimity in some way belonged to him.

WHEN THE COURT DAY was over, Susannah retreated to her chambers and welcomed the sight of Jill Fitzgerald coming in from the reception room on the other side.

"How's it going?" the secretary asked, reaching to help with the voluminous robe. As Jill peeled the gown back, Susannah raised a hand to the low neck of the peacock blue linen dress to adjust the flattened collar with a small sound of dismissal.

"Not much worse than I usually expect," she said, and gave Jill a quick account of the judge baiting that had been going on.

"Do you always get that?" the secretary asked incredulously.

"Not always, but it's definitely a 'shakedown' sometimes—the first two or three days of a trial—when an attorney hasn't been in my court before. Some lawyers can't seem to settle down to business until they've put me to test."

From the closet where she was putting the robe away, Jill asked, "Because you're a woman?"

"Well, a lot of them *do* come into court with sexist notions about how women are supposed to behave. They can't wait to see me do something irrational under pressure...maybe burst into tears. They can't resist giving it a try. But I don't really think that's what's been going on in this trial. Certainly not with Dan Sullivan. He knows me too well for that," Susannah confided dryly.

Her secretary's eyes widened with interest, and she waited for her to go on.

Susannah hesitated a moment before succumbing to the need for a sounding board. Her instinct told her she could trust Jill, who had thawed noticeably in the past two days.

"There's no question Dan was deliberately baiting me yesterday, but I suspect all he was really trying to find out was where he stands with me in court," she said at last. "He may have been having a little fun, too, but if he was, it wasn't sexist. It was personal."

"And Mr. Corwin?"

"Who knows? It doesn't matter. Now they've got it out of their systems maybe we can settle down and get on with the trial," Susannah said, a faint touch of amusement in her voice. "Actually, they're the least of my worries."

"How so?"

"I wish I could handle my own father as well," she said, her voice reflecting the new concern that had been troubling her since his phone call the night before.

Curiosity flashed for a moment in Jill's face and was immediately veiled by the mask of secretarial discretion. Aware that Jill was bubbling with unasked questions, Susannah took pity on the young woman.

But first she asked a question herself, "What would you think if I brought in a team of high-powered professionals to run my election campaign?"

The answer was in Jill's face and eyes as she replied in the old disapproving voice Susannah hadn't heard for a while. "It would cost you a lot of money."

"Suppose there were people in the city who were willing to finance it?" Susannah asked again, but seeing her secretary's look of shock and disappointment she carried her questioning no further.

"That's what my father has his mind set to do," she said. "I've got to stop him, and I haven't an inkling how." At the expression of sheer relief on Jill Fitzgerald's face, Susannah told her about her conversation with her father the night before.

"Politics has been his lifeblood," Susannah explained. "My grandparents left him reasonably well off. He used to dabble in insurance, but he's never had to work hard at a real career. Unfortunately, a whole new generation has taken over in San Francisco, and my father's nearly eighty. For the first time in his adult life he's out of politics and has nothing left but his vigor, poor man. If I don't get my own show on the road, he's coming up here to Cacheton with a team of public relations experts and pots of money to do it for me. Then what do I do?''

"Ohboy!" breathed Jill. "You've got to stop him. That's for sure!''

"Tell me how!" said Susannah. "After all, he's the expert. I don't know the first thing about getting myself reelected. Even if I did, I won't have time to work on it until this trial is over, and by then my father could be firmly entrenched.''

Jill's brows pulled together in a worried frown. After a moment she said hesitantly, "I don't know that much about campaigning either, since no one was ever fool enough to try beating Judge Randall. But if you think it would help, I can do some research. Find out how to go about running a successful campaign.''

Susannah felt a lift of spirit. She smiled her appreciation. "Thanks, Jill. I can't tell you what that vote of confidence does for me, but I won't let you do it, of course. I keep you more than busy during the day. You need your evenings and weekends just to go out and be young. I'm not about to encroach upon them.''

"Well, it's not as if I have anything fun to do," Jill said quietly, and Susannah was once more aware of the shadow of unhappiness she had seen before. It lay very near the surface and now darkened the clear blue of the young woman's eyes. She reached out to turn Jill around so she could look directly into the unhappy face.

"Something's worrying you, isn't it?"

For a moment a look of wariness masked the unhappiness in the eyes, and then a tear welled up and spilled over.

"It's just that . . . Oh, I know something really awful has—" Jill's voice broke on a sob, and Susannah took her into comforting arms and let the held-back tears pour out on her blue linen shoulder. After a minute Jill pulled away and reached for the box of tissues on the desk.

"Someone you care about, Jill?" asked Susannah gently.

Jill nodded, her eyes red rimmed. "A . . . lot," she said reluctantly, as if it were an admission she hardly dared make.

Susannah waited for her to go on.

"I didn't know how much until he was gone," Jill said woefully after a moment. "He wrote at first, but then I didn't hear for a long time. The last letter I wrote came back this morning unclaimed."

Susannah's breath caught in sympathy. "I think I know how you feel," she said, sensing that to ask more would frighten her secretary back into her shell. Even so, Jill seemed about to take off, the evidence of her outburst still marking her face, but she was stopped by Susannah, who motioned toward the judicial washroom.

"If you'd like to repair the damage, be my guest," she suggested, and was rewarded with a look of thanks.

Jill returned shortly, her face washed, her smeared makeup replaced with a skillful hand. Except for a quick, shame-faced grin cast at Susannah as she came back into the room and a bit of pink puffiness around her eyes, she gave no sign anything unusual had occurred.

"I know some people who have run successful campaigns in River County, and I'm going to hunt them up tonight," she volunteered, as if the election campaign had been the last thing they had talked about before her exit.

Susannah recognized that the gradual transition that had been taking place in their relationship since the trial began had reached a new plateau in the last ten minutes. This time she did not demur.

"And if you'll forgive my saying so, you'd better tell your father flat-out that what works for him in the city would be the kiss of death for you up here in tomato country," Jill went on briskly, the voice of efficiency once more. She headed toward the reception room, but when she reached the door she turned back.

"Listen," she said tensely. "If these River County yahoos turn you out at election time, they don't deserve you..." Curiously, her voice seemed to leave the sentence unfinished.

Then, after a long moment, she added the last word: "...Susannah."

CHAPTER FIVE

BREAKFAST WAS Dan Sullivan's favorite meal of the day—a hangover from his boyhood and a mother's firm conviction that her men and boys would never make it to noon without a good farm breakfast under their belts. Quentin's Café in Cacheton served buckwheat cakes and country sausage almost as good as his mother's. And better coffee, thought Sullivan disloyally as he stepped into the small Main Street eatery to fortify himself for the fourth day of the Minerva trial.

His hope to take a booth to himself by the window and read the morning paper with his breakfast, lingering on until it was time for court, was quickly dashed when he saw all booths were occupied. The only free place was a single seat at the counter, and he hurried to take it while it was still his to take.

"Cacheton wives must be on strike against making breakfasts today," he observed amiably to no one in particular as he slipped into the vacant counter seat between two men—both strangers—who looked up from their newspapers at his approach and grinned in agreement.

Sullivan ordered, folded his newspaper into a four-column rectangle to make it more manageable in the crowded quarter and began to read, sipping gingerly at the scalding coffee the waitress had poured for him

the moment he sat down. He glanced up in acknowl-
edgement when one of the customers beside him said
something about going back to the salt mines and left.
When no one seized on the empty place immediately,
Sullivan unwittingly let his paper encroach on the extra space.

"Excuse me," said a crisp voice behind him. "Are
you saving this seat for someone?" Not waiting to
look around, Sullivan began gathering in his newspaper, sorry to lose the space. It was a woman's voice.
The faint suggestion of fragrance was a woman's, too.

"Why, Mr. Sullivan, I didn't see who it was." The
voice was the same, but its crispness had given way to
a less challenging tone. Hearing his own name, he
glanced up. He'd seen the face before, but he couldn't
place it. The young woman seemed to know him, and
he owed her some form of apology for letting the paper slop all over the counter.

"In spite of appearances, I don't actually own the
counter," he said in apology, still trying to remember
where he had seen the woman before. And then he
knew. She was Susannah's secretary—the awesomely
efficient-appearing chatelaine of the judicial reception room. Out of her own domain she appeared considerably more approachable than up there on the
third floor of the courthouse.

"Won't you please join me?"

"Thank you," she said politely. It required a small
step up and a bit of strength to accommodate her
small, compactly shaped body to the high stool. Sullivan was surprised to see that she was much shorter
than her straight-shouldered, chin-up posture behind
the reception counter had led him to think. Settled in
her seat, she turned on him an uneasy smile, and for

the first time Sullivan realized that without the mask of reserve there was something winsome about the young woman—winsome and uniquely appealing. He saw too that underneath the overlay of assurance, the briskly competent secretary was really shy. Though physically they were totally unalike, there was something about her that reminded him of the young Susannah—something he couldn't get a hold on, but it got to him. Though his breakfast had still to arrive, he folded the newspaper into a newsboy-roll and crammed it into the pocket of his suit coat.

"Would you mind starting out by telling me your name?" he said with a smile for the look of uncertainty he saw on her face. "Well, you know mine, and if it will lend propriety to your telling me, I know you in the same way you know me—from the Superior Court office where you hold forth. What kind of conversation are we going to have if you call me Mr. Sullivan and I have to address you as 'Hey'?"

Her face loosened in a pleased smile. "I'm Jill Fitzgerald. Friends call me Jill." But she'd hardly said the words before her face turned serious again, her manner polite and reserved. "Please don't let me interrupt your reading."

"The paper's a poor substitute for talk. I was just checking out the sports page to see if The Woodsman has any recommendations on trout fishing in the Sierra around here. Unfortunately, anything that makes his column will be overrun."

The waitress arrived with his coffee and eggs and side order of bacon, took Jill's order for coffee and a prune Danish and was back with it in a minute.

When the waitress moved off again, Jill turned back to Sullivan and asked casually, "You are a trout fisherman, Mr. Sullivan?"

He detected an underlying note of hesitance, yet the question seemed eagerly asked. His curiosity was whetted.

"Of sorts," he said modestly. "I've done it all my life but have never fished the Sierra streams this far north. I thought I might try it while I'm here in the neighborhood. That is, if I can find someone to advise me on where to go."

"You're thinking about fishing this weekend?"

"If I find a good place to go."

Jill Fitzgerald's conversational well seemed to dry up after that. Sullivan threw out a few leaders, but the young woman didn't pick up on them for more than the few words politeness demanded. About to give up, Sullivan was wondering if he would offend her if he went back to reading his paper when she took a long swallow of coffee and turned to him again, having clearly come to a decision.

"What do you want to catch? Big fish? Quarter pounders and up? Or would you be satisfied with a limit of eight or ten inchers?"

"Would I!" exclaimed Sullivan. "Tell me more, *wunderkind*."

"The stream is about an hour into the mountains from here on the highway and another half an hour on a logging road that's full of chuckholes, but passable," Jill said. "Patch Creek. It's one of the prettiest streams in this part of the Sierra, and it's hardly fished at all. You can go up there early in the season like this and not run into another soul."

"How come?"

"Oh, there are lots of reasons. They don't stock Patch Creek, for one. Wild fish aren't all that easy to catch. Any fish larger than ten inches has been around so long it's too wily to be caught. Besides, you can only use flies—no bait, so the people who want to come home with a creel full of fish, or one they can mount on the wall, don't bother with it. There are too many streams planted with big fish you can go after with worms or grasshoppers and spinners. Baseball bats, for all I know."

"You talk like a fisherwoman," Sullivan remarked.

"Well, I'm not," said Jill flatly, "but I know Patch Creek. I used to take my camera up there and take pictures."

"Oh, *well*!" said Sullivan, deflated as he saw the fishing stream he had always dreamed about vanish into thin air. There was no way he could have managed to keep the sound of his disappointment out of his voice. He saw the chin rise and the blue eyes flash defensively, and he was sorry. But "take pictures," for God's sake!

"Look, Mr. Sullivan, I'm sorry I got into this." She was the straight-backed secretary again, her eyes as distant as the sky. "A boy...a man now...you can call him my brother if you like...we grew up under the same roof, and I guess even now he still thinks of me as his little sister..." She came to what was obviously a horrified halt. "Oh, my gosh, never mind. I don't know why I'm rattling on like this." She turned her head away, and as she picked up her coffee cup Sullivan saw her hand tremble slightly, and he knew she was near tears.

"You were just about to tell me where I can find the kind of trout stream I've been looking for all my life, and I'm not going to let you get away from me, Jill Fitzgerald, until you do," he said. "I apologize for not giving picture taking its due. It's evident that people who fish are not the only ones who know where to go to catch them. Now, are you going to tell me how to get to this Patch Creek, or are you going to make me get down on my knees and beg for directions?"

She turned to look at him again, and though a shadow of unwillingness lingered in the round blue eyes, her mouth struggled against a smile and lost. In the end she gave in to a reluctant laugh.

"I suppose what I said wouldn't exactly inspire confidence in my advice on fishing streams, but trust me. I've tagged along with an expert too many years not to know where the best ones are. He brought home enough fish to feed the whole family two or three times a week during the season. He let me go with him sometimes, because I like to do pictures of the mountains and the wildlife."

"I'm surprised you never learned to fish."

The small turned-up nose wrinkled fastidiously. "I tried it a few times, but I hated the thought of actually catching them."

Sullivan chuckled. "Did you ever catch one?"

"No. I lucked out." She finished the last bite of the Danish with a swallow of coffee and extended her feet to the floor in a move to leave. "I have to go, but if you'd really like to try Patch Creek, I'll draw a map for you."

"I'd appreciate that," Sullivan said.

She was on her feet now, fumbling in her wallet for money, which she placed on the counter with her check. Sullivan knew instinctively that an offer from him to pay her bill would not be well received. She seemed about to go, but after a moment's hesitation, she turned back.

"You think you might be going this weekend?"

"By all means. Saturday. If I can find some level ground to park the sports wagon, I'll probably camp."

"No problem," Jill assured him. "I'll draw you a map. Come by the office to pick it up, and I'll explain it all to you."

Nice kid! thought Sullivan as he watched her go. She made it sound almost as if he were doing her a favor by choosing to go to her fishing place. It was hard, somehow, to reconcile the bright, friendly youngster who had seemed inexplicably pleased with herself as she walked away with the model of aloof competence who presided over the judicial reception room.

IN THE JUDGE'S CHAMBERS Susannah was going over the transcript from the previous day in court when Jill's familiar light tap sounded on the door to the reception room.

"Come in, Jill," she called out, welcoming her with a smile as the door opened and the trim, round figure of her secretary appeared.

"Do you have a minute to talk about the election?" asked Jill.

Susannah gave a groan of resignation. "No. But I guess I'd better start *making* minutes."

"Would it make you feel better if I told you Jack Kramer has promised to start getting a campaign organized for you?"

A terrible feeling of helplessness engulfed Susannah—a feeling of inadequacy. She didn't even know who Jack Kramer was! She'd been in Cacheton five months, and she'd gone at everything wrong. She'd been so determined to prove herself to the people of River County, she hadn't taken the time to learn who the people were. When she was not in there on the bench, she'd closed herself in her chambers during the day, steeping herself in the law. And every night she'd gone home with an armload of books and papers she plugged away at until she fell asleep. Except for the people who worked in the courthouse, she didn't know more than a handful of others by name.

Even her own secretary! What did she know about Jill? That her parents had died when she was a child. That she'd lived with a River County farm family until she finished school and went to work for Judge Randall. That she now had an apartment of her own. Nothing more. Except for the recent hint that deep within, Jill suffered hidden pangs of unrequited love.

Her own secretary! Not that Jill had given her any encouragement to ask questions until the last few days. On the other hand, Susannah admitted, hadn't the thought that she didn't have time to listen to long answers kept her from asking the questions?

She suddenly felt deeply disturbed that she could have been so self-assured in her determination to be accepted for her capabilities as a judge that she hadn't made any effort in five months to get acquainted with anyone.

"I'm sorry, Jill," she said, and felt the color rising to her cheeks in embarrassment.

"Sorry?"

"I guess I should know who this Jack Kramer is, but I don't."

Jill stared at her a moment, as if in disbelief.

"It has just occurred to me that I haven't earned the right to ask you for your help in getting me elected," Susannah went on with a new sense of humility. "In the almost half a year I've been here, not once have I made an effort to get to know someone or something outside the court. Come right down to it, although you're the one person in Cacheton I can count on, the only one I can think of as my friend, I don't even know that much about you."

"Well, don't blame yourself for that," Jill said after a moment, color rising to her face now. "It's not you. I wasn't . . . particularly friendly. I would have resented anyone who tried to replace the old judge, I suppose, but when you turned out to be a woman…one who doesn't look any older than me…" With a shame-faced grin, she let her voice trail off. Then she added quietly, "I owe everything I am or ever will be to Judge Randall."

"Would it bother you if I asked why?" Susannah said cautiously.

Jill hesitated. "No," she replied thoughtfully, as if somehow the fact it wouldn't surprised her. "My folks . . . I suppose you might call them hippies or bohemians or free-wheeling artists. They made jewelry and leather goods they sold on the streets in cities, and my father would set up an easel and do pastels of people who passed by. We lived in a bus and moved a lot. . . ." Her brows furrowed as if she were trying to remember. Susannah waited, afraid a word from her would shut off the flow.

"I don't remember…I was seven or eight and some of it's not very clear," she began again. "It was all pretty casual. Like the day the truck hit the bus on the freeway. It seems we'd been staying at the campground outside of Cacheton all summer, and my parents had left me with some people in the campground and gone to San Francisco to sell what they'd made, when the truck hit them.''

Again Susannah waited. After a moment Jill gave a shake of her head and clearly brought her mind back to Susannah.

''I don't remember things very clearly after that,'' Jill said apologetically. ''I just know I ended up in River County's detention home.''

Susannah swallowed a rising gasp, but her dismay did not go unnoticed by Jill.

''Well, if it was up to you, what else is there to do with an eight-year-old orphan or a run-away, or a kid who's been abandoned?'' Jill said matter-of-factly. ''You can't turn her out on the streets or put her in Juvenile Hall with kids who do dope or are in there for real crimes.''

Though she knew there'd been no other choice, the knowledge did not abate Susannah's feeling of regret that such a practice had been applied to a young Jill.

''I'm sorry,'' she said again. It was all she could find to say.

''Don't be,'' Jill told her, and Susannah could hear no sound of self-pity in her voice. ''It was one of the luckiest days of my life. They brought me before Judge Randall. His daughter, Lucille, who already had three kids of her own, took me into her home. That's where I lived for the next twelve years, like a real member of their family. When I finished secretarial school I went to work for the old judge. I have my own apartment now, but I always think of the Kramers' farm as my home.''

Susannah picked up on the name. "Kramer? Is that who Jack Kramer is . . . Judge Randall's son-in-law?"

Jill nodded. "Jack farms several hundred acres to the north of town, but he gets involved in local politics when there's a candidate or an issue he really cares about. Jack would be just the right person to manage your election campaign, and when I asked him last night he said he'd be glad to."

"But he doesn't even know me," Susannah said doubtfully.

"But *I* do, Your Ho—" Jill began and broke off, her face flushed. After a moment, as if the syllables lay on her tongue, wanting to be let out, she corrected herself in an embarrassed fluster. ". . . Susannah."

THERE WAS A SPRING in Dan Sullivan's step as he walked in to take his seat at the plaintiff's table that morning, and the assurance in his bearing was that of a man in control. Yesterday he had been forced to admit that these daily encounters with Susannah were slowly breaking down the inner wall that had closed her out of his mind for the past ten years. He'd realized then it was high time he made up his mind just what direction he wanted to take and take it.

Driving out into the country, he'd hiked the foothills, scaring up an occasional rabbit or a covey of quail until darkness and a good, healthy physical tiredness overtook him. Later, after a shower at his motel and a scotch-and-water and hearty meal at Quentin's Café, he returned to the motel and was asleep almost as soon as he turned out the light. The long hike had brought him back to reality. Any future relationship they might foolishly try to work out together would demand more sacrifices than either of them would be willing to make.

The Susannah he had once loved was gone forever, replaced by Judge Ross up there on the bench. From now on he would not let himself forget it. Once this trial was behind him, he would go back to Fresno and the firm of Curtis & Sullivan. He'd ask the new law-yer in the Fresno County D.A.'s office—Helen some-thing, he thought—to have dinner with him, or Donna Prince at the bank, or Judy Harris maybe. Someone, anyhow. Now that he understood it was the shadow of Susannah that had stood between him and other women, he'd find a way to exorcise the old ghost.

It was just a matter of toughing it through the trial, and if he spent the days he wasn't in court fishing Patch Creek in the Sierra, he wouldn't be obliged to make the trip to Fresno weekends to avoid running into Susannah in this small town. For the first time since Susannah had made her unwelcome appearance in his life, Sullivan felt on top of things.

Or so it was until the voice of the bailiff announced across the courtroom, "The Superior Court of River County, California is now in session, the Honorable Judge Susannah Ross presiding." The muscles across Sullivan's abdomen tensed as the door to the cham-bers opened and Susannah entered and walked across to the dais, the flowing black gown that hid the woman giving delicious hints of the splendid body beneath.

And as he watched her, his heart remembered, and he was shaken with a helpless kind of rage. Who did he think he was kidding?

He'd be willing to risk almost anything just to see her alone again, but he knew he wouldn't. There was nothing ahead for them. He'd play by the rules and see her only in court, and when the blasted trial was over he'd be off.

The *real* reality, he thought, the irony of it bitter in his heart, was that she was a part of him and would always be, yet they'd both built lives away from each other that seemed almost designed to keep them apart.

EACH TIME SUSANNAH ENTERED the courtroom since that traumatic moment three days earlier when she had first looked down to see Dan Sullivan in her court, she had steeled herself against an uneasy feeling that if their eyes should ever meet she would lose herself and be unable to tear hers away. Even more disturbing was the certainty he could read in her eyes the sleepless nights she'd endured since he'd invaded her domain and would know what put the shadows there. He would know that she buried herself in work every night until she was sure nothing could keep her awake, only to have him appear like an old movie when she turned out the light and tried to sleep.

For three nights now, their past and present had reeled through her wakeful hours, mixed with new scenarios of her own making for a future that would include Sullivan. Nothing so contrived as Jill's flat-tire scheme. Feasible scenarios over which one or the other of them had control. Scenarios in which Dan would charge into her chambers when verdict and judgment had been rendered and demand that they talk, or in which she would send a message asking him to come to her at the end of the trial.

It was easy enough to imagine the meetings, the forgivings, the delicious rendezvous of love. But what then? The bottom line was *nothing*. A dead-end street.

In her role of judge, she had found fulfillment for the first time in her life. Once tasted, it wasn't something she could voluntarily give up. If she lost the election she would look for another career where she might find similar personal rewards. It wasn't something she'd find waiting for her in Fresno. There she'd be Dan Sullivan's satellite, no matter what she did.

As for the possibility that Dan might be willing to give up his law office in Fresno and start a practice in Cacheton, it just wasn't there. As an attorney in a county where she was the only judge, he would be hopelessly handicapped—hardly a solid premise on which to rebuild a relationship.

So went the waking hours of nights that ended in the same single, early-morning resolution: quit dreaming of post-trial meetings with Dan Sullivan and put her mind to winning the judicial election ahead.

Now, this fourth morning of the crop-dusting trial, she did not let her glance fall upon Sullivan until she was seated on the dais, where the judicial furnishings gave her an illusory sense of control. When at last she let his face come into her line of vision, she was both relieved and disappointed to find him looking down at a file in his hand, his eyes hidden by thick sandy lashes.

Thus began a court day marked by a singular lack of legal pyrotechnics as Sullivan put on technical witnesses one after another to testify to matters ranging from wind speed and thermometer readings during the morning of the fateful day to soil conditions of the field and the season's tomato prices per ton. Corwin seemed to have lost his zeal for cross-examination, dismissing them one at a time with no more than a few cursory questions. To Susannah's relief, both attorneys had given up their game of baiting the judge.

As was her practice, Susannah stayed on in chambers after the court adjourned for the day. The first hours of the following morning would be given over to domestic court and matters that had nothing to do with the trial. Jill had put on her desk papers she would need to look over in preparation for the cases she would hear. She began with the one that troubled her most—a settlement conference involving two otherwise apparently agreeable young people bent on destroying each other and their three children in a bitter divorce and custody fight. No matter which way her decision went, in the end the children were bound to lose, and the knowledge of it depressed her immeasurably.

It was the kind of proceedings that normally required no more than a brief survey of the material in advance, but it was two hours later before she put down the file. She wasn't quite sure why it held her. Leaning back in her chair, she closed her eyes. The counseling required by law in cases where child custody was involved obviously hadn't accomplished a reconciliation. Nevertheless, after reading the full report of the counselor, she had a gut feeling that neither husband nor wife really *wanted* a divorce. *If he/she really loved me.* It was like a theme running through the entire report.

If she really loved me, she wouldn't keep spending my money like it was going out of style. And *If he really loved me, he wouldn't be such a cheapskate.... If he really loved me, he'd want me to know how much money he makes.*

Love equated to money.

The fact was, if this couple expected to maintain their present standard of living, they couldn't afford a divorce, she thought wearily. The old foolishness about two living as cheaply as one applied only if they lived together, understood the conditions and the ground rules and were both equally committed to making the relationship work.

If he really loved me. If he really loved me. Like an old refrain, the words kept drifting back into her mind.

She rose from her chair and stretched her arms to relieve taut muscles, resolved to advise the husband and wife and their attorneys when they came into her chambers for the conference in the morning to postpone the proceedings until the couple had talked over their problems with a financial adviser—someone who might make them see they were on a collision course with realities neither of them really wanted to meet.

Preparing to leave, she paused in the midst of tucking the file into her briefcase for another reading—her usual practice to make sure she hadn't misinterpreted anything—and gave in to a cavernous yawn. Thank goodness she'd closed all thought of any future involvement with Dan Sullivan out of her mind once and for all. Maybe now she could get some sleep.

The day had left her drained. Her arms loaded with enough papers and books to keep her awake all night, she walked down the deserted corridor to the elevator, empty-minded, blind to everything on either side. Noting she had the elevator to herself when its doors opened, she stepped in and was reaching out from her load to press the button for the ground floor when she saw Sullivan emerge from the law library halfway down the hall and come striding in her direction.

The first glad leap of her pulse quieted and she knew that the last thing she was ready to handle was a sterile encounter with this man she had once loved. The strains of the day had left her too vulnerable. In her haste to reach the button that would immediately close the door, a book slipped from under her arm and dislodged the rest, spilling them on the floor. She stared down in dismay, paralyzed for a moment by ridiculous indecision. Should she take time to pick up the books or... She was astonished to find herself teetering on the dangerous edge of a giggle. She hunkered down to retrieve what she had dropped.

And then he was there. Towering over her. The eyes she had managed to avoid in court captured hers, and what she had feared was true: she could not pull herself free.

"Go away," she said weakly.

He pushed a button and the doors closed. He reached down and lifted her to her feet, gathering her into his arms. Her will to protest was lost.

Dan! a voice inside her cried out silently. Oh God, it had been so long. It was as if she had at last come home. She reveled in the prickle of his coat fabric against her cheek, in his clean, natural smell. Just under her ear she heard the hard, excited beat of his heart and, without willing it, pressed herself closer to his long, hard body. This was where she belonged.

But the sweet sensation could not put to sleep an underlying sense of hopelessness that brought tears to her eyes. When he held her away from him to look again into her face, they spilled over and rolled down her cheeks. With his forefinger, Sullivan wiped them away and pulled her to him again, taking her mouth in a deep, urgent kiss, as if to cancel all the lost time that lay between them. Completely disarmed, Susannah gave with all the passion of a long-deprived heart. Lost was any sense of time or place. For the moment she knew only the sensual pleasure of his caressing tongue and the fluid heat of longing deep within her.

Then with no more warning than a slight, unexpected stiffening of his body that barely touched her consciousness, he withdrew and let her go.

Unprepared, Susannah watched in dazed bewilderment as he turned abruptly away and without looking back made for the control panel of the elevator. The doors parted. Swaying slightly in a kind of paralysis of shock, Susannah watched him go. Somehow it didn't strike her as surprising that the elevator was still on the top floor, except to wonder absently what magic Sullivan had used to hold it there. It seemed an eternity had passed since she had seen him hurrying down that same corridor to catch her in the elevator. She watched him set off determinedly with that same long, urgent stride and accepted the harsh reality that this time he was hurrying to get away. While he was still within sight, she pressed the Down button and the door closed off the sight of his departing back.

Not until the elevator carried her down and away from him did she realize that except for the first moment, when she told him to go away, not a single word had been exchanged during the time they were together. She wondered wryly what the California Commission on Judicial Performance would say to that.

WHEN JILL FITZGERALD entered the judge's chambers from the reception room after court adjournment Friday afternoon, she found Susannah still in her black robe, slumped in her desk chair, staring disconsolately off into space. Jill cleared her throat, and Susannah gave a start, swiveling her chair to face her secretary.

Straightening her shoulders, she asked with a sheepish smile, "Would you believe I'm planning my campaign strategy?"

"No," said Jill candidly.

"Well, you're right," Susannah admitted with a sigh, "but that doesn't mean I'm not going to. Beginning this weekend. Starting tomorrow morning, I'm going to ring doorbells and kiss babies and pat dogs on the head."

"No you're not," said Jill.

Susannah raised her eyebrows in surprise. "That's the trouble with the help nowadays. You give them an inch, and they take a mile! But seriously, Jill, it's about time I get out and meet people. Or are you trying to tell me I'd be wasting my time?"

"What I'm trying to tell you is that it's about time you take a weekend off from being the judge, Susannah. I've been watching you for five months now, and I know from the work you bring in to be typed up on Monday mornings that you've been at the job every weekend since you were sworn in. If you keep that up, you're going to... to *congeal*!"

Congeal? In spite of herself, Susannah had to smile. The word was so apt. It exactly described what she'd suspected was happening to her. Jill was absolutely right. If she could just get through this trial and then the election...

"I appreciate your concern, and I'm *listening*. I really am! But my dad's right. If I don't get going on a campaign I'm not going to have this judgeship to

congeal *into*. I can't afford to let another weekend slip
by without getting at it.''

"You don't have to worry about that," Jill assured
her. "Remember, I told you how much the Kramers
love to be in the middle of an election campaign.
When I told them you could use their help, they
couldn't wait. To begin with, they've got a big barn
dance planned out at the farm for a week from Friday
night—a kind of meet-the-judge night. Everybody
that everybody else in the county listens to will be
there. That's the time and place to start your campaign.''

Susannah gazed at her in astonishment.

"So since you don't have to ring doorbells, you have
the weekend ahead of you to do whatever you like,"
Jill announced with a self-satisfied smile.

After a moment's thought, Susannah said without
enthusiasm, "I suppose I could drive to the city and
see my father. I'm going to have to talk to him about
all this one of these days.''

"I suppose," agreed Jill. "Unless maybe you think
you'd rather go fishing.''

"Fishing?" ... *crazy, self-indulgent, small rebellion?* Susannah's spirit was suddenly alive. This was a
found weekend! Why not?

She hesitated a moment longer. "I wouldn't know
where to go," she admitted with reluctance.

"Of course not, but I do," said Jill. "I'll draw you
a map.''

CHAPTER SIX

MONEY!

Like the aftertaste of a heavy condiment, the word insinuated itself into Susannah's mind next morning as her small car climbed the timbered mountain road toward Patch Creek in the high Sierra. Maybe not the root of *all* evil, she decided, but in the case of the couple currently at war in her court it was.

And wasn't it money, after all, that had caused the break between her and Dan ten years before? A lot of money dangled in front of Dan's nose by one of San Francisco's top law firms to which he had risen like a trout to a fly. She was shocked at the echo of bitterness that whispered through her like an old ghost. She'd never dreamed she still harbored resentment and was disturbed to have it come oozing from some dim recess of her mind. Had she learned so little in the interim that she could still hold a grudge over something that had happened ten years ago? More to the point, had her resentment even really been justified?

It wasn't as if she hadn't understood the tenuous nature of the storefront practice she and Dan had shared. They'd talked often enough about careers they expected to pursue in the "real world" in some vague, not fully realized future time. Why then, when Dan actually went for it, had she felt betrayed?

She looked back fondly on those first twelve months they had lived together. It had been a kind of never-never land, where every collected fee was a cause for celebration; where the practice was to put all money into a common pot from which either dipped when in need of funds—if there was any money in it, which wasn't always the case.

Even then, money *per se* hadn't mattered. When the pot was empty, they took the austerity route until something came in. In those days, an empty pot was an inconvenience—not a cause for a big to-do.

Which was why she had been so stunned when Dan announced he'd taken a job with the law firm of Bradley & Hammer and mentioned a starting salary hard to believe. The communal kitty could hardly serve with so much money coming in. It would have to go, he said. They would open a joint bank account in its place.

In retrospect, she hadn't handled the suggestion well, she thought. Maybe if he had let it go at that—if he hadn't in the next breath shown her a chauvinistic side he'd never let her see before—maybe she could have done better. He needn't have tried to play Daddy Warbucks with her. He didn't have to tell the little girl she didn't have to worry about the expenses anymore. Big Dan Sullivan would pay them all!

And he wasn't talking merely about the apartment they lived in together. *That* point she might have argued without getting so mad. The real put-down was his proposal to pay the secretary's salary and rental for the storefront office—though he, of course, would no longer be availing himself of either. And to top it off, he had rubbed salt in the wound by pointing out that without him, the income from the law practice was hardly enough to get by on.

The arrogant bastard! she murmured aloud with a stir of the old anger.

But if the years had done nothing else for Susannah, they had mellowed her. Her anger was only a wisp of what it had been at the time. Her memory quickly passed over the racking quarrel that had sent him storming out into the night and moved on to the solace of forgiving and champagne and passion later that same night when he came back.

Nor could she bring herself to recall the devastating rows and tenuous reconciliations in the embattled months that followed before the last big blowup put an end to it all.

Dan Sullivan—male chauvinist, money lover! Not the kind of man she wanted back in her life.

But somehow the indictment no longer seemed to fit. Unexpectedly her mind opened up to a new probability that had been closed out before.

It suddenly seemed possible that those outrageous proposals had sprung not from chauvinistic arrogance but from real concern for her and a determination to set things right. From Dan's own experience he'd known how impossible it would be for a person alone to make it in that storefront office without someone sharing the overhead.

She wondered if she hadn't unfairly blamed Dan all these years for keeping the money thing going. Might not her own demands for endless, picky accountings have had something to do with keeping their disagreement alive; her brooding resistance to even so small a thing as his dropping in a token on the bus for her.

Come to think of it, had money really been what their breakup was all about? Wasn't it just an accumulation of petty things that grew like a snowball into something bigger than money and had a lot to do with pride? Without volition, her fingers curled into two tight fists around the steering wheel.

He might at least have told her he'd been offered the spot with Bradley & Hammer before he took the job. She was dismayed at how much it still hurt that he had shut her out.

She almost missed the graveled logging road where it branched into the highway to the left. Halfway across the intersection she braked the car to a stop and looked at the map Jill had drawn, confirming her location. She backed the car to turn off into the graveled road and adjusted her speed to its uneven surface.

Underway, she rolled down her window and breathed in the fragrance of fir and pine and the fresh earthy smell of raw, red dirt from the embankments through which the road had been cut. Mountain smells laced with the spring scent of wild lilac, which turned the slopes blue with misty bloom, and the sweet, orange-blossom essence of white syringa, which hung heavily on the air around the occasional spot where one of the bushes chose to take hold....

A golden squirrel scampered across the road in front of her car and then another and another in a never-ending death-defying chase. She welcomed the distraction of their antics as she drove along. It was like watching a teenager's game of "chicken," she thought, as one saucy creature perched on a roadside rock ahead as if waiting for her car to reach some point of maximum allowable danger before darting under the very shadow of its wheels.

The narrow road snaked its way along heavily timbered slopes in a series of switchbacks, climbing steeply now. Far below she caught an occasional glimpse of a meandering stream she guessed to be the lower waters of Patch Creek. She dared not let her eye follow it. An able and confident driver on freeways, she had never been alone before on a mountain road and found the experience unnerving.

Giving full attention to the maze of potholes that pocked the road, she almost didn't see a flash of movement in the brush at the top of the sheared-off embankment on one side a short distance ahead. Her foot came down on the brake more from instinct than from judgment. An instant later, a spotted fawn came sliding down the almost perpendicular slope into the road bed directly in the path of her moving car. By the time she'd brought it to a full stop, the infant deer had come to a wobbly halt in the road's center less than fifty yards beyond.

Susannah sat watching the pretty creature, enchanted, and waited for it to move on so she could pass. When, after a few moments, it appeared evident it was in no hurry to do so, she honked her horn. When the animal still didn't budge, she turned off her motor and stepped out onto the roadway, hoping the sight of her would frighten the young thing on its way. For good measure, she slammed the door with a resounding bang as she went.

"Go home to your mama, Bambi," she called out. "You're much too young to be out in the woods on your own."

The liquid brown Disneyesque eyes stared back at her unblinkingly. She clapped her hands and yelled,

"Shoo!" and then "Scat!", and then, with a feeling of desperation, "Scram!"

The little fellow looked no more than a day old and bewildered, she thought, wondering if an accident to the mother had left it orphaned. If she could be sure the mother wasn't lurking somewhere on guard, she would simply walk over, pick up the fawn and set it down in the safety of the woods alongside the road. Her approach might even scare it into taking off on its own before she reached it. But tales of how deadly a doe mother could be when its fawn was threatened flashed a warning to her mind and in the end decided her against risking a rescue.

Except for her own car, the logging road seemed utterly deserted. There seemed little chance, if she left it there, of a car rounding the curve up ahead and hitting the animal before it moved on, she thought—providing she could inch around the fawn with her car, which she seriously doubted.

A moment's survey confirmed her fears. There was passing room on only one side—a rocky, deeply rutted shoulder that extended beyond the edge of the road and would present more challenge than she was prepared for, even if her car was equipped with a four-wheel drive. As it was, there was no way she could get it over the rugged terrain without hanging up on a rock. Moreover, she knew it wasn't in her to go off and leave the helpless fawn in the middle of the road, traffic or no traffic.

She took a tentative step in the direction of the small creature, and a sound came to her ears. As a bird dog lifts its nose to the scent of game, she turned her head to listen. A spurt of panic surged through her. It was the unmistakable engine whine of some large, powerful vehicle changing gears. It sounded close—no farther away than around the next curve, perhaps, and coming fast.

All thought forgotten of a protective mother deer lurking in the roadside brush, Susannah took off in a run to grab the fawn. It seemed to sense she was coming after it and with sudden coyness began to move backward in a quick little dance step down the center of the road away from her. Then, with still half the original distance between them for her to cover, an ominous crashing in the underbrush at the top of the bank on the far side of the road caught Susannah's ear.

Turning her head apprehensively, she caught a glimpse of a big dun-colored doe breaking through the thick growth of manzanita that fringed the top. It took off in a fearless leap and seconds later landed halfway down the steep embankment on the way to where Susannah stood frozen, her body gripped by a sudden, nightmarish paralysis.

She watched the powerful legs in helpless indecision, knowing they could not only outrun her but batter her to ruin as well. Quickly she weighed her situation. Would it be better to take her chances on a frontal attack or risk being hit from the back by those piston-like feet as she made a run for her car. The thought of being knocked down from behind was not a pretty one.

Then, unexpectedly, she suddenly felt relaxed. Common sense told her that even if she had begun to run when she first saw the doe come leaping out of the brush she could never get to the car and inside before the creature was upon her. It would be better to stand her ground and keep her eyes on it, she decided.

The enraged beast came inexorably on. Susannah's eyes darted around in search of some convenient weapon. Seeing nothing, she remembered the red windbreaker she wore. Swiftly she peeled it off. Maybe she could divert the animal by holding the garment spread wide open and off to the side in rough imitation of a bull fighter in the ring. With a lot of luck, she might even manage to drape it over the doe's head and cover the eyes. At best, a few seconds of blindness might confuse the animal long enough for her to get to the car. At worst, if it worked at all, it might serve as a distraction to gain her a few moments of time.

The bright jacket spread open in her hands, Susannah braced herself grimly.

FOR THE FIRST TIME since the morning he had walked into Susannah's court, Dan Sullivan felt at peace with himself. He had made a final decision to stay away from her except for their time in court, and he was firmly resolved to stick to it. Now, as if fate were rewarding him for what his every instinct told him to do, he'd had one of the finest mornings of fly fishing he could hope to enjoy.

Leaving Cacheton, he had headed into the Sierra before nightfall the previous evening, following the map Jill Fitzgerald had given him, with scant expectations. He'd decided on Patch Creek only because nothing better in fishing streams seemed to offer itself.

The sylvan beauty of the spot to which she'd directed him had come as no surprise when he reached it. After all, the young woman had frequented the place to take pictures. He'd assumed she appreciated the surroundings with an artist's eye, but that didn't necessarily mean it held anything for the fisherman.

The surprise was in the lazy little stream that meandered across the small, semicircular meadow where he stopped. It had looked so unpromising he had felt no immediate urge to put together his fishing rod and drop in a line. Instead, he had settled in and brewed a pot of coffee on the camp stove—noting it was nearly out of gas—and eaten a bite. His mind still teeming with the day in court, he'd smoked a pipe and mulled over ways to pull the Bancroft case out of the fire if the detective agency didn't turn up the missing pilot he needed to verify the crop duster's spray boom was leaky. By the time his thoughts turned to fishing it was nearly dark, and he'd rolled his sleeping bag out on the edge of the meadow. He slept late.

The first ray of sun had fingered through a mountain gap to touch the meadow that morning before he finally crossed over to the stream. Most fishermen would argue that the best fishing hours of the morning had already passed, but it was a tenet Dan didn't hold with, having learned from experience that fish bit or they didn't according to their own inclination and not the hour. Even so, he'd expected nothing from the meadow stream when he made that first practice cast. His fly had barely touched the water before it was snatched up by a beautiful little ten-inch native trout. The fight it put up sent his blood spurting briskly through his veins before he finally scooped it into his net.

Jill Fitzgerald had been right. Patch Creek was full of fish. The fact he seemed to have it to himself was no doubt due to the heavy coverage the press had been giving to a well-stocked lake and a much larger stream only a few miles away to the south.

Driving the Jeep down the mountain road two hours later, Sullivan reviewed the events of the morning with the deep feeling of contentment known only to a man who has just fished the stream he has dreamed about all his fishing life.

The meadow, which had proved to be a fisherman's delight, was merely the beginning. The real pleasure came when he left it a while later to explore the stream above and below the meadow. On both sides it cascaded down the mountainside in a long succession of riffles and pools from any one of which one or more trout would rise to his fly. All open, all accessible, he thought almost gloatingly. Free of the surrounding brush thickets that were the bane of fishermen of his ilk who refused to fish for trout on their bellies.

Though it was a stream to be savored he fished it sparingly, changing to barbless hooks from which he could release a trout safely without injury when he found out how good it was going to be. He believed in saving some of his limit to catch in the later hours.

Full of the morning's rewards, he was now on his way back down the logging road to get gas for the camp stove at a roadside store and gas station he remembered seeing on his way up, a few miles below the turnoff.

Patch Creek! It reminded him of a stream he had taken Susannah to when . . .

Susannah! Without warning, the way a slide appears on a screen, the image of Susannah popped before his mind. She was there but a moment, her body lovely and lithe, arm raised as she made ready to let her line carry a fly out and lay it gently on the water, the breeze riffling her hair. And then she was gone.

The euphoria of the moment before was lost as a terrible sense of bereavement washed over him. *God!* Did he really intend to go back to Fresno without *seeing* her? Walk out of her life for the second time? Surely he must be crazy. The old feeling was there as strong as ever. He wondered if she felt it, too.

A deep melancholy settled over him. He'd been over that ground a hundred times in the last few days and always came up with the same answer. There was no way. No way except to give up the law practice he'd spent ten years of his life building with Jerry in Fresno and settle for being Mr. Judge Ross in Cacheton. It was something he knew he couldn't do.

Any more than he could demean Susannah with the suggestion she retire as presiding judge of River County's Superior Court to become Mrs. Dan Sullivan in Fresno.

Stay away from her, Sullivan! There was no other answer. The fact the answer was always the same did nothing to restore the false contentment of the morning.

He drove on with a kind of gloomy detachment, hands wrapped tightly around the steering wheel, foot heavy on the gas, paying little attention to the passing scene until the machine rounded a wide curve in the road.

His foot drove down hard on the brake and his hand shot out and pressed steadily on the horn.

"Susannah! Good God!"

HER WHOLE BEING concentrated upon her oncoming attacker, Susannah braced herself as the angry doe bounded onto the roadway in a final leap then came to a sudden, unexpected stop a short distance away. Was it the jacket? Susannah wondered, and held it farther away from her, waggling it shakily at the deer.

Focused solely on the problem at hand, her mind failed to register the horn that had set up a loud, continuous wail up ahead. Her attention never wavered from the female deer that pawed the ground, preparing to charge, as the solid bulk of the Jeep came skidding out of nowhere and across the rocky shoulder of the road beside her in precarious imbalance.

Cutting in between herself and the deer, the vehicle came to a halt beside Susannah in a shower of gravel. She stared at it in confusion and then the door flew open and the voice of the driver yelled for her to get in. Startled at last into action, she half scrambled, half fell into the wagon, which was already beginning to move.

Eyes closed, her body trembling from head to toe in its sudden release from tension, she felt the driver's arm cross over her and pull the door shut a second before she heard and felt the full weight of the crazed doe hit the side of the truck.

In a burst of power the wagon was on its way. Susannah clung to the seat where she had thrown herself, sagging like an abandoned doll.

"For such a smart person, that was a very stupid thing for you to do," the driver observed, his voice cracking on the words as he brought the wagon to a stop on the other side of the curve. Susannah's eyes flew open to stare at her rescuer.

"Oh, my God!" she murmured hoarsely. Slowly she sat up straight. "What are *you* doing here?"

"I might ask the same question of you," Sullivan said, "but let's go into that later. Right now, would you kindly tell me just what the hell you were doing out there in the middle of the road making like a matador to a very angry female deer?''

"It was the fawn...it wouldn't move...I thought it was an orphan," she said weakly, gazing at him in dismay. What was he so mad about, she thought crossly. His voice was so angry it shook.

Her own voice grew stronger as she took a stand in her own defense. "If I hadn't been 'making like a matador,' as you put it so snidely, you would have come barreling around that curve and crashed into the poor little thing."

"If I hadn't come 'barreling around that curve,' that doe would have made mincemeat of you, my dear. Want to bet there's a dent in the side of my truck that was meant for you? That might convince you what a no-win situation you were in when I came along."

At his words Susannah felt her body begin to tremble again. She was appalled to realize that if she tried to answer him she would most certainly cry. She turned her head away in silence and made no effort to defend herself further.

Staring through the windshield in front of him, Sullivan seemed to have run out of words. He took his hand from the wheel and ran his fingers through the thick thatch of hair in a gesture of helplessness. When his head turned in her direction, she quickly lowered her eyes.

He let out a long sigh. "Damnit, Susannah, you scared the livin' be-jayzus out of me," he said as if in apology for badgering her, though a trace of anger still lingered in the words. There was another moment of uneasy silence between them and then he reached for the key to start the engine. "We might as well get back to your car."

He maneuvered the sport truck into a turn that reversed its course and took the curve slowly as he scouted the lay of the land. There was no sign of the mother deer or the fawn. Susannah's car stood in the middle of the road where she had abandoned it. Sullivan pulled onto the rough shoulder off the roadway and got out to explore with his eyes the wooded slope below. In a moment he was back in.

"She's down there in the bushes all right, licking the fawn and looking a little bemused. It must have stunned the old girl a bit when she bounced off the wagon, but otherwise she doesn't look hurt."

Relieved, Susannah reached for the door handle to let herself out.

"Stay where you are," Sullivan commanded, and rather to her own surprise, she found no will to disobey. "You've had a shock. You may find you're a little shaky when you get out and try to stand." She watched languidly as he left the wagon and walked around to her side, standing back for a moment to survey where the doe had hit before reaching to open her door.

What now? she wondered in a half-hearted effort to rally her forces for resistance. Surely Dan wasn't going to escort her to her car and let her go on her way without a struggle.

On the other hand, maybe he was. After their bizarre midweek encounter in the elevator, she had prepared herself for new advances on Sullivan's part. She'd given more thought than it deserved to thwarting any future attempts to see her alone. And then he never made any. Now at the end of the week she was ashamed to find herself disgruntled that he hadn't so much as given it a try.

The door beside her swung open and he was there, hand extended to help her out. Perversely she bypassed the hand and planted her feet firmly on the ground, only to discover that her legs had turned to spaghetti. Involuntarily she grabbed for the arm she had snubbed a moment before and clung to it to steady herself.

"Whoa now! You're not ready yet to take off on your own," Dan said quietly. "Sit here a minute and give your body time to forget."

"I'm fine," she protested.

"Well, it won't hurt to humor me," he said. "You'd better give me your keys and let me move your car off to the side."

"Don't bother," she said dispiritedly. "It's all right." But to save argument she relinquished the keys and steadied herself against the open door as he walked away. After a moment she forced herself to look at the concave dent in the metal body of the truck where the doe had hit. It was shallow and about the size of a large frying pan. When she thought of the force that put it there and what it could have done to her, nausea rose in her throat.

It took Sullivan a minute or two to get her car tucked in close to the embankment, safely off the road. By the time he returned, Susannah's natural resilience had restored her to a nearly normal state. Still, though she didn't try to define why, she was in no hurry to move on. She leaned against the side of the vehicle and watched him come, soaking comfort from the sun-warmed metal through the cotton of her madras shirt and old blue jeans.

"You really didn't have to do that, you know," she said when he reached her side. "We seem to be the only people on this road today."

"That's how much *you* know," observed Sullivan.

"You have to admit it isn't exactly Market Street at Montgomery and Bush!"

"Spoken like a true city person. Which reminds me. What the devil are you doing here, anyhow?"

"That's *my* question. You may recall, I asked you first. What the devil are *you* doing here, Mr. Sullivan?"

"Aside from rescuing beautiful dames in distress?"

"Don't equivocate. That's not what you came for."

"Fact of the matter, I'm here to fish," Sullivan said. "I caught a limit on dry flies already this morning and let most of them back in the stream."

Something teased at Susannah's mind. "Patch Creek?"

"How did you know?"

A suspicion, too preposterous to accept, began to take shape in her head. "Where did you find out about Patch Creek?" she asked intently.

"Jill...the girl in your office. What's her name? She drew me a map...." His eyes widened in sudden comprehension. "Oh my God! Don't tell me I've been poaching on the judge's own private reserve?"

Susannah eyed him grimly for a moment. "Not mine. Jill's. She didn't tell me you..." she broke off, hesitating to say more. *Drat Jill Fitzgerald's romantic little hide! If I could just get my hands on her,* Susannah thought, *I'd wring her neck*. Meanwhile, she could hardly tell Dan that it was due entirely to Jill's moonbeam machinations that the two of them were here at the same time. It would mean confessing that she'd discussed their past relationship with her secretary.

Sullivan groaned. "For God's sake, Susannah, don't tell me it's against your judicial principles for us to fish Patch Creek at the same time! I'm not about to give up the best fishing I've had in—"

"Don't be silly," Susannah said crisply. "The creek is as much yours as mine. We don't both have to be on the same part of the stream at the same time."

Tight-lipped, Sullivan withdrew a coin from his pocket. "Heads or tails? Heads fishes below the meadow. Tails above."

She fought down a swell of disappointment. He wasn't even going to *try* to spend any more time alone with her than he had to! Not even in this remote spot they had all to themselves! Not now. Not ever.

"Very well," she said stiffly, and the coin was tossed. It was heads. Dan told her how to get to the meadow from the logging road, and then there was a long moment when there seemed to be nothing further to say.

Tension built between them. She could almost imagine she could hear it crackle in the air around them. There was a heaviness in her chest, and she knew there was nothing to be gained by staying on any longer. She moved away from the truck and started across the road to her own car, Dan following.

When they reached the other side, he said with a faint touch of sarcasm, "I trust this little rendezvous will not rest uneasily on your conscience, Judge."

Susannah refused to be baited. She opened her car door and stepped in, closing the door behind her and starting the car. About to go, she thrust her head out

the open window on sudden impulse to have the last
word.

"I told you. You didn't have to move the car. In all
the time we've been out here, not one single thing on
wheels has gone through."

Sullivan seemed about to reply, then raised his head
as if to listen. Susannah listened, too, and recognized
the powerful sound of a logging truck, its pitch alter-
ing with every change of the gears. Stacked high with
logs, the huge truck and trailer rounded the curve and
thundered past. And after it, even before the echo of
the first had died away, there came another, and then
another.

When they were all by, Sullivan leaned into the
window and grinned at her smugly. "You were saying, Judge...?"

Susannah slipped the car into gear and moved off,
leaving him standing alone in the road.

"Oh, shut up!" she muttered crossly. Something
pressed heavily upon her heart.

SULLIVAN STOOD at the edge of the road and watched
her drive off, more full of frustration than he'd ever
been in his life. Lost was the enchantment of the
morning, and for a moment he was sorry he hadn't
stayed up in the meadow and cooked his fish over a
campfire the way he had before he got spoiled with the
gas camp stove. Then the picture of Susannah, with no
better weapon than a red windbreaker, bracing herself against a frenzied deer, flashed across his mind,
and he thanked God he hadn't.

Seeing her there, he'd known in sudden revelation
that if she were lost to him, much of what was important to him in life would be lost, too. He'd weathered

their parting ten years before because something inside told him that as long as she was around, he'd find her when the time was right. Faced with the stunning fact she was in mortal danger, and without the foggiest notion how he was going to do it, he was off to save Susannah from the charging doe.

Now as he watched her car disappear around the curve, he felt much the same way. The same something inside was telling him this was that right time, and if he didn't seize it, it would be his last chance.

He had an impulse to turn the Jeep back around and head after her. But for what? In the end, he could offer her nothing.

He shook his head and ran his hand through his hair. Then with a helpless shrug of the shoulders he crossed the road to his vehicle and set off down the mountainside on his errand.

At the Indian Camp General Store, Bar & Service Station ten miles down the highway, Sullivan filled up his tank, bought a can of gas for the stove and a box of yellow cornmeal and talked fishing with the combination storekeeper bartender, who joined him in a bottle of beer.

But all the time, a debate was going on in his head. He let the man do the talking, and though Sullivan took time to buy two of the trout flies the fellow recommended, he was impatient to be away. The debate was over. He knew that he was going back up there to the meadow and find Susannah. He'd wasted ten years.

When he had pressed one foot on the gas pedal and one hand on the horn this morning and charged off to the rescue, he hadn't known how he was going to go about it, either. There had to be an analogy there somewhere.

One thing he knew... he loved her. And if she still loved him... Oh, God, then what?

He didn't know. He didn't know. But for the moment it didn't matter. He only knew he had to go back.

CHAPTER SEVEN

A FEW MILES BEYOND, Susannah turned off the logging road into the meadow and stopped. When she had shut the motor off, she continued to sit for a moment, looking at without seeing the lush green clearing before her, her mind on what had just taken place. She gave an involuntary shudder and got out of the car, her eyes following a fresh double set of tracks made by heavy-duty tires that continued on past where she was stopped.

Sullivan, she thought, and was at once drawn to follow the tracks on foot. Some hundred yards beyond, the Jeep appeared to have circled and gone back out the way it had come, leaving nothing behind to indicate that the driver intended to return. She wasn't sure what she had expected to find but felt strangely let down that he hadn't left anything to show he'd even been there but for a wide swath of flattened meadow grass.

Where had he been headed? she wondered. Back to Cacheton? But if he hadn't intended to return, why all the nonsense of flipping the coin? Having served notice she was not to encroach on the territory he'd won in the toss, he obviously expected to be back to fish "tails."

A lingering annoyance with her secretary grated on her nerves. How dare Jill send the two of them up here, knowing they were bound to meet? In her mind Susannah framed a sharp reprimand. She would let Jill know in no uncertain terms that she hadn't done anyone a favor with her antics. Her performance as a secretary was flawless, she conceded grimly as she turned back to the car, but Jill might as well know this kind of meddling could get her replaced.

But she hadn't taken five steps before she began to demur. Replace Jill? Could she really do without her? She could replace the secretary, but never the friend. Susannah didn't have to think twice to know which of the two had cooked up this misbegotten scheme. Certainly not the secretary.

What a mess! she thought, and at the same time found herself grinning in spite of herself.

Her amusement was short-lived, but her forgiveness held fast. Walking on, she kicked disconsolately at the dirt, knowing it wasn't fair to have gotten so mad at Jill. If the whole thing hadn't gone sour—and she couldn't blame Jill for that—she might have overlooked her friend's indiscretion. Been pleased with it, in fact. She remembered the first thought that flashed across her mind when she had realized who her rescuer was. Not relief that he'd saved her, but a sudden gladness that in this remote spot they could talk to each other at last without corrupting the judicial process or compromising her judgeship.

The thought still made sense. If only Dan hadn't walked away without putting it to test.

She had no heart anymore for fly casting. But for a certain stubbornness that drove her to finish whatever she set out to do, she would have turned around and started back home. Even so, when she reached the car she didn't immediately take out her fishing tackle and head for the stream. Still feeling the hurt of Dan's rejection, she stood beside the car brooding, trying to adjust to what was now obvious: Dan wasn't looking for any conciliatory meeting between them. The golden opportunity had come and gone, and he hadn't bothered to seize it.

In a sudden fury she flung the car door open and got in behind the wheel. If a chance meeting on the stream bothered him so much, she'd be darned if she would spoil his day by parking here in the meadow, where he had presumably staked his claim. Heaven forbid they should accidentally run into each other, going and coming from their cars.

She started the car and drove back on to the logging road, heading in the direction from which she had come until she reached a narrow dirt road off to the side. She'd seen it on the way up without noticing its condition. The moment she was on it she regretted her impetuous departure from the meadow. The road was deeply rutted and almost straight downhill. There was no turning back until the creek bed at the bottom was reached. She gritted her teeth and rode the ruts all the way down to a small gravelly spot at the edge of the water. There she parked and took out her rod and tackle box without giving the stream more than a glance.

What in the world was the matter with Dan, she wondered moodily. He'd kissed her in a public elevator in the courthouse—not just a casual, for-old-times-sake kiss but a kiss that asked for and promised more. Now, two days later, alone on a mountaintop, he didn't even want to be on the same part of the stream with her.

Frowning, she fit one section of the fly rod into another. When she had it extended full length, she slipped the base of the reel into the two holding rings on the grip. As she pulled on the leader to thread the line through the eyes, the leader slipped from her fingers and circled back onto the reel. She grunted in disgust, remembering what she'd forgotten to do. None of the stuff had been used for ten years, for heaven's sake. For all she knew, leaders crystallized and lines rotted. She did know that even the best lines and leaders could become stiff if they were stuck away in a cupboard for a time. She should have dampened and stretched the line last night the way Dan showed her. Then if it didn't soften up, or if it broke, she could have bought a new one when she got her fishing license this morning.

Nevertheless, she continued to fiddle with the line and on the second try managed to string it out through the tip of the pole. She even succeeded in tying a fly on the stiff leader and reeling out a length of line. At that point she was thwarted. The line was as stiff as piano wire. It came off the reel into a series of concentric circles like a child's Slinky toy, quite impossible to send out in a cast. It was so unmanageable she didn't try to get it back on the reel again but spent a minute pulling it all out until it lay in a nondescript pile at her feet.

One thing was clear—she'd made a long drive and nearly gotten herself killed *not* to fish, she thought sourly as she disassembled her rod. As if that wasn't enough, she had the uneasy certainty that she shared her sylvan retreat with Dan! The day was definitely out to get her. She should have stayed in Cacheton where she belonged and got started on her election campaign.

Back in the trunk she put the tackle box and the net and the creel and her wading boots—all the appurtenances of fishing Dan had long ago assured her she couldn't be without. She scooped up the coils of fishing line, stuffed them into a back corner of the trunk and slammed it shut.

Straightening, she breathed deeply and viewed her surroundings. For the first time she took a good look at Patch Creek, sparkling before her, and listened to the music of the water as it splashed and swirled across the rocky stream bed, almost at her feet. She moved along the bank to where the stream poured in a froth of white water over a fallen log and into an iridescent pool, the spray a fine mist on her face. Her eyes followed its course on down the steep slope until the stream disappeared into the trees. A flash of silver in the pool below caught her attention and on closer scrutiny she detected the sleek dark sliver of a trout idling near the bottom.

That was one fish she wouldn't have to take off her hook, she thought, remembering the tangled line in the trunk of the car, and to her surprise realized she didn't care. A marvelous sense of release spread through her. She wondered then if she had ever really enjoyed catching them. She remembered she'd hated taking them off the hook and had done a lot of casting in unlikely waters just to avoid the risk of success.

And yet on those fishing trips she'd taken with Dan years ago she'd known some of the happiest times of her life. Had it been Dan or the surroundings or—because she'd never had time to learn game skills when she was growing up—the heady satisfaction that came with making a perfect cast? Could it be that the magic of the judge/writer's lyric prose had charmed her into imagining she'd liked to fish? If she was so crazy about the sport, why had she waited ten years to try it again? Perhaps the real seduction wasn't the fishing but the "small rebellion," the breaking away from the serious involvements of life to escape for a few hours into a serene other world.

The trout slipped out of sight into the shadows of the fallen log. Susannah gazed moodily into the pool another moment and then turned to go back to her car. After a few steps she laughed and came to a stop. Why go home just because she didn't intend to fish? Now that she understood the true nature of her own small rebellion, she should stay and make the most of it.

An immense flat-topped granite boulder, painted with lichen as colorful as an artist's palette, loomed up at the edge of the stream a short distance away, and she followed a faint pathway near the edge of the water to get to it. Once there, she scrambled up the side to the top, where she stood and surveyed the open woods around her, bending to sniff a wild rose blossom from a rambling bush that grew out of the hillside beside her. Stretching out on her stomach on the sun-warmed surface of the boulder, she hung her head out over the edge to watch the pool at its base, where two large rainbow trout lazed in its shade and a school of minnows chased across the sunny shallows. The breeze was cool, and the sun felt good on her back.

She thought of her father, who had called to say he had business in the state capital tomorrow and would drop by to see her on his way back to San Francisco. How could she tell him that she didn't want him interfering in her election campaign? She was on shaky ground as it was. He'd take over if she let him, and if she did, she'd lose for sure. Still she hated to hurt him. Somehow Dan had known better how to deal with her father than she did. If only she could talk to him!

Her mind turned to the court—the child-custody case and then, inevitably, the crop-dusting trial.

Up to this point the case had been all Sullivan's, but it was much too early to tell. Corwin's defense was still to come. If Dan didn't have somebody waiting in the wings to corroborate the field checker's testimony, it wouldn't take much effort from Corwin to cast doubt in the jurors' minds.

A small, prickly missile of some sort bounced off the back of her head and she rolled over and looked up. When her eyes adjusted to the brightness she sighted the smart-alecky chipmunk perched on a pine branch above her pedestal, scattering bits and pieces of debris from a brown, conelike morsel it was attacking like an ear of corn.

Dan...Dan. No matter what she tried to think about, she realized helplessly, her mind always homed back to Dan. She sat up and wrapped her arms around her jean-clad knees, gazing up at the overhanging limb from where a moment before the small animal had dropped a final morsel onto her shoulder and scurried away.

What did it matter that he hadn't tried to make something more of their unplanned meeting? Even if talk could heal the old injuries and erase the scars, there was no place for them to go from there. The truth of it was, there was no place for Dan in Cacheton, no place for a judge in his life. She wasn't even sure she would want to be a part of another person, the way they had been a part of each other before. But even as the thought took shape, she knew she lied.

She still loved him. She always had.

Seconds later she was scrambling down the rough side of the boulder. She hit the ground on the run, heading for the car. If Dan wasn't going to make the move, then she would. The thought of spending the rest of her life on the outs with Dan Sullivan was too much to bear.

She loved him. She wanted him with her whole heart . . . her whole being. She held no false hope of walking off into the sunset with him, but all the more reason that they should seize today.

WITH A PERFUNCTORY WAVE, Sullivan left the Indian Camp store and headed back up the logging road full throttle, torn by uncertainties. Not about what he intended to do. That was the one thing he was sure about. He was no closer to figuring out how to deal with their future than he'd even been, but he would worry about the future later. Right now they had to get the past turned around. And make the most of the present.

The immediate uncertainty was what to do if she wrapped the blasted judicial mantle around her and told him to buzz off. Go macho? Grab her in his arms and kiss her until she went limp? Go home? Whatever her reaction, he couldn't believe she would haul him before the disciplinary council or take it out on him through his case in her court.

At his first glimpse of the meadow, he scanned the area for her car. As he drew nearer and turned down the short roadway that led into the flower-strewn field, a feeling close to despair swept over him. Her car wasn't there.

Oh hell! She'd turned around and gone home. He'd scared her away. But if she had left the mountain she would have had to pass him on her way down, and he would have seen her. He felt a transient moment of relief, quickly lost when he realized she could have passed without his seeing her while he was in the store having a beer.

Anger simmered in him as he opened the door of the wagon and stepped out. Maybe it was just as well, he thought. Overblown scruples could be heavy to live with, he knew from experience. It had had a way of driving him crazy in those other days when the principles of the younger Susannah had gotten in the way of her common sense. But as soon as she quit taking herself too seriously everything had fallen into balance. Now it looked as if being a judge had changed her, he thought with a poignant regret. Maybe it was just as well she hadn't stayed. Except he knew it wasn't. It left everything still up in the air.

Abruptly his dissatisfaction shifted from Susannah to himself. He shouldn't have let her drive off. She had given him her keys. Why hadn't he hung on to them . . . at least until he had a chance to find out if there was anything left between them that was worth working on.

The roar of a jet from some distant airfield broke the quiet of the meadow, and he watched as a plume of vapor cut across the sky directly above him. The reverberating echo of the plane dulled his hearing, but as it died away in the distance he detected another sound, and his eyes turned up to the logging road along the hillside bordering the meadow on one side.

There was Susannah in her car, careering along the washboard road at an injudicious speed toward the meadow turnoff. She slowed sharply and a moment later came bouncing down the gradual incline and pulled up in the flattened grass a few feet away. Watching her come, Sullivan suddenly felt unsure of himself. A moment before he had wanted her here more than he wanted anything else in the world. Now that she *was* here, he wasn't sure what he was going to do about it.

He stood frozen to the spot as she killed her motor and opened the door. When she stepped out she stood where she was and came no closer. Silence lay heavy between them for a long moment. They faced each other, stricken with a sudden shyness.

Then Susannah blurted out the question that had waited ten years to be asked.

"Why did you do it without telling me?"

Caught off balance, Sullivan stared at her without understanding.

"Do what?" he asked. She eyed him with suspicion, then realized the question was innocent. He really didn't know what she was talking about.

"Sign the contract with Bradley & Hammer without even telling me you'd been offered one?" Hearing the words spoken aloud, she wondered for the first time if perhaps the question was petty. And yet she had to know.

"I *did*?" he said, forehead furrowing in a puzzled frown. "Does it matter?"

"Does it *matter*?" Susannah stared at him in disbelief, and all at once the issue assumed importance again. *After all they'd been to each other, did it matter?*

"I swear, I'd forgotten all about it," Dan said with new seriousness, disturbed by this unexpected turn, which threatened to undo his strategy. He went on slowly, trying to reconstruct the scene from the past for himself. "It was a long time ago. As I recall, from the minute I told you I had agreed to go with Bradley & Hammer, the situation became volatile. In the light of your outrage it didn't seem important right then, I suppose. Why didn't you ask me about it at the time?"

"I couldn't, Dan," Susannah said quietly. "I was too proud."

Stunned at the look of hurt and anger he saw in her eyes, Dan made no effort to defend himself. His mind continued backtracking to that other time as he sought desperately to put the pieces together. Why, for godsake, *hadn't* he told her? He honestly didn't know. He felt sick at the trauma his failure had clearly caused her, and with good reason. Their lives had been bound up in each other's as closely as two people's lives could be. She'd had the right to expect him to consult her in advance about a major move that would seriously affect her life. That he obviously hadn't done so seemed unconscionable to him now, as did the fact he could come up with no satisfactory explanation for why it had happened in the first place.

From where she stood, Susannah faced him, awaiting the explanation he didn't have. Maybe he had been afraid if he told her before he was committed, he might let her talk him out of what he knew he had to do. He raked his mind for something reasonable to say.

"Susannah . . . listen to me," he said, as the silence grew uncomfortable. "I remember a lot of other things you brought up that night, but this is something you never mentioned. In the midst of all the verbal pyrotechnics I didn't realize it mattered. It was stupid and insensitive of me to have overlooked it. I only wish you'd told me *then*, instead of letting it eat at you for the past ten years. All I can say now is, I'm sorry.''

In the pause that followed, he could see she was thinking over what he said.

"I'm sorry, too," she said softly, without rancor. For a moment Sullivan was relieved, thinking she had let him off the hook. Then she sighed. "I would still like to know what made you shut me out."

The thought crossed Sullivan's mind that his profession had lost a good trial lawyer when Susannah went on the bench. At the same time he caught a note of sadness in her voice that stabbed his heart. In a fervent longing to comfort her, he gave the only answer that came to him at the moment—one he didn't honestly believe himself.

"I never intended to shut you out, Susannah. Believe me." That much of it he knew was true. He drew a deep breath and went on. "Blame it on the fact I was a coward. I *had* to have that job, and I was afraid if I didn't sign a contract before I told you, you would have talked me out of it."

The beautiful dark eyes stared back at him, round and unblinking. He saw that she was troubled by what he'd said.

"I wouldn't have, Dan." Her voice was quiet. "It was an opportunity most young lawyers would kill for."

"Not you."

"Yes, me. That is if I had been you. Being *me*—a woman—the temptation wouldn't have been so great," she said wryly.

"How so?"

"In the first place, they wouldn't have offered me a whopping salary or the prospect of such a glowing future. In the second place they would have started me out as a gofer. Twenty-five years later I would still have been doing research for associates young enough to be my sons."

Sullivan couldn't argue it. The inequities he'd seen at Bradley & Hammer were one of the reasons he had left the firm as soon as he could.

"You might have had a little more faith in me," she said, but the bitterness was gone from her voice. "I wouldn't have tried to talk you out of it, even if it were possible."

Sullivan couldn't help darting her a challenging grin. "Not even a *little* bit."

In spite of herself she had to grin back. "We-ell, maybe, a *little*," she admitted, then added virtuously, "All I ever wanted was what was best for you."

"That's all I wanted, too. That's why I quit Bradley & Hammer in the end."

"You didn't like it?"

"Hated it. That kind of high-pressure, unprincipled dehumanized practice is not my style. This is not a complaint, understand. I'd been around enough to know what I was signing up for. They bought me, and I knew I was being bought. They wanted it all. There wasn't much left over at the end of a day or a week or a month to share with you, you may recall."

Susannah nodded broodingly. "You went into it with your eyes open...but *why* Dan?"

"For the money."

She felt strangely disappointed. "I still don't understand. I never thought money mattered to you."

"I *had* to have it, Susannah. I didn't say anything about it at the time, because...well, because I didn't want you to know. My kid brother got into a scrape that put the Sullivan family in a financial bind. Associated with Bradley & Hammer I could borrow on future earnings and help get Brian out of a jam. Otherwise it could have made things hard on my folks and probably would have ruined him."

"Oh, Dan. I wish you'd told me. I'm so sorry."

"Don't be," he said reassuringly. "Basically he was a good kid. He came out of it all right."

"But did you?" she asked softly.

Seeing her there before him, almost near enough to reach out and touch, Sullivan wanted desperately to close the distance and gather her into his arms. Still he held back. He sensed a new structure of trust building around them and feared if he moved too soon it would all come tumbling down. At the same time the aura of sexuality that surrounded her was almost too powerful to resist. Somehow it was hard to remember that this beguiling, womanly creature in snug-fitting jeans and running shoes, dark eyes glowing from some inner warmth, was the same serious-visaged, black-robed judge who held sway over the court during the week.

She had removed the madras shirt she'd been wearing when he came upon her in the middle of the road. The yellow T-shirt under it showed the twin mounds of her breasts in bewitching bas-relief, reminding him of the ivory satin flesh beneath, and for a moment, before he pulled his gaze away, he thought of cupping them in his hands. As the logo on the front of the T-shirt registered upon his mind, the thought was lost. The shirt looked brand-new. The message on it read, Bay to Breakers, 1982.

Her voice broke in upon his line of thinking.

"I don't know about you, but I've been buried in chambers and this is my first time out in the sun. I've got to get out of it or my face will be shedding skin by Monday when I get back to court. Could we move this summit meeting to the shade?"

"Sorry," said Sullivan, coming back to reality. "There's plenty of shade by the stream, but the ground's rough and may be a little damp. I'd better bring something along for us to sit on." He turned back to the wagon and hauled a rolled-up sleeping bag out of the back. His heart beat faster. He dared not think ahead. The thunder of anticipation within him made it difficult to think at all. He seized her hand and started off at a dogtrot toward the upper reaches of the stream, Susannah keeping up with him at his side. After a short way, their pace slackened to a walk. Still they did not speak. It was as if, having said so much, they had to regroup before going on.

Sullivan's anticipation gradually cooled into dread. Nothing had been settled between them. She seemed to accept his dubious excuse for not having consulted her before he signed up with Bradley & Hammer, but they hadn't even touched on the real problems—the things that had turned their living quarters into a battleground those last six months. He wasn't even sure he understood what they were about himself.

All he knew was that his whole being cried out from the need to make peace with her, to love her, to somehow find a way to go on loving her without tearing them both apart.

Susannah, walking beside him, was busy trying to reconcile herself to what he had just said. He'd given her a plausible answer, and she believed it. Whatever Dan's flaws, she'd never known him to lie to her. But somehow it didn't ring true. There had never been anything cowardly about Dan Sullivan, and if she'd ever had the power to talk him into doing something against his better judgment, this was the first she'd heard of it.

Her heart went out to the young Dan, torn between loyalty to his family and his feeling of responsibility to her. If only his pride had let him tell her about his brother, they could have worked it out, she was sure. He might still have been obliged to work for Bradley & Hammer, but she would have understood what was happening. Instead, bitterness had festered in her until she'd misread everything he'd done in his efforts to make amends for pulling out on her.

A few yards above the spot where the stream came out of the forest into the meadow was a small clearing beneath the trees, not much bigger than the sleeping bag Sullivan rolled out upon it. Susannah sat down without waiting for an invitation and stared up at him thoughtfully. He watched her for a moment with a bemused expression before he dropped down beside her.

"You've still got some things on your mind, lady. Let's have it."

"Well, if you must know, I have this terrible feeling I shouldn't *be* here."

Dan groaned. "Damnit, Susannah! We're going to have to do something about that paranoia. There's nothing wrong with what we're doing, and you know it."

"Not *we*. Me. I shouldn't be here."

"Even if someone were to see you here with me, which is hardly likely, there's not a chance in the world they'd know us," he said impatiently. "Besides, you have as much right to be here as anybody."

"Well, Mr. Sullivan, I'm mighty glad to hear you say that," she teased. "My order was to stay in 'heads' and keep strictly away from 'tails.'"

But Sullivan refused to play. Locked in frustration, he said testily, "Cut it out, Susannah. Before we go any further I've got to know where we stand. The last time we were alone together there were a lot of words said that we'd better get cleared away before we go on. Words like 'chauvinist' and 'sore-head,' and that I was the kind of person you didn't want in your life."

"You know I never meant that, Dan," she said softly.

But Sullivan pressed on doggedly. "Sore-headed, I'll admit to. You had beat me in court that day, and old Bradley had chewed me out for losing it, and..."

"He had no *right* to chew you out, Dan," Susannah broke in indignantly. "It really was a lousy case on your side. I could have won it in my sleep."

"You won it because you did a great job. I've waited ten years to tell you I didn't mean it when I accused you of winning the case with your feminine wiles, and I'm sorry." He looked uncomfortable. "That one time notwithstanding, I hope you don't think of me as a male chauvinist.''

"You know better than that. I said a lot of things I didn't believe in those last six months," Susannah admitted. "I wish there were a way to unsay them."

Unexpectedly Dan reached over and rumpled her hair teasingly. "Couldn't you issue an order declaring those last six months null and void? If you can't, what good is there in being a judge?''

Susannah's eyes were filled with laughter. Dan's hand came down and lifted her arm away from where it covered her T-shirt.

"Where did you get it?" he asked curiously. "It looks brand new."

"Bay to Breakers, '82? It's five years old. It so happens that in my line of work, I don't get much chance to wear it. It's mine, though, honestly come by."

"Somehow I can't picture you running a marathon."

This time she laughed aloud. "Don't try. Once a year for as long as I lived in San Francisco I used to watch those hordes of people running over the hills from the bay to the ocean on the other side. So there came a day when it occurred to me it might be fun to see if I could do it."

"And did you?"

She shook her head and grinned. "After the second hill I looked around and all the runners were grim. I didn't see a single person with a face that said he was having fun. So I asked myself if I was, and I wasn't. At that point I decided to hell with it."

Sullivan chortled aloud. "That's my love. You remember what I taught you. Glad to see you still give fun a high priority."

With a soft moan, Susannah rolled over on her knees and took his face between her hands, pulling it so close their noses were almost touching.

"Oh, Sullivan," she crooned. "I've *missed* you."

CHAPTER EIGHT

A CHOKED SOUND rose from Sullivan's throat, and he caught her in his arms and brought her close to him.

Wrapped in the wonder of his embrace, Susannah buried her head in the curve of his shoulder and let her senses soak in the clean male smell of his body. She burrowed her face in the shallow indentation that lay between the sinews of his neck, and her pulse quickened to the virile strength she could feel beneath. She explored the hollow with her tongue, tasting the salty sweat that filmed his skin. For a moment of mindless rapture, she reveled in remembered tastes and smells and feelings she had barred from her thoughts for so long.

Holding her hard against his heart, Sullivan fought to stem the desire rising in him, knowing the drive of passion was ill-timed, but even as he struggled to hold it in check, his whole being cried out to him to take to its fullest the moment's promised fruit.

When the inner struggle became intolerable, he lifted Susannah's head and held her where he could look into her eyes and search their dark, enchanting depths for some sign that would strengthen his will to resist—hoping he would not find it.

With a soft cry of homecoming, Susannah reached out and clasped her hands around his neck, so unbalancing the two of them they toppled together onto the spread-out sleeping bag. Lips met, pulled apart and met again, thirsting, moist and swollen with desire. Feverishly their tongues touched and caressed, and his went on to stroke the warm, dark sweetness of her mouth. Deep within her Susannah thrilled to the poignant heat of her own sensual reawakening. With it came an instinctive sense of commitment she could not rationally justify.

At the same time Sullivan, ripe with desire, took the honey of her lips and knew, with a kind of desperation, that if he went on he would soon reach the point of no return. With deep reluctance he lifted his mouth from hers. He resolved inwardly to go no further, but fingers stroked his cheek, and as if by a will of its own his hand played lightly at the fabric of her T-shirt until it came free from her belt, leaving a large enough opening for his hand to slip through. His pulse surged. He had no will to resist.

Then as his fingers smoothed across the bare flesh of her stomach, their eyes met, and he saw in the warm, dark pools he gazed into an open renewal of trust. A lump of emotion swelled in his throat. He was filled with tenderness and a deep yearning to protect her. Where a moment before he had wanted her with an urgency beyond anything he had ever known, now to indulge his passions and put Susannah at risk had become unthinkable.

Reluctantly he withdrew his hand and poked the T-shirt clumsily back under her belt. In the act of doing so he sensed she had grown suddenly still. Calling on all his will, he sat up and leaned over to kiss her cheek lightly, trying not to see the bewilderment in her eyes as he straightened again.

She lay quietly beside him for a moment before she spoke. "What are you going to do?" she asked quietly. He could hear the sound of hurt in her voice.

"How about going fishing?"

Susannah rolled over abruptly and pulled herself up on her knees. Bracing herself with both hands flat on the ground, she faced him, her brown eyes shooting fire.

"If this hot-and-cool stuff is your idea of fun, Dan, I'm afraid my sense of humor has gone flat."

He groaned. "Fun? Oh God, Susannah, if you only knew..." The words caught in his throat.

She gazed at him suspiciously and then her face lost its anger. She hesitated a fraction and then moved from her knees to sit beside him. Reaching out, she touched his face as if to comfort him, her own face making no secret of her disappointment, her dark eyes smoky with unsated love.

"Is there something I've forgotten that still needs to be covered?" she asked anxiously.

It was all he could do then to keep from taking her in his arms, but he dared not. He doubted his will could be trusted a second time to let her go.

"Susannah...love...no," he said quickly. "Don't look so worried. This has nothing to do with the past. It's just that...I didn't come up here expecting...anything like this."

His words brought a wry smile from Susannah. "Nobody expected it—with the probable exception of my secretary."

"Why her?"

"You don't know Jill," she said dryly. Before he could question her she continued, almost pleading. "Please, Dan. What's the matter?"

"I...uh...I'm not prepared to make love, Susannah," he said, his voice quiet. "And I doubt if you are either."

"Prepared?" she echoed with no understanding. Then she said slowly, regretfully, "Oh... *that*." Her eyes were still luminous from the tender interlude of a minute before. "Preparedness, in that sense, hasn't been a major concern of mine since...oh, never *mind*!"

Sullivan reached out and drew her hand to his lips, filling her palm with kisses. She gazed at him dreamily and gave him a reproachful smile.

"I wish you hadn't reminded me," she said.

"Don't think I wasn't tempted not to."

She raised her face to his, her dark eyes sultry with longing.

"This is supposed to be a safe time of the month for me," she ventured.

He smiled at her skeptically. "By what scientific method of calculation did you arrive at that specious conclusion, Lady Judge?"

"We-e-ll, maybe I *am* guessing a little, but if *I* don't think the risk is too great..." she murmured, leaving the sentence hanging in the air as she tipped her head to offer him her rosy lips, still moist and full from the press of his own shortly before.

His groan of self-denial only half repressed, Sullivan moved away from her, not trusting himself to the seduction of her nearness.

"Don't, Susannah!" he said harshly. It was a moment before he could think straight enough to go on. "Suppose you are wrong. Suppose the 'safe time' isn't safe. It could cause...complications even if you were a private person, but nothing we couldn't handle. The real problem is that you are not a private person. You are Judge Susannah Ross and you occupy a position of public trust."

The smoky languor faded from her eyes. After a minute's thought she drew a deep breath and slowly let it out.

"Oh-h damn," she said quietly. "You're right . . . I guess. No, *of course* you're right." She gave him a weak grin. "I suppose I should thank you for reminding me, but that'll have to wait. At the moment it would be an act of hypocrisy."

There was an awkward silence that stretched out uncomfortably until Sullivan glanced at his watch and saw it was well after one o'clock.

"Have you had any lunch?" he asked, and when she shook her head he reached down and pulled her up beside him.

"Care to join me? I brought some . . ."

"Don't tell me—let me guess!" Susannah broke in shakily but laughing, reminding Dan of the way she had always been able to throw off an unwelcome mood like a piece of unwanted clothing when the occasion demanded. "Crackers and Vienna sausages and canned sardines."

"How did you guess?"

"And those remnants of your childhood—a package of Oreo cookies and a Snickers bar. How could I forget? I have sandwiches and a thermos of coffee back at the car," she added. "We might pool our resources."

After they had eaten, Dan announced he was ready to have another go at the stream. Susannah pleaded a fouled-up line and declined Dan's insistent offer of tackle from the redundant supply he carried with him

in the back of the Jeep. Together they struck off across
the meadow, walking cautiously to avoid sinking into
marshland left from the recently melted snow. When
they reached Patch Creek they followed its bank
through a stand of aspen up into the evergreens that
covered the mountainside.

To Susannah, the air around them seemed charged
with their compounded desire. When their arms accidentally brushed as they made their way upstream, she
felt a shadow of the lovely, quivering pain deep inside
her that had driven away all caution but a short time
before.

When Dan found a fishing spot to his liking, Susannah settled herself against a nearby boulder, the
ground around it snugly cushioned with grass. She
clasped her knees with her arms and watched him send
his line upstream and across from him in a flawless
cast, then pick up the slack line with his left hand and
raise the rod tip to lift the floating fly off the surface
in perfect form. It was like watching a big-league
pitcher throw a perfect curve ball, she thought, as the
lean, sinewy body brought the fly into the air and cast
it out again.

Her eyes followed him as he moved on upstream,
but she stayed where she was. His chino pants and
fishing vest and his dark green shirt blended into his
surroundings. Each time she turned her eyes away she
had to look hard to find him when she turned back.

It was the way things were with them, she thought
restlessly. He was here, and yet he was not here. Deep
in her heart she could see no chance things would ever
be different, considering the changes that had come
over their lives since San Francisco.

She wished for a moment that Dan had never come to Cacheton to try the case. Until he showed up, she'd almost forgotten. Maybe not *forgotten*, but she had seldom thought of him anymore. When she did it was without pain, or at least the pain had dissolved into a kind of wistful regret for what might have been. But here he was back, and it was as hopeless as it had ever been, though now in a different way, and the forgetting was all to do over again.

When her eyes could no longer separate Dan's figure from the shadows upstream, she stretched out on the wild grass at the base of the boulder and soaked up the warmth of the sun sifting through the trees, her thoughts on what Dan had told her a short time before in the woods. The causes that had driven them apart seemed surprisingly unimportant now, and she wondered if their relationship might have been undermined not so much by circumstances as by something basic in their characters that sooner or later would have surfaced under any conditions. Like pride, she thought. Wasn't it Dan's pride of family that had kept him from telling her he needed money to get his brother Brian out of a scrape? And her own pride, which had kept her from asking the moment he broke the news to her why he hadn't consulted her before he signed?

She thought of Dan's admission that he had been afraid she would talk him out of the job with Bradley & Hammer with a vague disappointment that bordered on disbelief. Dan Sullivan *afraid* of her power to persuade him? Not anytime she could remember! The Dan Sullivan she thought she knew had been strictly his own man. It was one of the qualities she'd admired in him.

Her thoughts skittered back to the sweet, sensual moments in his arms a short time before. Her body stirred with the echoes of desire and she knew nothing else mattered. The only thing that mattered was there would be no more.

What was she doing here now? she asked herself restlessly. The renewal she'd looked for in the quiet of the mountains was lost to her. In a moment she would get up and go back to the car, she thought. She might as well go home and get started on the election campaign. She'd slip a note under Dan's windshield wiper to let him know she was gone.

But still she lay where she was in the sun, talking herself into actually making the move, when the strains of the week that had etched into her nights finally caught up with her and she fell asleep.

The sun had dropped behind the mountain when she awakened. She sat up and looked around her blearily, disoriented for a moment before she remembered where she was. Through the trees she could see that the sun still shone on the distant slope to the east. A glance at her watch told her it was a few minutes after five o'clock. She couldn't believe she had been so near exhaustion she could sleep away more than two hours. And on a hard bed of wild grass that sparsely covered the irregular ground. She yawned and stretched and realized she was cold. But for that she might have slept until Dan awakened her, she thought as she got stiffly to her feet, her head still fogged with sleep.

When she was fully awake she peered upstream into the deep shadows beyond. She didn't really expect to see him in the dappled light, even if he was in range of her sight, so she cupped a hand to her mouth and called his name. When a second call brought no answer, she dusted herself off and started back down-stream toward the car.

Her knees and neck creaky from her long nap on the ground, she did some limbering aerobics along the way. When she reached level ground she set out at a jog to get her blood circulating and her body warmed until she reached the marshy land of the meadow and slowed to a walk.

Plodding across the uneven ground, she composed a note she planned to tuck under Dan's windshield wiper. A note that would tell him how glad she was the resentment between them had been laid to rest, but now, she would say, she was going home. There would be no need to explain. He understood the problems.

Halfway across the meadow she glanced up toward where the two vehicles had been parked and saw only her own car. Apparently Dan had taken off, she thought, quickening her steps, not sure what to think of this new development. He might have at least wakened her and said where he was going and when he planned to be back.

She had no doubt he would return, but with no place to secure a note she gave up the thought of leaving one. She wanted suddenly to get away before he came. She wanted to avoid the inevitable awkward parting.

Coming up to her car she saw a folded piece of paper clipped to her own windshield, and when she pulled it out and opened it she recognized Sullivan's big sprawling handwriting, remembered from long ago.

"Don't go. I'll be right back. Dan."

Susannah gazed at the note a long time before she folded the paper and put it away in her jacket pocket.

What good would it do to stay? It was far more frustrating to be here alone with Dan than to face him across the courtroom.

With a heaviness in her heart for lost moments of happiness that had been doomed from the start, Susannah climbed in her car and started the motor.

No more! she thought. Today was over, the chance lost and no likelihood of there being another. The memory hurt. She should be glad it hadn't gone further. Anything more than those few lovely moments in the woods would only have made the memory more poignant, that much harder to forget.

She didn't bother now to write a note. When he got back he would have no trouble figuring out that she'd gone home. She had to get away before he got here— while she still had the will to go.

She drove the car out onto the logging road as if something were after her. Oblivious to the deep ruts that had intimidated her on the way up, she charged straight ahead, slowing a bit when the wheels lost traction in loose dirt and skidded slightly. It was not until she left the logging road to turn into the highway that she realized she had a death grip on the steering wheel. What was she running away from? she asked herself scornfully, and knew she was running away from herself. She forced her hands to loosen their hold on the wheel. Lightening her foot pressure on the accelerator, she let the muscles of her neck and shoulders go slack.

A mile down the road her newly called-upon composure fled at the sight of Dan's Jeep rounding a curve a short distance ahead. He sounded his horn in a succession of short blasts and stuck his arm out the window, motioning her determinedly to stop.

Susannah's heart pounded fiercely in her breast. *Oh God,* if only these unexpected appearances of his wouldn't tear her apart this way, she thought desperately. Then, knowing it was not in her to ignore his signals and continue on her way, she searched for a road shoulder wide enough for her car and, finding one, pulled off the road. When she had come to a stop she looked back to see Dan loping toward her, a swatch of unruly hair blowing across his broad forehead in the late-afternoon breeze.

"Where the devil are you going?" he called out as he drew nearer. She waited for him to get all the way to her car before she answered.

"Home," she said flatly.

"You mean you just came up here for the day?" he asked, adding almost accusingly, "Don't you like camping anymore?"

"I haven't done it since…oh, I don't know when," she finished on a note of impatience.

"Yes you do," Sullivan disagreed pointedly.

"All right, the last time was with you," Susannah admitted, and added reasonably, "I don't have any camping equipment."

"Well, your old lover Sullivan has, Susannah honey," he said with a grin. "And a sleeping bag that'll hold both of us."

She gave him a withering look. "Don't be cute. I believe that issue was settled this afternoon. Now if you'll kindly move away from the car, I'm going home." She let the car roll forward a few inches, but Dan grabbed hold of the window edge and went along with it.

"Don't go, Susannah. I'm sorry," he said, huddling down again to peer in the window, his eyes teasing. "Forget I ever said that. There's plenty of time to go home after you've eaten. Come on back to the meadow and I'll cook you a trout *amandine* that'll be the envy of Maxim's."

Trout *amandine*? Not the Sullivan she used to know, she thought and laughed aloud.

"It would serve you right if I held you to that unlikely promise," she said. The memory of Dan hunkered down beside a campfire, holding a skillet full of badly charred fish over the flames, flashed across her mind in loving detail. His invitation suddenly seemed irresistible. It would be their last chance to be together, and the logistics of putting the meal together would keep their libidos in control. After they had eaten, she would drive down the mountain and, in a very real sense, out of his life.

But in her heart she knew she could never do it. She was asking too much of herself. She hesitated a moment, then said what she'd known all along she must.

"You make it sound tempting, but that logging road's a killer, Dan. I really don't want to drive back over it at night."

"You don't have to."

"Be real, Dan," Susannah said, almost crossly. "It won't work. Even if we spent the night at opposite ends of the meadow from each other, it wouldn't work. All it would do would be to lay up a whole new stack of frustrations for both of us."

"There'll be champagne," he said, wheedling.

Something in his voice caused Susannah's mind to come to a sudden halt and back up. She peered up at him from out of the car window and realized for the first time that he seemed immeasurably pleased with himself.

"Wait one little minute," she said suspiciously. "Would you mind telling me where you've been? You were supposed to be up there fishing."

"Oh, I limited out about three-thirty. When I came back to where I'd left you, you were sleeping like an owl in the sun. I didn't have the heart to wake you up, so I went on down to the Indian Camp store."

"Hmm. Sounds like you're still running true to form. What did you forget this time?"

He gave her an injured look. "Now I *ask* you! Is that fair? I took you to a concert just once and left the tickets behind, and I still get reminded of it. No, I didn't forget anything. I just hadn't anticipated the need."

Susannah felt her pulse begin to race. She gazed at him, her eyes round. "Oh," she said.

He gazed back at her solemnly. "Champagne for a lady judge . . . among other things."

"Champagne? At that funny little out-of-the-way store?"

"Lots of tourists come this way. They stock a little of everything."

She hesitated a moment before she asked the question uppermost in her mind. "Were you able to get . . . everything you . . . needed there?" Without knowing it, she held her breath as she waited for his answer.

"Every last thing."

For a moment Susannah felt as if she were melting into the warmth she saw in his eyes. His mouth quirked up in a half smile, and his face somehow seemed different to her. And then she remembered. It was the way he used to look at her in those early days together, before the bitterness set in. There'd been an underlying resentment in everything they did the last six months before they parted—even when they were making love.

He smiled at her now with a tender humor. Folding his hand into a loose fist, he reached in the window and chucked her lightly under the chin. There was something almost bashful in the gesture that caught at her heart, and she took hold of his hand and held it for a moment against her cheek.

"Oh, Dan," she murmured, and at that moment she knew she would go back with him to the meadow, whatever the cost. It was something that had to be—a last time together.

When she let his hand go, he leaned into the window and kissed her lightly on the cheek. As he stood up to go, her emotions were too close to the surface for her to venture to speak, but he seemed not to notice.

As if everything was settled he said, "There's a place just after you come off the highway onto the logging road where you can park your car safely for as long as you like. You can save some wear and tear if you leave it there and ride on back to the meadow with me."

Sorry now that she'd made such a fuss about the road when she actually thought she'd managed it rather well, she said, "Never mind, Dan. That's a lot of bother. The road's not all that bad!"

But Sullivan shook his head, and before she could say more turned and headed back across the road to where his Jeep was parked.

"The road's clear in both directions," he called over his shoulder. "Make a quick U-turn and follow me."

WHEN THEY REACHED the meadow, Dan drove past the spot where he had parked earlier and continued an uncharted course through the wild grass to the edge of the woods. He pulled alongside the place they had been that morning, marked by the still-flattened grass where they had spread the sleeping bag and talked. He shut off the motor and turned to her with a smile that sent a thrill of pleasure along her spine.

"I hope you don't mind coming back to the site of our summit meeting," he said.

"I can't think of a better place."

"Then I'll start unloading the stuff, and we can settle in."

Susannah followed him around the vehicle and watched him open up the back end and start pulling things out—a small ice chest, a box filled with cooking utensils, a collapsible table on which he placed a three-burner gas camp stove.

"Aren't we going to have a camp fire?" Susannah asked, disappointed.

"Don't we always have a camp fire," Sullivan said, as if they had been doing this regularly for the past ten years. "At least we do when I remember to get a permit to build one, and it so happens this time I did. What we don't have anymore is charred fish."

Quickly they fell into a routine established years before when they had spent most of their summer weekends in the mountains and when there was no gas stove or ice chest and the cooking utensils were a bent iron skillet and a granite coffee pot, both blackened with use.

The sun had already gone down by the time they reached the meadow and dusk was closing in. It didn't have to be said that there would be no time for amenities until the camping chores were done.

Susannah had forgotten the feeling of exhilaration that came with racing against the coming night. It was nearly dark by the time they had dug a shallow pit for the fire and gathered wood and kindling and carried water from the creek. They laid out the sleeping bag by the light of the blazing fire.

That done, Dan brought his bottle of champagne from the ice chest, popped the cork and poured the wine into coffee mugs. He touched his cup to hers and then was strangely silent.

After a long pause, he groaned. "Oh God, Susannah," he said. "I'm tongue-tied. I wanted to make a toast that would send you to the stars, and I can't find any words—" He hesitated, and when he went on there was a quiet emotion in his voice that took her breath away. "Except that I'm happier tonight than I've been in all the years since San Francisco."

"Dear love, have you forgotten?" she said unsteadily. "There's a much surer way than a toast to send me to the stars."

She heard a small rumbling sound in Dan's throat, and the heavy mug of champagne was lifted from her hand. Next thing she was in his arms, and Sullivan was murmuring broken sounds of endearment and his mouth came seeking hers. She lifted her face and their lips met in a long, hungry kiss, still fruity with the taste of the wine. Deep inside her quivered the lovely pain of awakening passion, and she wrapped her arms around him to bring him closer.

The need for each other was suddenly so demanding it drove everything else from their minds. They found their way to the sleeping bag next to the fire. On their knees, facing each other, he began to undress her, and she raised her arms to let him skin the T-shirt over her head. Its abrupt release threw him slightly off balance. Rolling back on the sleeping bag, he carried her down on top of him, slipped his arms around her and unfastened her bra, freeing her breasts.

Before he could take her to him, Susannah leaned over him where he half reclined and, with a small, sensual back-and-forth movement, let the firm tips of her breasts graze his lips until he captured one, taking all the breast his mouth could encompass softly in his mouth and laving it with his tongue.

In that deep, hidden part of her a wrenching quiver—half pain, half ecstasy—wrung from her a fluty, incredulous cry. When she was sure she could bear it no longer, he let her breast slip away. His hands worked feverishly at the fastening on her jeans, and the zipper gave. He pulled her down beside him, slipping a hand inside the opening.

"Oh darling, oh Dan...oh wait," she cried. Her hurrying hands found their way to his shirt, nimbly unfastening the buttons and then his belt and then the fly to his chino pants. Her fingers slipped inside and she clasped the remembered hardness lovingly at the same moment Dan's hand moved down her belly and his fingers closed convulsively upon the soft, wiry triangle of hair at the secret entrance he once had known so well.

With a moan of endearment, he flattened his hand to cover the small mound and pressed on it lightly, reaching beyond with his fingers to the other lips hidden there, now moist and swollen with passion. At his touch she felt herself open to him and cried out aloud.

"Oh come, Dan...come to me, love," she moaned, and then, remembering, she rolled away from him. When she had removed the last of her clothing, she lay in the light of the full moon, her eyes closed, her whole body aching with desire, and waited for Dan.

At the sound of the sharp intake of his breath, her eyes flew open to find him standing over her, his naked body in full arousal, silver in the moonlight. He dropped to his knees astride her and buried his face between her breasts.

"Oh God, Susannah," he said hoarsely, "I had no hope this would ever happen again."

He raised himself and the sweet, hot throb in her loins became more than she could bear. With a cry of yearning she reached out and guided him to her.

"Take it slow, Susannah," he murmured, his voice thick with emotion. "I'm trying to hold back. It's been a long time, love. I don't want to hurt you."

But she pulled him to her, her hands on his buttocks, and in the final instant his resolve was forgotten. With the full force of his passion he plunged, again and again, carrying her each time to a new height until they lay together, spent and fulfilled.

After a time Sullivan touched her face and found it wet with tears.

"Susannah, you're crying. Oh God, darling, I've hurt you."

"No, no... never," she protested muzzily. "I never thought I would ever be so happy again. Oh, Dan, I've missed you so!" To the complete bewilderment of Sullivan, who had never before seen her cry, she buried her face in his shoulder and wept.

As their bodies cooled they became aware for the first time of the sharp breeze that bit into their flesh. The night air had grown cold. They took shelter in the sleeping bag—a down-filled sack designed for a single body, yet it still managed to accommodate them with room to spare. As close as is possible for two people to be, they took warmth from each other's bodies, made love one more time and at last fell asleep.

SOMETIME TOWARD MORNING Sullivan awoke from a sound sleep with a feeling something important lay just beyond the grasp of his mind. The arm on which Susannah was lying had fallen asleep, and he pulled it gingerly out from under her, trying not to waken her. Once the arm was free, he could find no place to rest it without turning over. This proved to be no easy feat, but in the midst of the maneuver the elusive something that had escaped his mind suddenly struck him.

"Oh, my God...of course!" he muttered, sitting as nearly upright as he could.

"Dan, dearest, please lie down," Susannah murmured sleepily beside him. "You're letting the cold in."

"I just remembered the real reason I didn't talk the Bradley & Hammer offer over with you before I took it," he said, pulling the sleeping bag snug around her shoulders as he lay down.

"Not what you said?" Susannah asked, yawning herself awake.

"That happened to be the first thing that came to my mind when you started pushing for a reason," Dan said sheepishly. "The real reason came to me out of the blue just now. They didn't give me a chance. Remember? A client of mine was involved in a case Bradley & Hammer were working on too, and I'd been consulting with both partners at the time. I had no idea they had an opening until they called me into their offices that afternoon and said 'Take it or leave it.'"

"Why all the rush?"

"It's the way they worked. As I remember, they told me they'd been interviewing lawyers for the position during the month they'd been working with me and for some reason decided at the last minute that they would offer the job to me. Typical Bradley & Hammer style, they put pressure on me. The guy they'd been thinking about hiring was coming in shortly, they told me, and if I wanted the job I'd better sign then and there or they'd let him have it. They told me the starting salary, and I signed on the dotted line without giving it a second thought."

"*Why* did you wait all this time to tell me that, Dan?" Susannah asked plaintively.

Sullivan maneuvered himself around again in position to run his tongue around the shell-like intricacies of her ear and sent a delicious shiver racing down her spine.

"Think back, my darling. Did you give me a chance that night?" he asked gently, raising his head to speak. "And after that you never mentioned it. I never thought of it again until today."

"Hmmph," she grunted, not ready to accept full blame, but she believed him and was satisfied. She wriggled contentedly in his arms and yawned, and in the next moment all her senses reawakened with desire.

CHAPTER NINE

SUSANNAH AWAKENED to the first rays of the morning sun in her face and a deep reluctance to face the day. She blinked into the bright light and closed her eyes tightly again, taking comfort from the enveloping warmth of Sullivan's body, until she remembered it was probably for the last time. As if a cold hand touched her heart, she shivered and lay still, trying to pump up her courage for the moment drawing depressingly near, when they would say goodbye.

He moved and she felt the cold from outside edge in along her shoulders. A shadow came between her and the sun. She opened her eyes to see Sullivan looking down at her with a kind of wonder in his face. When he saw she was awake he greeted her with a faintly apologetic smile.

"Just trying to get you fixed in my mind as you are right now. Give me something to remember tomorrow when you turn back into a . . ."

"Pumpkin?" Susannah interjected.

"Some pumpkin!" said Sullivan argumentively. "Don't tell me that calling you what you are would violate your judicial etiquette."

"It's not that," she said unhappily. "I . . . oh, Dan, I'd just as soon not be reminded of it this morning, if you don't mind."

He ruffled her hair lovingly and touched his lips gently to hers in an affectionate kiss bereft of last night's passion. She could see a shadow of her own inner grayness in his eyes.

"Stay, Susannah. Who knows when we'll be together again," he said with sudden intensity. "Stay the rest of the day. You can go back late tonight."

"I can't, Dan. I told you. My father is coming to see me this afternoon. I can't very well let him arrive at an empty house."

"No, I suppose you can't," Sullivan said with a resigned sigh. He lay back with a kind of quiet detachment, as if learning to live with the situation. After a minute he began to disentangle himself from the sleeping bag.

"Stay where you are," he told her. "I'll get dressed and start the gas stove. No reason for you to get up until the coffee's brewed."

Her eyes were closed again against the piercing light of the early sun, but she could hear him scrambling into his clothes. A minute later she heard a startled grunt and raised her head to see what was going on. Sullivan stood a few feet away by the stove table with a bemused expression on his face and a coffee mug in his hand.

"What's the matter?" she asked, propping herself on her elbow to take in the full picture.

"We didn't eat." He dropped to his knees on the sleeping bag and showed her the mug filled to near the top with flat champagne. Reaching out far enough so they wouldn't be splashed, he tipped the mug and they watched the contents pour out on the ground.

"We didn't even drink the blasted champagne." They stared at each other a moment in disbelief and

Sullivan began to laugh. Susannah blinked at him in astonishment and the next instant was laughing too. Clinging to each other, they welcomed the release their laughter brought from the shadow of their imminent parting, and soon they were gasping for breath and tears came to their eyes.

Then, to her mortification, Susannah began to cry, and had no more power to bring it to a stop than she'd had with her laughter a moment before. Sullivan took her tenderly in his arms and let her cry until she gave a last hiccupy sob and raised her head from his chest.

"I don't know what's the matter with me," she said, managing an apologetic smile. "I never cry."

"So I remember. It probably has something to do with the fact you haven't been fed for something like eighteen hours," he replied lightly, but when she looked in his eyes she saw a sorrow that matched her own.

"Oh, Dan, what are we going to do?" she asked hopelessly.

"God, Lady Judge, I wish I knew."

They held each other fiercely for a second, and then Sullivan pulled the sleeping bag up around her shoulders.

"Any objection to trout for breakfast?" he asked as he got to his feet.

She stuck her face back out from under the down covering.

"*Amandine*?"

He grinned at her. "I just said that last night to get your attention. I only know how to cook 'em the same old way—covered with cornmeal and fried with bacon."

"And burned black on the outside," finished Susannah wickedly.

"Not since I got the stove."

She lay still for a while, watching Dan get the gas stove going, the coffee pot on and a pan of water heating on one of the burners. When the coffee began to perk, she reached for her clothes in a pile at the foot of the sleeping bag and dressed quickly. The morning was still chilly and her teeth were chattering by the time she was fully clothed. She headed into the woods at a dogtrot, hoping it would start her blood circulating.

When she came back she found Dan putting a skillet of meal-covered trout on the gas burner to cook.

"Sorry about the accommodations," he said. "There's hot water for your hands and face, though. Pour the hot into that basin with some cold so you won't get burned, and I'll be right back."

Leaving the fish sizzling on the burner, he went to the Jeep and returned a few seconds later with a towel that said Cacheton Motel on it and a bar of soap.

"No toothbrush?"

"Have a cup of coffee and you'll never notice."

The coffee and the face wash warmed her body if not her spirit. When she was finished with her ablutions she came back to where Dan stood tending the trout. Slipping her arms around his waist, she laid her cheek between his shoulder blades and rested the weight of her head on his back.

"Don't let me interrupt you," she murmured. "You've no idea how good you feel."

He turned away from the stove and took her into his arms. His cheek pillowed on the top of her head, and they held each other closely, rocking gently back and forth together on the balls of their feet. With all their senses fully alive to each other, the pain of impending separation overshadowed the erotic. It was as if they must store up the full essence of each other against uncertainties they saw ahead. The seconds ticked into a minute. Suddenly Susannah raised her head.

"Something's burning!"

Sullivan snatched up a towel, and as he pulled the smoking skillet off the stove behind them it burst into flames. He smothered it quickly with the towel. When the crisis was over, he dumped the remains in the trash and was about to start over when Susannah called a halt.

"It's all right, I've got plenty of fish," he told her.

"Dan, honey, I'm not all that crazy about fish for breakfast, even when it's not burned," she said. "Haven't you got anything else to eat?"

In the end they ate pork and beans and a bizarre assortment of canned goods out of Sullivan's pantry box for breakfast. With frozen orange juice from the ice box and the rest of the champagne that was going flat, Susannah concocted mimosas to add a festive note to the occasion.

For all their efforts to keep their last moments together light, they found themselves again and again engulfed in long, funereal silences. What was there between them to talk about, thought Susannah sadly, now that they had covered the past? The future didn't offer much conversational material—not with two hundred miles and two irreconcilable careers standing between them for all time.

When the stillness became so oppressive she couldn't stand it any longer, Susannah got up from the camp chair Dan had brought out from the Jeep and announced her intention to leave. Dan did not demur. He turned off the camp stove and stowed it in the wagon along with the table and chairs and the sleeping bag, which he took a moment to roll up.

"I'll clean up when I get back," he said, glancing around at the untidiness they were leaving behind.

"You're coming back?" she asked, surprised.

"It's a nice place. I'd like to get a little more fishing in."

They left the meadow and drove down the logging road to where Susannah had parked her car. Though they hardly spoke, there was no rancor between them. Then as Susannah was about to get out of his vehicle, Dan reached across the seat and took her hand.

"Stay awhile longer, Lady Judge," he urged. "Maybe we need to talk about it."

"Talk about what, Dan?" she said wearily. "Getting married? Trying to start a new relationship? Even if we weren't firmly established two hundred miles away from each other, there's no future for us. I hear it in the way you keep calling me 'Lady Judge.' It all shakes down to that. You don't like the fact I *am* one, and I don't like the idea of giving it up."

Sullivan released her hand thoughtfully. He sat for a moment, gazing out through the windshield at the forested land around them. Still not speaking, he opened his door and stepped down on the ground. Susannah got out and came around the wagon toward her car, meeting him halfway.

Without realizing she was going to do it, she flung herself into his arms and pressed her face against his chest.

"Damnit, Dan...oh, damnit. It hurts to love you like this."

He held her away from him, staring down at her thoughtfully. After a moment he gave her a light kiss and turned and walked her to her car, closing the door behind her without speaking when she got in. She didn't look at him again, though she knew he was watching her.

"Drive carefully," she heard him say quietly. "You've got the woman I love aboard."

A minute later Susannah was on the main highway on her way back to Cacheton, and Sullivan headed back up the mountain road to the meadow and Patch Creek, his mind caught up in what Susannah had said.

He'd found it hard to believe she could think his calling her "Lady Judge" implied anything but a term of endearment. He'd called her that the way he used to call her "Counselor," because he took pleasure in what she was. If she thought he did it because he envied her the job, she couldn't be more mistaken. He was comfortable with what he knew himself to be—a damn good trial lawyer. The last thing he aspired to be was a judge. He wasn't cut out for it the way she was.

Nevertheless, her words had given him pause for thought. It brought him flat up against the hard reality that no matter how lovingly he used the sobriquet "Lady Judge" the fact she *was* a judge threatened any future relationship between them. In that sense he guessed she was right. If she hadn't gotten the judicial appointment and was still working for the state in Sacramento, she might even consider coming into the law firm of Curtis & Sullivan in Fresno, and the problem wouldn't exist.

As it was, there was no future for him in Cacheton even if he could break up his partnership with Jerry, which was out of the question. When he'd come back from Washington to Fresno at loose ends eight years ago, he and Jerry had taken up where they'd left off when they went off to different colleges. Over the years they'd let their friendship lapse, but once they'd met again, Jerry had offered him a full partnership in a practice it had taken him fifteen years to build on his own. Sullivan hadn't even been sure he could bring in enough new business to pay his way.

They turned out to be a natural team and did better together than either of them could have done alone. They had established a solid reputation for the firm of Curtis & Sullivan in agricultural cases all over the state.

Apart from the matter of loyalty, he couldn't imagine walking out on the partnership. Going into trial without Jerry to work up the case would be like going into a tennis match without a racquet.

So the whole situation was an impasse, and what the devil was he going to do about it? he asked himself as he turned the sport wagon off the logging road and down the incline that took him back to the meadow. He parked at the edge of the woods where they had spent the night. As he stepped out on the trampled grass he glanced around him. Wherever he looked, he saw Susannah. The essence of her was everywhere.

"It hurts to love like this." Her words came back to him, and he knew they were as true for him as they were for her. Without her, he was incomplete. For all its sweetness, the night they'd had together had only sharpened his desire. It was like a new wound, and unless he could find a way to get around the basic problem of her judgeship, seeing her alone would do nothing but keep the wound open.

He set about cleaning up the camp spot before turning back to the vehicle to get out his fishing gear. But trout fishing had now lost its savor. With a last look back at where they'd lain together, he started the motor.

God, how he loved the woman, he thought, with a feeling of hopelessness. Life without her had suddenly become too burdensome to contemplate. But if he had any sense he wouldn't try to see her alone again until he could come up with an offer she couldn't resist. It was like too much champagne—lovely while you were drinking it, but the hangover was sheer hell.

AS SHE HEADED down the mountain on her way to Cacheton, each mile carried Susannah that much farther from where she wanted with all her heart to be. She wondered with a feeling of dread when, if ever, she would see Dan alone again. There was a cruel irony, she thought grimly, in knowing that all the years it had taken to make peace with each other had been spent arranging their lives in ways that might forever keep them apart.

Looking back on their last minutes together at the edge of the meadow, she wasn't even sure what she had said. One thing she *was* sure of: she'd closed the door resoundingly on any possibility of Dan's trying to see her alone again. At the time, all she'd wanted was to put a quick end to the pain. All she'd thought of was that she couldn't go through this ever again.

Oh, she'd made sure of it, all right, she realized now with dismay. She'd managed to make it sound as if she thought Dan *begrudged* her the judgeship. Dan, of all people! A man of action who loved his adversary role; the last person who'd want to be a judge. It was the kind of sedentary, cerebral job he loathed . . . and she thrived on.

And which she was going to lose on election day if she didn't get her campaign act together pretty soon.

For a fleeting moment she wondered if, after all, that could be the solution. If she didn't campaign there was no doubt she'd lose the election—and probably the likelihood of ever being a judge again. She could start a law practice of her own in some town in Fresno county and . . .

But she knew she was thinking nonsense. She was a good judge and she knew it. Furthermore, she'd be darned if she'd let someone else take by default the job she loved better than anything she'd ever done in her life. She'd give the campaign her best shot, and *then*, if she lost the election . . . If she lost the election she'd be sick about it. She couldn't even consider the possibility.

She thought of her father, who would be here that afternoon, and what she was going to say to him. If she didn't have something tangible at hand to convince him she had a definite plan of action, he'd take over, and she couldn't have that.

With this in mind, she called Jill as soon as she got back to Cacheton.

"Jill, hello, I'm back," she said. "This is Susannah."

There was a second's pause and then a pleased chortle at the other end of the phone.

"Susannah? Not *Judge Ross*?" Jill's voice came back to her. "You must not be *too* mad at me."

"Mad?" The last thing on Susannah's mind at the moment had been Jill's romantic meddling. When it dawned on her what Jill was talking about she made a half-hearted attempt at a reprimand.

"I was ready to skin you alive when I discovered what you'd done," she said. "You're forgiven, but don't try anything like that again."

She could almost hear the crackle of Jill's anticipation across the wire.

"How...did things go?"

"That's not what I called you about," Susannah said crisply. "I want to talk to you about my election campaign."

She heard a resigned sigh at the other end of the line. Jill's voice, when it came, was all business. "I'll help in any way I can," she said.

"I'm expecting my father this afternoon, and I really have to get something together before he gets here or I'm going to have him in my hair."

"Well, I've got a few things set up. What is it you want to know?"

Susannah paused for a moment to collect her thoughts. "First, what can you tell me about the two lawyers who have filed against me?" she asked. "They've both been in court, so I have a fair idea of their competence and their grasp of the law, but I need to know how they stack up on the outside."

"Well, there's Elmer Fairchild, the one everyone expected to be appointed when the governor appointed you," Jill said. "He comes from one of Cacheton's old families and is well liked but definitely no ball of fire. On the lazy side, maybe. I doubt if even his best friends think he'd make a very good judge, but they'll vote for him anyhow unless you can convince them they'd be better off voting for you."

"What about this man Parker?"

"Mel Parker? Listen, Susannah, he could give you a bad time," Jill said in a reluctant voice. "He's tough and aggressive, and he wants to be judge. He's out beating the bushes for money and trying to plant the idea in people's heads that River County doesn't want a woman judge."

Susannah drew in her breath sharply. "All right. You've told me the bad news. Is there any news that's good?"

"The good news is that since there are two of them, they split the vote against you," Jill told her. "Of course you have to win by a margin that's greater than the votes for the two of them put together or you'll have to go up against the one who gets the most votes next fall."

"God forbid!" muttered Susannah.

"Don't knock it," advised Jill. "You'd have the whole summer for River County people to get to know you personally and find out what a good judge you are."

"Thanks, Jill, I don't know what I'd do without you," Susannah said gratefully.

"Don't go away. There's more. You might want to tell your father that the invitations will be in the mail tomorrow for a county-wide barn dance next Friday night at the Kramers' ranch to launch your campaign. You can be sure, with Lucille in charge, all the people who influence other people will be there."

"That overwhelms me, Jill," Susannah admitted. "I hardly know Judge Randall's daughter, and here she and her husband are planning this huge undertaking for me. Who sold me to Lucille?" But even as she asked the question the obvious answer struck her.

"As if I didn't know!" she said. "Which over-whelms me even more. You didn't build this kind of support for me overnight, Jill."

"Don't give *me* any credit for it, Susannah," Jill told her. "It was really Lucille and Jack. Lucille was terribly worried about who would replace her father on the bench. They were afraid it would be Elmer Fairchild, and when it turned out to be you, they couldn't wait to find out all about you. Every time I went out to the ranch that's all we talked about."

Susannah groaned.

"You needn't groan," Jill said in an injured tone. "I told you I resented you, but give me credit for a little sense. After the first week I had to admit to them that you were intelligent, hardworking and fair. By the end of the first month the only thing I could do, in honesty, was tell Lucille that you are the kind of judge Judge Randall would have wanted to take his place. Ever since then they've been working on how to get you reelected. I told you, they love nothing better than to be in the middle of an election campaign."

Susannah drew in a deep breath, then let it out slowly. "I never would have believed it! You went around looking so darned disapproving! I just assumed you thoroughly disliked me."

"What was there to dislike...or to like, for that matter? You didn't give me much to warm up to, so I just did my job and kept my distance."

"You are an enigma, Jill," Susannah said on a note of wonder. "In spite of how cool you felt about me as a person, you could still recommend me as a judge to the Kramers."

"As a matter of fact, the Kramers weren't inter-ested in whether or not I liked you. All they care about is getting the best judge possible for the River County bench, and no matter what my personal feelings were, I couldn't lie to them about that."

"Thanks for the limited endorsement," Susannah remarked dryly.

"Don't mention it," Jill replied breezily. "It was the best I could do for you at the time. It was another four months before I discovered that when you weren't being judge you were an honest-to-God real person with a sense of humor and everything."

"Wait a minute!" interjected Susannah. "I can say the same about you, Jill Fitzgerald."

There was a momentary silence, then Jill laughed.

"I'll let you go," she said. "I know you want to get ready for your father. Good luck."

Susannah hung up, but as she turned away the phone rang.

"Hi, it's me again," said Jill. "One more thing I forgot to tell you. The last two months Lucille and Jack have been raising a war chest from the judge's old supporters to pay for campaign stuff."

Her words brought a small wail from Susannah. "God, Jill, what am I going to do?" she cried in a flurry of panic. "This is all foreign to me. I wouldn't know what to do with the money."

"Don't worry about it. The Kramers are old hands. They're already getting flyers ready to send out and someone working on posters and signs."

"Already?"

"If it had been up to Jack, he would have had your campaign kickoff a month ago, Susannah," Jill told her, and Susannah thought she detected a faint trace of disapproval in her secretary's voice.

She felt a bit ashamed. "I'm sorry, Jill. I suppose I've resisted the whole political idea of selling myself because I've grown up in the dead center of a big-city political ring. I have no right to sit back and depend on generous strangers to get me elected to the job I love."

"Don't get carried away, Boss," Jill cautioned. "The courtroom needs you. Just give those 'generous strangers' the green light and they'll gladly hustle the campaign for you. They've got a stake in it, too, remember."

"It's in your hands, Jill. I'll be available anytime from now on to do whatever the campaign experts want me to do, except when there's work to do for the court."

MANFRED ROSS, Susannah's father, was the archetypal San Franciscan. Born to comfortably well-off San Francisco parents from two "forty-niner" families in the hours immediately following the 1906 earthquake—which people like Manfred spoke of as "The Fire"—Fred Ross had all the bona fides it took to be a part of the bay city's political scene. He'd graduated from the University of San Francisco when it was still St. Ignatius College, had played outfielder for the Seals for two seasons in the old Seals Stadium and for the past twenty years had done the annual New Year's swim with the Dolphins from the Maritime Museum to Ocean Beach.

Except for a slight bulge in the area of his belt, he was trim and tall, and his back was as straight as a flagpole. Though Susannah didn't consider her father to be rich, he had been left well enough off by his family to retire from the insurance business in his fifties and devote his life to his real love, which was politics.

Watching him come up her walkway that afternoon, Susannah thought he looked ten years younger than his eighty years. He appeared handsome and alert and in full control. It never occurred to her to question whether he should be driving his own car in heavy traffic at his age.

She greeted him at the door with a hug and a kiss on the cheek.

"Dad, you're looking great," she said. "It's wonderful to see you. I really appreciate your driving so far out of your way to see me."

"Well, it *is* quite a distance, but I decided I might as well get used to it," her father declared. Susannah blinked, not sure for a moment what he meant. When she was, she chose to misinterpret the remark, hoping to ward off anything pertaining to her election campaign as long as possible.

"I *hope* so," she said warmly. "When you get used to it maybe you won't mind driving up now and then on a Sunday to spend the day. Come sit down and let me bring you something to drink. Coffee? Tea? Wine? Beer? . . . a highball?"

"I wouldn't mind a highball, but I suppose not, since I'm driving," her father said. "Have you got some coffee brewed? Not any of that instant stuff."

"I put on a fresh pot, just for you," she told him, "and how about a piece of cake . . . chocolate on chocolate? The kind you can't resist."

"Did you make it?" her father asked dubiously.

"You know I didn't," she said with good humor. "You have only yourself to blame for letting mother turn me into an academic whiz kid instead of teaching me domestic skills.''

He looked at her uneasily, as if to make sure she was teasing, before he gave her an uncomfortable smile.

''My secretary, Jill Fitzgerald, brought it when I told her you were going to pay me a visit today,'' Susannah assured him.

They settled down at the small dining table with coffee and Jill's cake and talked about small things of little consequence that had taken place since they were last together. Her father told her plaintively that things weren't what they used to be in the city. Politics was being run now by upstarts who weren't dry behind the ears, he said, and Susannah read that to mean her father's old cronies were no longer around or running for office. For the first time in his political life, her father had no campaign to manage in an election.

Watching him as he talked, Susannah saw for the first time that he did look old, and her heart ached for him. She felt almost physically sick knowing that before they parted today she must take away from him the only campaign he had left.

The moment came and caught her off guard.

''Now, Susie, about this election campaign of yours,'' he said, setting his empty coffee cup back in its saucer. ''I could drive back and forth from the city every few days, I suppose, but I've about decided the best thing will be for me to take a room in a motel here in Cacheton for a few weeks.''

She stared at him, round-eyed and speechless.

''I suppose you have a spare bedroom you'd rather have me stay in, and I don't want to hurt your feelings by refusing, but a room downtown is better,'' he continued, seemingly unaware of his daughter's distress. "If they don't have suites in these small-town motels, we can take adjoining rooms and use one of them for campaign headquarters."

"Dad . . ." Susannah said, getting her voice back at last.

But her father was on a roll now.

"We've got to start running TV spots as soon as we can get them lined up," he went on. "Who owns that big billboard I noticed coming into town? Your name and your face on that billboard, bigger than life, with nothing else but white space and the words, 'For Judge.' Then they'd *know* who you were by election time."

"Dad . . ." Susannah tried again.

"I know. I know. You're going to say all that costs money. Don't worry about the money. There are plenty of people with money in the city that I've helped out in the past who'd feel honored to make a contribution to get you elected judge."

"Dad! You've got to listen to me," Susannah said, raising her voice on a note of desperation. "The surest way to lose this election is to bring in a lot of outside money and make the kind of splash you're talking about."

"Now, Susie . . ."

"I *mean* it, Dad," she insisted, her voice taking on a new firmness. It was now or never. She was sorry she had to do this to her father, but she couldn't let her sadness at the thought he was drawing to the close of a successful and rewarding career jeopardize her own future.

"There probably isn't anybody in the world who understands San Francisco politics better than you do," she said warmly. "If you took a count, you've probably been more instrumental in getting more candidates elected to city offices than anyone in the state.''

"Oh, I don't know about that," her father demurred with a modest smile.

"Don't be coy, darling. You know it's true," she said, gently teasing. "That's San Francisco, and in San Francisco you're the best. But River County is not San Francisco. It is a small out-of-the-way county a hundred and fifty miles away from there, and the people here are proud of the fact they *are* small-town. They resent anyone coming in from outside to tell them how to run their show, Dad.''

"Now look here, Susannah, you aren't thinking of putting a bunch of amateurs in charge of this campaign, are you?''

"Yes, that's exactly what I'm doing," Susannah said flatly. "Have already done, in fact." She laid her hand on his arm and went on earnestly. "Just listen a minute, and I'll tell you about the plans and the people who are already working on it. They know about River County politics, Dad, just like you know about San Francisco.''

It was an hour later when Susannah's father pushed back his chair and rose to leave. The threat of storm was gone from his eyes, and Susannah reached up to kiss his cheek with a feeling of new affection. There was a hint of wistfulness there she found hard to face. At the door he paused and looked down at her with a crooked smile.

"I'd be lying if I said I hadn't been looking forward to winning my daughter's first election for her," he said ruefully. "But I'm an old pol', honey, and I've been in the business long enough to see what'll work and what won't work in this game. You've given me a pretty clear picture of the situation, and I have to say, you're right. These people sound like they know what they're doing. You're lucky to have them. I'd do you more harm than good."

Susannah's eyes flooded with tears, and she reached to put her arms around her father's neck.

"Oh, Dad, I do love you," she said.

CHAPTER TEN

"THE SUPERIOR COURT of River County, California, is now in session, the Honorable Judge Susannah Ross presiding," called out the bailiff. "Please stand."

Every day for a week now, Sullivan had been through the ritual twice a day, but he felt little better prepared for it this Monday morning than he had been that first day a week ago. Maybe less, he thought as the door to the judicial chambers opened and Susannah emerged in her black robe. On that other Monday, the only picture of her he had in his mind was ten years old and distorted by the memory of anger.

Today she appeared more beautiful than she'd ever seemed before, her velvety cheeks the color of a ripe peach from Saturday's touch of the mountain sun. The dark eyes, alert and serious, passed over him without a flicker of acknowledgment as she crossed to the bench.

As he watched her, his vision was blocked by the memory of her body's alabaster beauty in the pale light of the full moon.

"You may be seated," said the bailiff when the judge had taken her place.

Sullivan sat down mindlessly in reflex to the bailiff's instruction, but as the sound of movement in the courtroom quieted, he had to quell the sensual rise within and come back to the stern reality of the black-robed woman on the bench.

Focusing his attention on the yellow legal-size note pad before him, with reminders jotted for today's questioning, he concentrated on how to make the most of the next witness's testimony and waited for his pulse to slow down to normal.

"Mr. Sullivan, is your next witness ready to be sworn?" Susannah's voice came down to him crisply from the bench. He looked up from his notes. Their eyes met. He could find no hint in hers that she remembered the hours spent recently in his arms. He wondered uneasily if he was as successful as she at keeping the memory of it from showing in his face.

"Yes, Your Honor," he said, rising to his feet. He gave a nod to Len Barron, Minerva Farms comptroller, his first witness of the day, to indicate Barron should step up and be sworn in.

Up to this point Sullivan's goal had been to convince the jury that a chemical spilled from an Ag Dusters spraying plane had destroyed a bumper crop of Minerva Farms' tomatoes. Today he would launch the second phase of the plaintiff's case. His purpose now was to fix in the jurors' minds what the loss of the crop had cost Minerva Farms in terms of actual dollars.

This was not only the most difficult part of the case to prove, he knew, but also the hardest in which to keep the jury's attention. Times before, when trying such a case, Sullivan had watched the faces in a jury box and seen eyes glaze over when the questions and answers turned to the breakdown of damage costs. When you asked them to award a client a damage total in six figures they thought it was too high, but give them someone on the stand to break down the figure and explain to them how it all adds up, and they fall asleep, he thought dourly. His biggest job now was to keep the jury awake.

Three witnesses and a number of charts and graphs later, Sullivan finished the case for Minerva Farms in time for the midafternoon recess. The jury had paid reasonable attention to the figures, and he was glad to have all the facts out on the table. Nevertheless, as he put his papers into his briefcase to leave the courtroom for the break, he was deeply dissatisfied.

He was relieved to see that his client, Bancroft, who had been in and out of the courtroom watching the proceedings from the beginning, hadn't chosen to be there today. After the third day of the trial, Bancroft had been boasting gleefully that the case was as good as won. Sullivan knew better. The defense was yet to come, and he felt uneasy. He was in no mood to talk to his client right now.

If he only had another witness who could say positively that the Ag Dusters plane had spilled the chemical on the tomato field. One wasn't enough, especially when the one happened to be a longtime employee of Minerva Farms.

If the jury hadn't already taken note of the lack of a corroborating witness on that single, most important testimony, Corwin would point out the oversight.

By the time Sullivan left, the courtroom had emptied. He walked out into the corridor and paused to speak for a moment with his final witness, who was on his way to the elevator. When they had shaken hands and parted, Sullivan bent over a nearby fountain for a drink of water. As he raised his head, Jill Fitzgerald came out of the door to the Superior Court reception room down the hall and walked toward him. From the sheaf of papers she carried, he assumed she was on an errand. He was about to walk on without detaining her when he suddenly stopped short. He hadn't had a chance to thank her for sending him to Patch Creek.

And then he remembered the fish. *The damned fish!* When he left the meadow the day before, he'd forgotten he had a limit of trout, cleaned and ready to cook, in his ice box in the back of the Jeep. He hadn't thought to offer them to Susannah or to give them to the owner of the Indian Camp store on his way back down. He'd forgotten about them until he got all the way back to Cacheton.

Now he was stuck with them. He had to find someone to give them to in this town of strangers or else throw them away.

Throw them away where? The motel would about as soon have him fry them in one of their rooms as dump them in one of their trash cans.

That left Jill Fitzgerald. He hurried to catch up with the compact little figure in high heels and a blue dress as she clicked up the corridor away from him. With his long stride he quickly reached her and slowed down, matching his step to hers.

"Ms. Fitzgerald, could I talk to you a minute?" he said as he came up beside her. He was surprised to see her face take on a look of alarm when she saw who it was. The alarm was covered by an uneasy smile.

"Why...uh, Mr. Sullivan! Hello."

"I want to thank you for sending me to Patch Creek," he said.

She studied him a moment, and he watched the smile change from uneasy to dubious.

"You . . . liked it?"

"Liked it? I had the best fishing I've had in a long time, and not another soul on the stream. We had the place to ourselves." Too late he realized his gratuitous use of the plural and knew that to correct it now would only make matters worse. Except for a quick blink of her eyes, Jill showed no sign she heard it.

"I'm glad you had a good time," she said primly, but at the same time she beamed at him.

"The fishing was so good I came back with a limit in my ice box and no place to cook them," he told her. "I was hoping you'd take them off my hands. If you're not a fish eater you might know someone who is."

"As a matter of fact, I do," Jill said delightedly. "The Kramers—Lucille and Jack—the people I used to live with. They're crazy about trout and never have time to fish."

"You'll be doing me a favor," Sullivan told her. "How about meeting me in the law library after court adjourns this afternoon? You can come down to the parking lot with me and I'll give you the trout."

"That'll be great," said Jill in agreement. "Now, if you'll excuse me, I've got to run. I've got to see the court reporter about a transcript."

Sullivan headed back to the courtroom grinning. *Why the cheeky little rascal!* he said to himself, feeling a warm glow of affection for the pretty, freckle-faced matchmaker who was evidently responsible for his meeting with Susannah on the mountain. He now understood what Susannah had meant when she'd said, "You don't know Jill Fitzgerald." Jill was obviously a force to be reckoned with, and a good one to have on your side.

SHORTLY AFTER COURT RECONVENED, the bailiff brought Sullivan a note from Oliver Fox—the detective he'd hired to locate the missing pilot—asking Sullivan to contact him as soon as possible. Reading it, Sullivan felt a stir of anticipation. Could it be Fox was on to something? He pocketed the note and turned his attention to the proceedings.

With his first witness, Corwin had set the tone of the defense. The witness was experienced in the development of hybrid plants and was there to testify that hybrids such as the Minerva tomatoes were sometimes more susceptible than commoner varieties to outside factors such as weather, soil and water conditions.

On cross-examination by Sullivan, the witness admitted he had not seen the Minerva crop at any time, nor had he any knowledge that what he had sworn to was necessarily applicable to it.

Undaunted, the defense attorney next brought to the stand a specialist who testified that the temperatures during the period in which the crop was damaged had been excessively high. A soil expert was then called on to leave a suggestion in the jurors' minds that the soil was too shallow to support tomato plants so heavily loaded with fruit. A doctor in chemistry next turned their attention to a high boron content in the irrigation water.

The only way to cope with this, Sullivan decided, was to bring in rebuttal witnesses who could testify that the same tomatoes in other fields had not been damaged by the same heat and boron. He would also call on a soil expert to verify the quality of the soil in the field. An arduous way at best. Flood soil deposit in the field was both rich and deep.

It was plain to Sullivan that since Corwin lacked real evidence to refute the testimony already presented, the best he could do was to throw such a barrage of counter possibilities at the jury he would confuse them into a defense verdict or a hung jury.

Sullivan sat through the remainder of the afternoon session with a faint new hope that Ollie Fox was at last on the trail of his missing witness. A glance at Bancroft, who had chosen to drop in for the opening salvos of the defense, told him his client was not happy with the way things were going. Nor was Sullivan. Long before the time came for court to adjourn for the day, Sullivan's impatience to call the detective seemed to be eating a hole in him. When the tap of the gavel signaled the end of the court day, Sullivan was the first on his feet.

"Hey, wait a minute, Sullivan." Bancroft's nasal voice behind him brought him around with a start. "What the hell's going on here? You didn't even *try* to cross those turkeys up on cross-examination. You keep on like this and you're going to lose this Goddamn lawsuit for us."

"Later, Hubert," Sullivan said, trying to keep his voice placating. "Trust me. I haven't got time to talk about it now."

Leaving his client glaring after him angrily, Sullivan hurried out of the courtroom and down the stairs to the pay phone he knew was in the basement. Bancroft was mad enough at the moment to ask to have him removed from the case. Sullivan would have to mend those fences later. Right now, the matter of first importance was to make connection with Ollie Fox.

As the courtroom cleared, Susannah made her customary unhurried exit into the sanctuary of her chambers, yet it was all she could do to hold back from making a dash for it. When Dan had rested his case with no witness to back up the field checker's testimony in regard to the boom, she knew for the first time how much she wanted him to win. And for the first time she was seriously afraid he wouldn't.

With the door to the courtroom safely closed behind her, she threw herself full length on the couch and covered her eyes with her arms.

Dan! she cried inwardly. *What am I going to do?* Like it or not, he was part of her. Without her wanting it to happen, it had become a personal thing. She wanted him to win as much as she had wanted herself to win when she was a lawyer trying a case. She almost wished she had disqualified herself in the beginning and been spared the repeated agony of having to rule against him. Each time it placed her in a moral dilemma, one she would endure again and again to the bitter end of the trial.

A discreet rap on the door adjoining the reception room brought her arms down from her eyes. She sat up, placing her feet on the floor.

"Jill?"

The door opened enough to let the piquant face peer around the edge.

"You okay, Boss?" Susannah managed a grin for the name her secretary had recently bestowed upon her.

"Fine," she lied, making a determined effort to look as if she were.

"You don't look it," her secretary observed bluntly. "Bad day in court?"

Susannah shrugged her shoulders. "Until this case is over, they're *all* going to be bad days, I'm afraid," she admitted with a sigh. "I'm too close to it."

Jill gave her a speculative look. "Do I take that to mean that you got things worked out at Patch Creek?"

"No . . . sorry, Jill," Susannah said abruptly. "You gave it your best shot. Now let's forget about it."

After a moment's awkward silence, Jill asked cheerfully, "How's it going in court?"

"Moving right along," Susannah told her, trying to keep her tone breezy. Then, giving in to her concern, she said, "Dan's got a problem, I'm afraid. He closed his case today and he still hadn't put on anyone to back up the witness on whom his whole case hangs."

"You don't think the jury'll believe the witness alone?"

"A trusted employee of Minerva Farms for umpteen years? What would you think?"

"I'm sorry to hear that. Mr. Sullivan's a nice man. You really think he's lost the case?" Jill asked, and Susannah could hear the genuine concern in her voice.

"He could still put someone on in rebuttal maybe, or I might even be able to let him reopen his case. But he doesn't have anyone," Susannah insisted. "Dan would have used him early on if he had." A new thought entered her mind and caused her to digress. "Incidentally, would you mind telling me where you two met?"

"Over coffee at the counter at Quentin's Café last week," said Jill with a grin.

"And the subject of fishing came up, and you just happened to draw him a map to Patch Creek?" Susannah asked accusingly.

Jill bypassed the question by changing the subject. "Have you anything country and western to wear to the Kramers' barn dance, Susannah?"

"Oh, that's right . . . the barn dance," she said absently. "When did you say that was, Jill?"

"You don't remember?" wailed Jill. "It's Friday—the end of this week."

"That soon!" Susannah said with a groan, then hastened to add, "Don't worry, my friend. I'll be there and appropriately dressed. The groan was because I should have gotten in touch with the Kramers long before this. What must they think?"

"They're beginning to think you don't really care all that much about winning the election," Jill said candidly, her voice faintly reproachful.

"Look, Jill, would you please call the Kramers for me and see if I could come out and talk to them after dinner tonight?" she asked.

"They'll be happy to see you, I know, unless they're tied up with something else."

"It's the old ostrich syndrome, I'm afraid," Susannah admitted. "Bury your head and it'll go away. All I can say is it comes from a lifelong aversion to politics. It's just occurred to me that I'm going to have to do this periodically as long as I want to be a judge, so I'd better get used to it."

"It also occurs to me that how I feel about politics is *my* problem, and both self-centered and irrelevant. The voters have a right to as much of me as it's possible for me to give them, whether I like it or not," she went on seriously. "They have a right to see who I am and how I think and what my philosophy is as a judge. It's the only way they can decide intelligently whether they want me to stay on or not. It's not fair to the voters for me to expect other people to get out and sell me like a . . . used car!''

Jill clapped her hands in applause. "Great speech, Boss."

IN A PHONE BOOTH on the ground floor of the courthouse, Sullivan gave the operator his credit card number and the phone number of Ollie Fox and waited impatiently for the call to go through.

At the third ring, the familiar voice of the detective came over the line.

"Fox speaking?"

"This is Sullivan, Ollie. What's up?"

"It looks like I may have a lead on your missing witness," Fox said. "It seems he lived with a family by the name of Kramer in Cacheton for a few years as a teenager. I talked to them on the phone this afternoon. They say the last they heard he was in Alaska."

Sullivan's spirits took a plunge. Alaska was a big place.

"They don't have an address for him?"

"They seem to have lost touch somehow, but they gave me the name of a woman they say corresponds with him regularly. I thought I'd better talk to you about it before I follow through on it, in case you might know her."

"Not likely. I don't know anyone here."

"Well, she happens to be the judge's secretary, name of Jill—"

"Fitzgerald!" Sullivan broke in with enthusiasm. "She happens to be one of the few people I do know in this town. Matter of fact, I'm going to be seeing her in about an hour."

"You want to take care of it?"

"Glad to. Thanks a lot, Ollie. Any more leads, in case this doesn't work out?"

"This is it. You want me to keep at it?"

"Time's running short. We'll see. In any case, I'll get back to you."

Sullivan hung up the phone and stepped out of the booth, running his hand through his hair, quite unaware of the disarray he was causing it. *Jill Fitzgerald!* Right here under his nose all the time. He wondered if she had any idea what an important piece of information she was holding, and if she did, had she been deliberately keeping it to herself? And if she was, why?

From each question leaped another until he shrugged them away and headed back up to the third floor to research a point of law in the law library, where he had agreed to meet her when she was through work.

Shortly after five o'clock he looked up from his books to see Jill in the doorway of the library. Motioning that he would be right with her, he got up and returned the books to their places before ushering her out into the corridor.

"Come with me to the parking lot, and I'll move the trout from the wagon to your car," Sullivan told her as they started down the hall.

"I'm sorry," Jill said. "Mine's not in the parking lot. It's at my apartment. Until I could afford a car I walked everywhere. I still walk back and forth to work if the weather's right."

"If you don't mind giving up your walk, how about letting me give you a ride home?"

"That would be fine, thanks."

She directed him to a two-story U-shaped apartment complex built around an inner courtyard and swimming pool a few blocks from the courthouse. So near, in fact, they arrived before Sullivan had framed the question uppermost in his mind.

"My apartment's in the back," Jill told him as he pulled up in front of the entrance.

"Fine," said Sullivan. "Wait a minute while I get the trout out of the ice box..."

Before he finished his sentence Jill was out of the Jeep and waiting for him at the rear of the vehicle. She peered curiously into the back end with its load of fishing rods and camping equipment, boots and waders.

"Do you carry all this stuff around with you all the time?" she asked curiously.

"Usually," he admitted with a grin. "One never knows when you'll find yourself near a good fishing stream? Why?"

Jill shrugged and gave him a sad little smile. "Oh, it just reminds me of someone I know." Then, seeing that Sullivan intended to carry the plastic bag of fish to her apartment, she protested, "I can manage. You needn't bother to bring them in."

"No bother. Lead the way."

When she had unlocked the door and turned again to relieve him of his catch, Dan still didn't relinquish it.

"I may as well take them in to your refrigerator," he said. "If you don't mind, I'd like to stay and talk to you for a bit."

The secretary darted him a wary look but didn't protest. When the package of fish had been stowed in the refrigerator and, after a moment of obvious indecision, she had offered him a drink, which he declined, Jill at last asked him to sit down. Sullivan dropped into the lap of an overstuffed flower-print sofa. Jill took an upholstered chair nearby, from which she eyed him uneasily.

"I hope you're not going to ask me anything about Judge Ross, because I'm not going to tell you anything," she said. "Besides that, she'd be furious if she knew you were asking."

The idea was so preposterous, so unexpected, Sullivan laughed aloud.

"Relax," he said. "Of course I'm not going to ask you about Judge Ross. Why the devil do you think I would?"

The pretty, freckled face flushed. It was a most disarming one, thought Sullivan.

"Because she's all I can think of that you might want to ask me about," she said with complete candor.

"What about a young man by the name of Oreste Kerns, Jill?"

Her face suddenly went pale and the blue eyes were shot with alarm.

"Oh my God! Resty! Something's happened to him!" She flew out of her chair to the sofa beside him and seized his hand, her own hands as cold as ice. "What's happened to Resty, Mr. Sullivan?"

The efficient, self-contained secretary seemed to him all at once a frightened child who needed comforting.

"Calm down, honey," he said, rubbing the cold fingers. "Nothing's happened, at least as far as I know. I'm just trying to locate him, and I was told you might have his last address."

The young woman breathed a shuddering sigh and withdrew her hands. He watched in silence as she struggled to pull herself together, afraid that anything he said might destroy her fragile control. After a few moments she got up, walked over to the refrigerator and poured a glass of white wine for herself with a hand that shook.

"Would you care to join me?" she asked unsteadily.

"If you have a beer."

By the time she poured the beer and brought it back to him, her hand was steady once more.

"Before we go any further, Mr. Sullivan, I have to know why you are looking for Resty," she said firmly. "If he's in some kind of trouble..."

"If he is, I certainly don't know about it," Sullivan assured her. "I need him as a witness in this Minerva lawsuit I'm trying in Judge Ross's court. If I don't find him, I may jolly well lose the bloody case."

"Resty? *He's* your missing witness? Oh, I don't think..."

"Oreste Kerns, the pilot of the crop-dusting plane with the malfunctioning boom that dumped a lethal load of chemicals on Minerva Farms' tomato crop," Sullivan insisted.

Jill stared at him with dawning comprehension. "So *that's* why he just took off," she said in a stunned voice. "All he would say was that he'd gotten in a terrible row with Mr. Ashton, the owner of Ag Dusters, and was going to cut out. But that was nearly two years ago."

"That's right. It's been nearly two years since the whole thing took place. Young Kerns must have left not too long after it happened, because we couldn't find him when we took depositions. It didn't seem important enough at the time to go looking for him."

"What makes it so important now?"

"A former employee at Ag Dusters has told me the reason Kerns left was he couldn't get Ashton to keep the equipment in shape. The guy says Kerns told him that he'd warned Ashton about that leaky boom at least three times before it dumped on the tomato crop, and when your friend Resty heard that the tomatoes he'd made his return over that day were destroyed, he quit."

"That's Resty," Jill said.

"If I can get him to swear to that on the stand, I've won my case," Sullivan told her. "That's why I'm asking you to tell me where he can be found."

"The trouble is, I don't know," she admitted, her voice breaking. "He's not real good about writing. I have an address for him in Ketchikan, Alaska, but the last letter I wrote came back."

"When was he in Ketchikan?"

"Not more than a month ago, but I don't know where he went from there. He didn't leave any forwarding address."

Sullivan pretended not to see the tears that filled her eyes and rolled down her cheeks.

"How long have you known Resty, Jill?" he asked gently.

She thought a minute. "Going on twelve years, I guess." She hesitated, as if unsure whether to reveal more. Then she gave an embarrassed laugh and added, "We were both in the county detention home."

Under Sullivan's kindly, discreet questioning, Jill gradually unfolded the story she had told Susannah of her own unorthodox upbringing. The dominant thread woven through it was Resty Kerns, a sixteen-year-old runaway when they met. Gradually a picture took shape of the lonely youth from an upper-middle-class San Diego home of career-oriented parents unsettled by divorce and remarriage who made himself Jill's self-appointed protector at the detention home.

It didn't take Sullivan long to see that to Jill, Resty had been her White Knight from the beginning. He also surmised that to Resty, she was the little sister he'd never had, which was not at all what Jill wanted to be.

As Jill told it, they had both been wards of the court. The late Judge Randall had found a home for Jill with his daughter and son-in-law, Lucille and Jack Kramer, and tried to send Resty back to his parents in southern California, but young Kerns had balked and the parents had not seen fit to insist. He had remained under Judge Randall's guardianship and gone to live and work on the Kramer farm until he discovered Ag Dusters, the flying operation down the road. The owner, Lloyd Ashton had hired him as a flag man for the company's crop-dusting planes and later taught him to fly.

"Everybody said Resty was the best crop-dusting pilot in the business," Jill told Sullivan proudly. "He loves to fly. That's what he's been doing in Alaska. Making charter flights into the fishing country."

Sullivan felt a load lift off his shoulders. "If that's what he's doing, we'll have no trouble locating him through Alaskan aviation and sportsmen sources. I'll get the detective on it right away."

"What are you going to do?" Jill asked anxiously. "Subpoena him?"

"There's no point in that. If he didn't want to come we couldn't make him. They don't extradite except in a criminal case,'' Sullivan explained. "No. We'll ask him nicely and pay all his expenses. He'll be glad to come. Wouldn't you like to have him home for a visit?''

"Oh, Mr. Sullivan, there isn't anything I'd like better," Jill said with a deep sigh. "But he won't come. He's not about to come back here and testify against the man who taught him to fly.''

"I think we can persuade him, Jill, once we get him on the phone,'' said Sullivan positively. "If that doesn't work, we'll send somebody up there to convince him it's the right thing to do.''

"Mr. Sullivan, you don't know Resty. You can't *get* him to testify against Mr. Ashton, and that's all there is to it.''

"But you just said they'd had a falling out. Apparently because of the faulty boom. When I point out over the phone what a lot of damage the leak caused, surely he'll—''

"Mr. Sullivan, if you find him, *don't* try to talk to him about it on the phone,'' Jill pleaded, tears in her voice. "If you do, you'll lose him for all of us. *Please*, not over the phone.''

"I don't see—''

"You don't know Resty. You'll lose him for good, if you do. If he thinks you're coming to try to talk him into it, he'll take off again, and next time he won't even let *me* know where he is.'' Again she was almost in tears. "That's the way Resty is. If he can't figure out what to do about something, he takes off.''

"You mean he'll run away?''

"He's been doing it all his life, when he thinks things are getting to be more than he can handle.''

Sullivan was finally convinced. He didn't like it, but he was convinced she knew what she was talking about.

Getting to his feet to leave, he said gently, "It'll be all right, Jill. I'll get Fox to find him for us, and then I'll let you know." Maybe by that time he could figure out how to get Kerns back here on the witness stand, he thought. "Whatever we do, I promise you we won't risk his running away."

CHAPTER ELEVEN

THE KRAMERS' BARN was big and red and had a high arched roof to accommodate a hay loft on either side within. Tonight the floor had been swept clean for the barn dance, which was designed to draw a good sampling of the River County populace to meet Susannah. The Kramers were confident these same people would subsequently sway others to vote for Susannah on election day. Susannah wondered how they could be so sure.

Huge track doors at both ends of the barn had been rolled back to open it up and let the evening breeze blow through, carrying with it the pungent smell of citronella from lanterns suspended from the rafters to keep mosquitoes away. Around the walls, bales of hay had been arranged for seating, leaving a huge center circle of empty floor space for square dancing, which was soon to begin.

Standing with the Kramers at the front of the open barn, Susannah looked around her in awe. Already the place was alive with people who had begun to arrive some fifteen minutes before the appointed hour and had continued for the next half hour. Only now had the stream of newcomers thinned to a trickle.

When Jill had talked of a barn dance, Susannah had envisioned thirty or forty people drinking cider and dancing to taped country-western music. She'd spent almost every night of the past week talking campaign strategy with Lucille and Jack Kramer, but she wasn't prepared for this. Two hundred people at least, a group of hoe-down musicians playing live music, a barbecue supper, a wine-and-beer bar; the thought of the money that had gone into the affair staggered her. Her first thought was that she wasn't going to her father and his political cronies for funds. Even if it made her the most impecunious judge in California, she'd pay for it somehow.

The first chance she got during a break in arrivals she whispered to Lucille sickly, "How much will this all cost?"

"Not to worry," Lucille told her amiably. "Everybody here anted up fifteen dollars—all in advance. Ten dollars goes for food, drink and entertainment. The other five goes into the campaign coffers."

Susannah gazed at her in astonishment. "I didn't know you could do that."

Lucille laughed. "I don't know that it would work except in a place like River County. We're a long way from big-town entertainment. People work hard, and they jump at anything that looks like fun. They expect to pay for it, and they don't mind as long as it gives a chance for friends and neighbors to get together."

"What makes you think all these people want to contribute to my campaign fund?"

"I don't. Some of them probably would just as soon not, but they'd rather do it than miss a good party. It's up to you to see that they don't begrudge the extra five dollars."

Susannah looked at her aghast. "How on earth do you expect me to do that?"

"Just be yourself. Make a point of singling people out to visit with. Talk to everyone. Ask them about their work and their kids. Find out what they expect of a judge."

Meeting the people now as they came in, Susannah strove to record names, faces and pertinent data in her mind, and in the proper order: *Ellsworth Brock, banker, heavy jowled, balding; wife, Elise, blond hair, dark at the roots, chic blue dress. Dorothy Lewis, fortyish, school teacher...*

Fortunately Susannah had learned the art of remembering people and their names at an early age from her father and was quite good at it. She was reasonably sure that when she saw Ellsworth Brock later in the evening she would not call him Mr. Honeywell or ask him how his corn was doing, or address Dorothy Lewis as Mrs. Brock.

Except for an occasional straggler, the stream of arrivals at last had run out. To one side on a platform of loose wooden planks, the musicians in Western garb were now assembled and showing signs they were about to begin. The two fiddlers were tuning their instruments at the upright piano, and a tall, thin fellow with a cowlick like Alfalfa in the *Our Gang* comedies was studying a handful of three by five cards.

Jack Kramer excused himself to tend to the barbecue.

"I've got to go give the beans a stir," Lucille said. "Come with me, if you like, or I can send Jill out to keep you company. She's holding forth in the kitchen."

"In this crowd of thousands?" Susannah said with a laugh. "Let Jill take care of the kitchen. I'm here to meet my constituents, and by crackee that's what I aim to do."

When Lucille was gone, she stood looking after her, wondering what would have become of her election campaign if it weren't for this hearty, plump-bosomed woman and her energetic, jovial husband.

"Why me?" Susannah had asked from the depths of her appreciation the first night she had gone to their farm to discuss election plans.

And Lucille had said, "Because I didn't grow up the daughter of Judge Homer Randall without learning that the person who holds the most power over every other person in a county is the judge. Therefore you want your judge first of all to be wise and second, honest . . . or vice versa."

"We happen to believe that one of your opponents is not very honest," Jack had added, "and the other one is not very bright."

"What makes you think *I* am?" Susannah had asked.

"We have Jill's word for it," Lucille had said seriously.

When Lucille had disappeared in the direction of the house, Susannah turned her attention back to the crowd, where the preliminary strains of the music were playing and couples were beginning to take positions on the floor. It was a colorful scene, the men dressed in plaid Western shirts and denims, the women in traditional square-dancing garb—bright, full-skirted, calf-length cotton dresses or blouses and swirling skirts. A few of the younger women wore Western shirts and skin-tight jeans, mostly blue, though there was one mauve pair and one white.

Susannah had been hard-pressed to find something suitable in her own rather limited wardrobe. Taking measure of the dancers now, she felt reasonably sure her sheer apricot cotton dress with its banding of cotton lace around the full-swinging skirt was not too much of a "city dress" to be taken as a put-down by the natives.

The lanky fellow with the cowlick stepped to the front of the platform and began to call: "Honor your partners and circle to the right, now gents swing your ladies and keep those buzz steps light."

Watching, Susannah felt strangely isolated. She wondered for a moment where Dan was and what he was doing tonight, and in the next moment refused to let herself think about him anymore. She had finally accepted the fact that since there was no future for them together it was sheer folly to imagine seeing him alone again. To fill every momentary lull with thoughts of him didn't make it easier for her to forget.

She turned her attention to the dancers, who were now in full swing.

The caller sang out: "Ladies circle left, gents circle right, grab the prettiest gal in sight."

How was it possible to make personal contact with these people? she wondered helplessly. Those who were not cavorting in the square-dancing circles were congregated around the bar, which had been set up in the barn opening at the far end, and showed no inclination to come to her. As she debated whether it would be considered improper to join the people at the bar—mostly men—by herself, she noticed a late-comer, a man, approaching from where the cars were parked.

"I thought I knew everyone in River County, but I have never seen *you* here before," a mellow male voice remarked over her shoulder a moment later. She turned to find a squarely built man, a few inches taller than she, smiling humorously at her. His face was pleasant but rather homely, and he had a shock of iron-gray hair and warm gray eyes that peered at her from a crinkle of laugh lines.

Susannah smiled, but before she could speak, Jack Kramer came hurrying up beside them.

"I see you two have met," he observed. "I'm sorry, Susannah, I left you without even a drink. Nathan, why haven't you taken care of that?"

"I just got here, but I'll be glad to," the man said amiably. "And as a matter of fact, we haven't met, although I rather imagine this is the guest of honor."

"You're right about that. This is River County's now-and-future judge, Susannah Ross."

The man bowed his head slightly in acknowledgment. "Judge Ross, it's a pleasure to meet you. I'm Nathan Richards, and may I say you don't *look* like a judge—at least not like the ones I know."

Jack Kramer gave a hoot. "Look who's talking! You don't look like one, either. Susannah, this guy's a native of River County. Still owns a house outside Barnstown but lives in Sacramento. He's a superior court judge there."

Susannah smiled and held out her hand in welcome. "I'm delighted. I hadn't expected to meet another judge here tonight. You make me feel not quite so outnumbered."

Nathan Richards laughed. "It's not often we get a chance to talk shop. Especially where the population's the size of River County."

"This guy knows as much about the people of this county as anyone around here," Kramer said. "He's supposed to see that you get to know the ones who will bring in the vote. He can give you a rundown on everybody. Now, if you'll excuse me, I'm going to turn you over to Nathan and get back to the barbecue."

Uncomfortable and apologetic after Kramer was gone, Susannah said, "This is a terrible imposition on you. I'm embarrassed."

"Don't be," Richards said with a smile. "Jack Kramer is a lifelong friend. Probably as good a friend as a man can have. I would have come here willingly for the Kramers when they asked me under any circumstances. Now that we've met, I'd like to change that 'willingly' to 'gladly.' "

What a nice man, thought Susannah. *I really think he means it.*

While they had been talking, the dance set ended. Now the fiddler was retuning his fiddle and dancers were changing partners and beginning to regroup for another set. The crowd seemed to be divided into two groups, the dancers and those who stood and visited around the bar.

"Square dancing is a remarkably good way to get to know your constituents," Richards observed. "There's a kind of camaraderie about it. Would you care to get into this one?"

"Oh no, I couldn't," said Susannah in alarm. "I've never square danced. As a matter of fact, I've never done a lot of dancing of any kind. I grew up too fast, I'm afraid."

The humorous eyes watched her a moment. "Then

let's have a glass of wine and visit with the nondancers. If later you decide you'd like to try it, this is a good place to learn."

And so the evening went. It was midnight when the fiddler pulled his bow across his strings for the last time and the caller called the last sashay.

The evening had been a political success and more, Susannah concluded sometime later as she turned out her light and settled herself in bed. It had been fun. And something else. For the first time since Dan Sullivan had sallied back into her life, she'd been able to shut him out of her mind for a while. From the moment she had gone with Nathan Richards to mingle with the people around the bar, she'd been swept up in such a variety of conversation there'd been no room for any wool gathering on her own. Even less after she let Nathan talk her into entering the square-dancing arena.

Remembering, she smiled in the dark, rather pleased with herself. Square dancing had turned out to be not so different from the folk dancing she'd done in gym at school. Once he had taught her the basic vocabulary, words like *do-sa-do* and *promenade*, and she could understand the directions of the caller, her feet did what they were told to do.

And her first impression had indeed been right. Nathan Richards was a really *nice* man. One of the nicest men she'd ever met, maybe; a man she felt easy with. They had much in common and no conflict in careers. He was forty-one years old and a widower who lived and worked less than forty-five minutes away. And she had agreed to have dinner with him the following night.

So why wasn't she elated?

She buried her head in her pillow and cried a few tears... and fell asleep thinking of Dan.

AT THE EDGE of the Patch Creek meadow in the high Sierra, Sullivan lay wide awake in his sleeping bag, staring up at the sky full of stars and wondering what tomorrow would bring.

As time for adjournment had drawn near that afternoon, his mind had been made up to head home to Fresno for the weekend. It meant a long drive, but he had told himself that because Ollie Fox still hadn't turned up his missing witness he was edgy and needed to get away.

The truth of the matter, he now told the stars, was that he'd known he had to get out of Cacheton or he would find himself battering down Susannah's door. He'd taken the highway out of town that connected with Interstate 5 south to Fresno some miles out of Cacheton, and next thing he knew he was driving due east, heading into the Sierra. It was as if the Jeep had developed a will of its own.

He'd stopped at the Indian Camp store and had a couple of beers and exchanged fishing yarns with the proprietor, taking a counter stool where he could keep his eye on the highway outside, though he didn't know why.

The hell he didn't know why! he confessed to himself now. It was for the same reason he'd left the Indian Camp store and come up here to the meadow once it got too dark to recognize her car if it passed by—even knowing if she did come, it probably wouldn't be until the following morning, as she had done the week before.

And what made him think she would come at all? In those final minutes before she had driven away last week there'd been a tacit understanding it was a last goodbye. And yet as he lay there now, something told him she would come in the morning. Intuition or wishful thinking? He refused to question which.

Bleary-eyed from the restless night, he rose with the dawn, ate a peanut butter and jelly sandwich with a cup of coffee and took off to the stream below the meadow. He felt little zest for fishing today. After he had landed three ten-inch rainbows and released them back into the stream, he spent some time working to improve his roll-casting technique. When it neared ten o'clock, he packed up his tackle and headed back up the hill, his heart quickening with anticipation.

But the Jeep sat alone at the edge of the meadow. For a moment his disappointment was like a sickness. He'd been a damn fool to imagine she would change her mind.

He sat down on a log and propped his head on his hands, staring blindly at his boots, still wet from the creek. One thing was sure, he thought. He had to work out an answer to the dilemma they were caught in. He could not spend the rest of his days knowing he'd lost the most important person in his life because he hadn't gone the limit in looking for a way to keep her.

Eleven o'clock came with no Susannah. And then it was noon. He knew then she wouldn't come. He ate a can of sardines with crackers and drank a can of tomato juice, still stalling. Finally he stowed his fishing tackle and sleeping bag in the rear of the vehicle and started back down the logging road to Cacheton.

By midafternoon he was at his motel, where he found a message from Ollie Fox. In his room, he put in a call to the detective.

"I've located your man," Fox told him. "He's in Juneau, Alaska, working as a pilot-guide for a private charter company that takes fishing parties into the wilderness."

"You didn't talk to Kerns?"

"He wasn't there. Anyway, you told me not to. I talked to the owner, and he said Kerns was due back in Juneau Tuesday, so I told him I wanted to talk to Kerns personally about a fishing trip. The guy said I could call him at the company airstrip Tuesday. Now what do you want me to do?"

"Go get him, but I don't think you can do it alone."

"Hey, listen. You didn't tell me this guy was dangerous, Sullivan. You know I don't much like—"

"He's not dangerous. He just may not want to testify. You can stick a subpoena in his fist, but if he wants to stand pat there's no way on earth we can get him back here. Our only chance is to talk him into coming voluntarily. There's one person who might be able to do it," Sullivan told him. "Stick around. I'll call you back as soon as I can."

"So, JILL, the plan is for you to fly out of Sacramento Monday morning for Juneau, Alaska, with Ollie Fox, and on Tuesday you will see your old friend Resty again."

It was an hour later and Sullivan was sitting on Jill Fitzgerald's flowered sofa in her living room. Jill was in a chair across from him, gazing at him with a look both hypnotized and alarmed.

When she appeared disinclined to speak, Sullivan prompted, "Well, what do you think?"

Jill blinked and shook her head as if to clear her mind. "I think you're crazy, that's what I think," she said, straightening her shoulders, clearly getting a hold on the situation. "In the first place, what ever gave you the idea I could talk Resty Kerns into anything he didn't want to do?"

"I have a hunch Resty feels as great an attachment for you as you seem to feel for him," Sullivan said. When she eyed him skeptically, he went on, "Maybe not the same kind of attachment, exactly, but one that is just as strong."

"I'm just his kid sister," Jill replied disdainfully.

"A very intelligent and capable kid sister who must have had a strong influence on his attitudes when you were with each other," Sullivan told her. "All I'm asking you to do is talk to him. Tell him what's at stake here, and try to make him see that he has an obligation to himself to see that the truth is out. You can tell him Ashton doesn't stand to lose personally if the verdict goes against him. Ag Dusters is well insured. You might also tell him there's a rumor going around that Ashton plans to get out of the crop-dusting business as soon as the trial is over. I understand he is already looking for a buyer."

Sullivan could see he was making progress. He kept still and let her think about it. After a minute she got up and started for the kitchen.

"Coffee?" she asked absently, her forehead furrowed with worry.

"That'll be fine," Sullivan said, but doubted the words had gotten through to her until she came back and handed him a full mug, black and steaming.

"I'll admit, I really want to see Resty," she began slowly when she was seated with her coffee. "What you want me to do sort of makes sense. I used to talk him out of doing things that meant trouble sometimes, but I certainly can't guarantee I could get him back here for you, Mr. Sullivan. If I didn't, you'd be spending a lot of money for nothing."

"Not 'nothing' as far as you're concerned," Sullivan said with a grin. "You'll get to see your Resty. You let me worry about my end of it."

"I'm not saying I'll go, but suppose I decided I might. I can't just take off and leave Judge Ross without a secretary."

"What does she do when you're sick or take your vacation?" Sullivan asked.

"She hasn't been here long enough for that to happen, but with Judge Randall we always got a secretary from one of the other county offices to fill in."

"You could be back by Thursday. Do you think you could find someone to take your place till then?"

"I suppose so," Jill said without enthusiasm, "but what can I tell her?"

"What's wrong with the truth?"

"That I want time off to help one of the attorneys find a missing witness for a trial in her court? I can't do that. Think what a spot it puts her in."

Sullivan thought about it a moment. "I don't think any of us would actually be breaking any laws, but I suppose she might look on it as out of line."

"And there's another thing." Jill hesitated, then went on in a small voice that sounded suspiciously like a wail, "I've never been in an airplane."

"Then you're in for a treat," Sullivan assured her.

"The very thought of flying to Alaska scares me to death," she confessed, and the truth of what she said was there for him to hear in her voice.

Steeling himself against the unmistakable quaver, Sullivan got to his feet. "Then it's all settled," he announced positively. Jill stared at him in astonishment and rose to face him.

"Now wait a minute, Mr..."

"I'll have Ollie make all the travel arrangements," he continued. "I'll call you back later and fill you in on the details." He saw her draw a deep breath and then was relieved to see the pretty, freckled face shape itself into a bemused grin.

"I think I'm going to do it," she told him. "I must be out of my mind."

WHEN THE PHONE RANG, Susannah was lying stretched out in the sun on her patio, struggling with a melange of private worries that were doing their best to distract her from the Sunday paper.

"Susannah...uh...Boss?"

She knew it was Jill, but the voice sounded troubled and uncertain. Unlike Jill. Very strange, thought Susannah.

"Jill? That *is* you, isn't it? It doesn't sound like you. Is something wrong?"

"No... Well, yes...well, no, not really. It's just that... Listen, would it be bad for you if I got somebody...Helen Perkins...she used to come in for me on vacations when Judge Randall...*you* know her."

"Jill! Of course I know Helen Perkins. She works part-time as a court reporter," Susannah said, trying to make sense of the words coming at her over the wire. "Jill, please! Would you mind telling me what you're talking about? I can't believe you called me to find out if I know Helen.''

She heard a nervous laugh at the other end of the line, and then there was a pause. When her secretary spoke again it was in the stilted voice Susannah had grown accustomed to in the early months of her judgeship but had seldom heard in recent days.

''Something has come up. I have to be away for a few days, if it's all right with you.''

''It *is* all right, Jill. Surely you know that. How long do you think you'll be gone?''

''I expect to be back sometime Thursday. I've already talked to Helen, and she said it would be fine with her. She said unless she heard from me otherwise, she would be in the office tomorrow at nine o'clock.''

There was a sound of apprehension, almost fear, in the voice of her secretary that disturbed Susannah.

''There *is* something wrong, isn't there. What can I do to help?''

''There's nothing wrong, really,'' Jill insisted, but Susannah didn't believe her.

''This is your friend you're talking to, Jill. Not the judge. Please tell me what's going on.''

''Remember the...the fellow I told you I...hadn't heard from, and the letter came back?'' Jill said, after a moment. ''Well, it's . . . him.''

''Oh, Jill! You've found him.'' Susannah was about to express pleasure when she realized there was nothing in Jill's voice to encourage celebration. ''I hope it's nothing bad.''

''No, it's nothing bad,'' said Jill in a flat voice. ''I have to go. I'll see you Thursday.''

Slowly Susannah put the phone back in its cradle. There was something going on—had been for several days. Jill had tightened up and become more than usually close-mouthed. Susannah racked her brain trying to come up with something she herself might have done to cause the change but couldn't think of a thing. Nevertheless, her secretary seemed almost to be avoiding any conversation between them outside of court business. At the barn dance, she realized suddenly, her own secretary was probably the only person she hadn't visited with that night. She would notice Jill across the barn, but by the time she'd made her way through the crowd to the spot where she'd last seen her, Jill would have disappeared.

With a glance at her watch, Susannah rose and went inside, her mind still on her secretary. She felt troubled to discover Jill didn't reciprocate with the same trust and openness Susannah had shown freely to her.

In her bedroom she peeled off the shorts and halter she'd worn out in the sun, showered, then changed into a cool, butter-yellow cotton dress and a pair of buff espadrilles. She was going with Nathan Richards to an outdoor fund-raising concert and supper on the grounds of a turn-of-the-century mansion that had been bought by the county and was gradually being converted into a historical museum to house River County's past.

It was to be the last of a series of electioneering junkets Richards had taken her on. They had spent Saturday driving around, talking to people—all of whom Nathan knew—on the streets of the county's outlying towns and calling on what seemed an unlimited number of his lifelong friends.

She was almost sorry the pleasant weekend was drawing to a close. Nathan Richards was an intelligent and entertaining companion, and there had even been a moment when she had wondered if he might in time be able to fill the deep, empty hole in her life left by Dan.

But it had been only a moment, and in the next, her heart was keening for Sullivan. She had known then that there might never come a time when she could settle for somebody else. Still, she dreaded the moment when Nathan would ask for more than companionship. She needed him. She needed him as her friend, and she knew from experience that all it would take to ruin their friendship was to say no.

THE AFTERNOON EXTENDED into a long evening at the old mansion and was as much education as pleasure, Susannah thought when Richards pulled his car to a stop in front of her house some hours later. Campaigning was easy in the company of this man who not only seemed to know everybody in the county he'd been born and raised in, but still maintained a genuine affection for most of them, an affection that was clearly returned.

"I must say I'm glad you didn't decide to come back here to practice law after you graduated," she said with a laugh as he escorted her to her door. "Anyone running for judge against you in this county wouldn't stand a chance. I can't begin to express my appreciation to you for devoting yourself to me these past two days."

Richards smiled his appreciation. "You don't have to. It's in the best interests of all judges to do what they can to get high-caliber judges elected all over the state.

Besides, I wouldn't have missed it for the world. If Jack Kramer hadn't asked me to introduce you around I might never have got to know you.''

Oh-oh, here it comes, thought Susannah with a feeling of regret as she turned the key to unlock her door.

"Do you mind if I come in for a minute?" Richards continued. "There's something I'd like to talk to you about."

Hiding a strong desire to postpone the conversation she could see coming, Susannah said, "Then do come in. I'll fix us some coffee."

"Not for me, thanks. I've got a full day in court tomorrow and need my sleep. Don't let that stop you from fixing it for yourself."

"I don't really want any, either," she said. "Do sit down."

But he made no move to be seated. Looking at her directly, he said, "I'm sure you must know, Susannah, that I find you a delightful companion and one of the most...well, *decent*, persons I've ever known."

"Thank you. I feel exactly the same about you," Susannah said with equal directness, refusing to play coy in the face of his obvious sincerity.

Richards gave a self-deprecating chuckle. "Well, I didn't intend this to be a fishing expedition, but thanks." He paused a moment before he went on. "You will have to forgive me for being blunt about what I am about to say, but I don't see how else I can handle it."

Susannah looked at him, puzzled.

"I've been a widower for five years, and to be perfectly candid with you, Susannah, I've grown very comfortable with bachelorhood. Furthermore, I don't have the time or temperament for all that male-female posturing we used to call dating.'' He came to a stop and seemed uncertain how to go on.

It didn't sound like a proposition, thought Susannah curiously, much less a proposal.

"Damnit, Susannah," he said at last. "What I'm trying to tell you is I'm reluctant to give up the good companionship we've shared the last couple of days, but I'm not sure I've got anything much to offer except what you've already seen. I had a very good relationship with my wife. After she died, I . . .''

Susannah laid her hand on his arm and brought him to a stop. In response to the concern she saw on his face, she laughed with genuine amusement.

"Would you feel more comfortable if you knew that ever since you asked to come in and talk I've been afraid you were about to spoil a fine friendship by wanting a commitment of some kind? Your friendship is all I want from you, Nathan. I hope to see you now and then for a long time to come.''

"Until the right man for you comes along, Susannah.''

An unexpected feeling of melancholy cast a shadow across her smiling face.

"He's already come," she told him, and added tonelessly, "and gone.''

After a moment of silence Richards said, "Ah, so.'' He moved to the door, Susannah following.

"I'll keep in touch with you and Jack on your campaign. If there's anything I can do to help, let me know.'' He bent his head and dropped a kiss on the top of hers. "Good night.''

Susannah closed the door on his departing figure and stood for a moment, her mind on Nathan Richards.

He really was a nice man. But he was not Dan.

CHAPTER TWELVE

SHE WAS A LONG TIME getting to sleep. Exactly twenty minutes later, 12:15 by her digital clock, the insistent clangor of the telephone bell by her bed startled her awake again. Struggling to collect her wits, she propped herself on one elbow and reached for the phone. If it was some lawyer wanting her to sign an order to get a drunken client released from jail, he was out of luck, she thought with the crankiness of the rudely awakened. Let the miscreant spend a night on a jail bed. Wasn't it better than sending him home to some long-suffering wife?

"Judge Ross speaking," she said in her best no-nonsense voice.

"Susannah..."

"Dan! Oh darling...oh, Dan. Is something the matter? Something's wrong," she cried out in alarm, suddenly alert.

"Of course something's wrong. You *do* love me, don't you?"

"You don't have to ask. You know I do."

"Well, and I love you. So if the two of us can't come up with some way to break this deadlock and spend the rest of our lives together, we don't deserve each other." His voice was husky with determination. "It's true, we've got some obstacles between us, but it's no time to abandon each other, sweetheart. It's time to close ranks."

She couldn't see the logic in what he said but felt no inclination to argue it. All that mattered was that he was there at the other end of the line.

"Oh, Dan, I *need* you," she said intensely, her voice hardly more than a whisper.

Across the wire she heard Sullivan's groan. "Oh, God, Susannah, do I ever need *you*," he said grimly. "Stay right where you are. I'm coming."

"You can't, Dan. The trial...someone will see..."

"It's not going to affect the trial any more than it did up on the mountain," argued Sullivan, almost crossly. "And nobody's going to see. I've already cased your house. It's dark as a pit. The street light's way up at the end of the block. With all those trees and shrubs, who's going to know?"

Susannah thought a moment. "Maybe not my neighbors to the north. The landscaping takes care of them, but I'm not so sure about the ones on the other side." She hesitated, reconsidering. "No. I just remembered. They're gone. They're in San Diego to see their son."

"I'm as good as on my way. Don't turn on the porch light."

"Suppose somebody sees your car?"

"They won't. I'll walk. Expect me at your front door in ten minutes."

The line went dead. Still holding the phone, Susannah lay back on her pillow and stared into the darkness again.

Dear God, how she loved the man! He was so positive, he could make her believe anything. And yet for all his talk, she knew they didn't have a prayer of breaking what he called "this deadlock." Not as long as she remained judge.

She didn't even bother to reconsider the alternative now. She'd been over that ground too many times before and knew instinctively that as much as she loved Dan, if she gave up the bench to be with him, she would give up a part of herself.

Nothing had changed. It was insane to let Dan talk her into letting him come. She put out her hand to touch the phone base for a dial tone. She must stop him before he left his room.

She looked for the motel number in the directory and picked up the phone to dial, then paused. After a moment she hung up. She wouldn't be truthful if she tried to convince herself she had really wanted him not to come.

WITH THE FAST, steady stride of a man taking a nightly walk for exercise, Sullivan passed under the street light at the end of the block and out of its arc into the deepening darkness beyond. He resented having to see Susannah on the sneak and was relieved that the occupants of the houses he passed all appeared to be asleep. Except for an occasional car, he had the street to himself.

As he entered Susannah's driveway a car turned the corner at the end of the block. Feeling a bit ridiculous, he fled to the protection of the shrubbery and stood still until the slow-moving car rounded the next corner at the end of the block. When it was gone he moved hurriedly on, staying close to the garage wall, which formed an L with the house. He was reasonably sure he hadn't been seen. If he had, there would no doubt be a patrol car along pretty soon to check out a reported prowler.

The house was dark, but when he reached the front door it flew open and his heart started fiercely pounding. She stood in the doorway, the light-colored garment she wore taking on a luminous look in the darkness. It gave him a passing illusion of some exquisite lunar creature. As if to make sure she was real, his hand reached out to touch her and brushed across the silken fabric of her kimono. Instantly he was aware of unfettered breasts beneath, and at his touch he heard the quick catch of her breath.

He stepped inside after her, murmuring words of endearment as he circled her body with his arms and curved his hands around her buttocks to pull her hard against him. Her arms reached up to clasp his head and pull his face down, and their mouths met and held in a deep, welcoming kiss. In time he found and untied the sash to the kimono and slipped it over her shoulders, only to find as it fell to the floor, the short, silk shift that was her nightgown.

"Too many clothes," he muttered, in too much of a hurry to remove it. Instead, he eased his hands under its loose folds and up the satiny surface of her body. Finding the soft globes of her bare breasts, he curved his fingers around them. The budding points firmed and thrust against his palms. As on the night in the meadow, he felt his restraint slipping away.

He wanted her. He wanted her more now than ever before. The very depth of his wanting made him steel himself to hold back and wait for her.

He made his hands drop to her waist and then withdraw from under the silken folds.

"Unless you enjoy making love on cold tile floors, do you think we . . ." She interrupted with a laugh—a laugh that was ripe and throaty and stoked the heat that burned within him. Leaving her kimono where it had dropped, she put an arm around him and guided him down the lighted hallway to her bedroom. She left him to turn on a pale, indirect light, then came back to stand beside him.

In her eyes he saw the soft, smoky look of desire, and with a small, wordless cry, he pulled her to him. Her hands pressed against him, pushing for her release, and for a moment he feared she was rejecting him. Rejecting him because she refused to believe they could find a way to go on together?

His heart heavy he let her go and stepped back, but her fingers curled around his for an instant before she pulled away, and once again his heart took wing.

"It's time for bed, Dan Sullivan," she said in a voice husky with desire. "I may hate myself in the morning, but right now I don't much care."

There was an unabashed invitation in the sultry heat of her eyes and the full moist curve of her lips as she pulled the silk shift over her head and began impatiently to unbutton his shirt. Their hands met at his shirt front and they worked together.

With a soft purr from deep in her throat, she caught herself to him when the shirt came off, pressing the cool points of her breasts against the heat of his bare, hairy chest. Clothing discarded, he lowered himself to the bed, bringing her with him until she rested half on top of him. Their mouths joined in searching kisses, murmuring endearments that were not words but the throaty, erotic sounds that come from men and women when they make love.

But even as they touched and fondled and caressed, he fought a wild urgency to roll her over and drown in her exquisite flesh. In an effort to slow down he drew a deep breath and then another. More than the climax his whole being keened for, he wanted to carry her to a fulfillment she would remember with joy.

His hands slipped along the soft inner surfaces of her thighs and Susannah felt an ecstatic, wrenching quiver and a frantic need to close the distance between them. Lifting her hips, she brought the full length of her body directly over his. Her long legs slipped between his, and as her body pressed against the fevered staff that came to meet her, the quiver within her became a white-hot pulse.

He lifted her away so she lay beside him on the bed and knelt over her. Taking the full dome of one of her breasts into his mouth, he played upon it with soft, rhythmic contractions of his lips that brought a small, earthy cry from deep in her throat. Her hands reached up to seize his buttocks and pull him down between her open thighs, her body arching to meet him as he came.

Only then did he let himself go. In his last moment of exquisite release, he heard her cry out—a strange husky moan, wrenched from her again and then again. Up, up, up they soared together into a blinding sunburst, and slowly together drifted down.

IT WAS MONDAY AGAIN, and the third week of the *Minerva* v. *Ag Dusters* trial continued with Attorney Robert Corwin for the defense. On the stand at midmorning was a pioneer tomato grower in the county, an eminently successful one who had sold his farmland fifteen years before to a developer for a shopping center and retired early and rich.

"Mr. Haas," Corwin began after the witness was sworn in, "during your years as a tomato farmer, did you ever have any experience with the chemical in question, commonly known by the commercial name of Harvest Helper?"

"Yes, we used it on the fields every year when the tomatoes were ready to be picked."

"Now let me be sure I understand you, Mr. Haas," Corwin said on a note of astonishment. "Are you saying that you actually *applied* this chemical—this chemical the plaintiff says is deadly to tomatoes and swears destroyed his crop? You put it on your tomato fields as a routine procedure?"

"At harvest time. Yes. You see—"

Corwin cut him off with a question. "Did this chemical ever at any time damage your tomatoes or cause you loss?"

"No sir. We used it to—"

"Thank you, Mr. Haas, I believe that is all," Corwin broke in quickly, but not quickly enough. Sullivan took his cue for cross-examination from the two sentences Mr. Haas had not been allowed to finish.

"Mr. Haas, I believe when Mr. Corwin dismissed you, you were about to tell the jury what you used to use this chemical for," he said smoothly. "Would you mind telling us now?"

Corwin jumped to his feet. "Your honor, I object," he protested.

"Objection overruled," said Susannah. "However, I am going to ask you to rephrase the question, Mr. Sullivan."

Sullivan obliged. "For what purpose did you use the chemical, Harvest Helper, on your tomato fields, Mr. Haas?"

"To make the leaves on the plants dry up, so the tomatoes were easier to pick," said Haas. "But that was twenty years ago, before the days of the tomato harvester when the tomatoes were picked by hand."

"You are saying, then, that now that tomatoes are picked by mechanical harvesters they are no longer treated with Harvest Helper?"

"Yes."

"Would you mind telling the jurors why, Mr. Haas?"

"Objection," called out Corwin. "Irrelevant and immaterial."

"Objection overruled. You may answer the question, Mr. Haas."

"Because it's a dessicant—that is, it kills all the leaves and exposes the tomatoes to the sun and does something to the stems so the harvest machines can't shake the tomatoes off the vines, which is what a harvester does," explained Haas. "That stuff's the last thing you want around your tomatoes, the way they're harvested now."

"Thank you, Mr. Haas," said Sullivan. "You may step down."

Bravo! Susannah cheered silently from the bench, and tapped her gavel for the morning recess. For a man who hadn't reached his own bed until well after 2:00 a.m., Dan was on his toes in court. And he'd better be, she thought grimly. He was up against an exceedingly crafty lawyer who would squeeze everything he could out of a bad case. So far he had produced witnesses to blame everything from poor farming practices to the weather for the Minerva crop loss: high temperatures, powdery mildew, sandy soil, boron in the water, poor nutrition, overstress, too many tomatoes and too small roots—everything but the chemical.

In effect he was asking the jury, Can you blame Harvest Helper when there is a myriad of other hazards that could play havoc with a tomato crop?

But the worst was yet to come. Corwin's next step would be to get them wondering if the chemical had actually fallen on the Minerva tomato field. If Dan didn't produce a witness to back up the checker's story about the leaky spray boom, he was going to lose his case. She could see it on the jurors' faces. They were confused by the huge volume of testimony Corwin's army of witnesses was pouring into their ears and beginning to wonder if some of it might be true. The old "where there's so much smoke there must be fire" reaction. It was in their eyes.

Entering her chambers, she rang for Jill before she remembered her secretary was away. Her substitute, Helen Perkins, came in a minute later with a folder of papers in one hand and a small tray with a carafe of coffee and a cup in the other.

"Jill says you drink your coffee black, Judge Ross."

"Fine, Helen, and thanks. I guess I needn't ask you if you have any questions," she said, amused at the lengths to which her secretary's efficiency reached. "Knowing Jill, she probably left you with detailed instructions on everything."

"You're right," the other woman told her with a smile. "I brought in some letters you'll want to look over and sign."

"Thanks. Just put them there on the desk, and I'll get to them during the lunch break."

Alone again, Susannah let herself luxuriate in the memory of the early hours of the morning spent with Dan, regretting only that it had ended on a small note of disagreement. The time together had been heavenly, but to let it happen again while the trial was on was simply asking for trouble. Dan accused her again of being paranoid.

"It's that bloody conscience of yours," he'd said grumpily when she told him not to try to see her alone again until the trial was over.

And she'd admitted he was partly right. Strictly speaking, last night's meeting had stretched the ethical boundaries of their respective professions beyond all reasonable limits. But the purely practical reasons he should stay away was the possibility he would be seen slipping in and out of her house at strange hours of the night.

"Count up the number of people involved in this trial—jury, witnesses, litigants, employees of the court, relatives, friends—and you're talking about fifty or so people, Dan, who at the moment are interested in Dan Sullivan and Susannah Ross," she'd argued. "Sooner or later, in a town this size, one of those people is going to see you come or go. And when that happens, there goes your case."

"And there goes the election?"

"That, too."

In the end they had struck a bargain. Dan would stay away until the trial verdict was in and the case ended. In return, she would go with him to Patch Creek the weekend after it was over.

Dan had this crazy idea that if they just got back up there in the mountains together, they could talk away all the problems of their future relationship.

"I'll be damned if I'll come back down until we've found a way to spend the rest of our lives together," was the way he'd put it as he sat on the edge of her bed in the early-morning hours and bent to tie his shoes.

If only they *could* talk it out!

To spend a weekend away from the rest of the world alone in the Sierra with Dan was as near pure bliss as she could imagine. The mere thought quickened her pulse. Why couldn't he just be willing to embrace the moment and not spoil it by trying to talk about a future they couldn't make work!

Dan, Dan, what's there to talk about, love? she questioned him in the silence of her mind. A future of nightly long-distance calls? Occasional weekends... vacations together... long holidays? That was all the future held for them. The longer they postponed it, the harder the last goodbye would be.

She almost wished she hadn't let him talk her into a last trip to the meadow. There was a kind of mountain bewitchment up there that played mischief with her senses. Dare she risk giving Dan such an opportunity to persuade her that somehow they could make it work?

But they couldn't. Maybe two other people, but not she and Dan. In San Francisco they hadn't been just a man and a woman who shared sex and an apartment for a time. They had been a *family*. There was no family in what they were looking at now.

SULLIVAN WELCOMED the morning break to go to the coffee counter in the basement of the courthouse.

There he filled a heavy mug to the top with the bitter brew and found an empty table where he sat down.

His energy level was low this morning, his eyelids gritty. It had taken his full power of concentration to keep his attention from straying from Corwin's seemingly endless string of witnesses. He'd had the strongest urge to tip his chair back, put his feet up on the table and relive last night's hours with Susannah.

From the moment she entered the courtroom, he had wanted her to look at him. He had willed their eyes to meet, hoping to see in their darkly exciting depths an acknowledgment of what they had shared a few hours before. When she walked straight to the dais as always and her eyes had traveled around the courtroom without pausing when they came to him, he'd felt a little let down.

What the hell had he expected? he wondered now, smiling faintly, feeling a trifle foolish. Had he expected her to wink at him?

As the week moved on, Corwin gave him no chance to coast. Just when he thought all the loose ends in his case were tied up, Corwin would present a witness who would unravel a different strand. By the time Sullivan had done the work it took to make sure he could put it all back together in rebuttal, Corwin would unravel yet another strand.

Tuesday was a typical day. It opened with a defense witness, Granville Dexter, directly contradicting the testimony of Sullivan's key witness, Martin, the field checker.

Sullivan went looking for Martin when court adjourned for the day.

"This man Dexter swears he was out there the same time you were and didn't see anything leaking from that boom," he told the field checker. "I didn't get to first base on cross-examination. There's got to be an answer."

Martin's brow furrowed in thought. "That's crazy. He was there all right. I remember he stopped on the road in his pickup, and we talked a minute. He drove on, but then he stopped a little ways up the road when the dusting plane came over and stuck his head out the window—maybe to see how close it had come. Sometimes they sound like they're right on top of you, even though they're not."

"How close was it?"

"Not real close. If it had been, the way it was leaking we'd have both got wet."

"Dexter said he didn't see any leak from the boom."

"I can't understand why not," Martin maintained, his expression genuinely puzzled.

"Would he have any reason to lie about it under oath?"

"Naw, I know Gran. He's kind of a macho show-off, but he'd be scared to lie."

"There's got to be an explanation."

"I just thought of something," the field checker said suddenly. "Maybe he *didn't* see the leak. Maybe he *couldn't*. I went all through school with him, and the teachers always made him wear glasses in the classroom. As soon as he'd get out he'd take them off. He always said he could see as good as anybody. He said the teachers had it in for him."

"He wasn't wearing glasses on the witness stand," Sullivan observed thoughtfully.

"Oh, he does all right without them, I guess," Martin said, "but you have to see pretty good at a distance to notice liquid leaking out of a boom."

And so it went. After more time with the field
checker and a visit with the Department of Motor Vehicles—where he learned Dexter had been issued a re-
stricted driver's license that forbade him to drive
without glasses—Sullivan eventually had another
strand of his case tucked back into place, but it gave
him little satisfaction. The defense was still on the
march.

Expecting to hear from his Alaskan expedition late
Tuesday afternoon, Sullivan went directly to his room
at the motel after court adjourned for the day and
waited for a call from Ollie Fox. When eight o'clock
found him still waiting, he sent out for pizza and beer.
By nine he'd reached the floor-pacing stage. A knot of
anxiety was beginning to form in his stomach, and in
an effort to relax, he stretched out on the bed fully
clothed and turned out the light.

He lay in the dark, his eyes wide open, and a string
of possibilities for what could have gone wrong began to roll across his mind like credits on a TV screen:
They couldn't find Resty Kerns in Juneau. They'd had
to go looking for him in some godforsaken other
place. They wouldn't get back in time for Kerns to go
on the stand Thursday. By the time they got here the
trial would be over and the jury out.

At nine twenty-seven, the telephone rang. In his
rush to get it and at the same time turn on the light, he
pulled the phone off the bedside table.

"Sullivan? What the hell's going on down there?"
Fox's voice yelled at him from Juneau.

"Have you got Kerns?" Sullivan blurted out impatiently without taking time to retrieve the phone
cradle.

"We found him," said the detective in a normal voice. "I can't say we've *got* him, though. He says he's not going to come."

Sullivan muttered an expletive.

"Matter of fact, I've got a kind of mutiny on my hands," Fox said.

Sullivan groaned. "I suppose there's no way to keep you from telling me about it."

He heard a grunt of laughter from Fox a thousand or so miles away.

"Well, when he refused to come, I was all for serving him with a subpoena on the chance he didn't know it wasn't enforceable, but that darn woman said nothing doing," the detective explained.

"You mean Jill?" Sullivan asked, momentarily distracted by a picture of the feisty young woman locking horns with the burly Fox.

"She says if I do, she'll tell Kerns that a person can't be subpoenaed and extradited from out of state unless it's a criminal matter. She says if she can't talk him into it, we'll come home without him. Maybe if you talked to her..."

Sullivan thought about the suggestion a moment then shrugged it off. He'd be damned if he wanted to win the case by luring his key witness here under a false implication.

"No. Let her do it her way. We'll just have to hope she can bring him back."

And she'd better make it snappy, he thought unhappily as he hung up. Corwin was about finished with his list of witnesses. After that it would be rebuttal time, and if he didn't have Kerns by then, it would be too late.

He considered how long he could prolong his rebuttal questioning before Corwin began to holler, or Susannah got wise he was stalling and told him to knock it off.

For the first time he was grateful to the defense attorney for the numerous and varied witnesses he had put on the stand, many of whom gave testimony Sullivan had rebuttal witnesses to refute. It would all take time.

Getting Oreste Kerns back to Cacheton was one thing. Getting him on the stand was another. All day long the situation had nipped at Sullivan's consciousness like a mosquito in the bedroom when you're trying to sleep. The problem was, you couldn't bring in a witness to give new testimony after the plaintiff's case had been closed, and unless one of Corwin's remaining witnesses testified that the boom had been in good working condition, he couldn't put Kerns on the stand as a rebuttal witness. He had assumed he would, but the defense was getting down to his last witness. It was something to worry about.

At 6:30 a.m. the telephone awakened him from a nightmare in which Susannah, in her judicial black, was clinging to the topmost pinnacle of a glistening iceberg and he was trying to climb up the face of it to reach her. It was Ollie Fox, sounding vastly pleased with himself.

"We got him, Sullivan. We got him. That Jill Fitzgerald is something else," Fox announced triumphantly. "We're leaving Juneau for Anchorage in about twenty minutes, and then on to Seattle and home."

"How soon can you get here?"

"That depends on what time we can get a plane out of Seattle. We'll see you sometime in the early evening. We'll tell you all about it then."

The conversation ended, Sullivan lay back on the bed and began to worry seriously about what he was going to do with Resty Kerns now he had him. He wished he could talk it over with Susannah—the way they used to put their heads together over legal intricacies in the San Francisco days.

He was half tempted to pick up the phone and call her at home.

"I've just found this witness whose testimony is the key to my case," he could say. "If Corwin doesn't give me an opening to use him in rebuttal, will you let me reopen the plaintiff's case?"

And—soft and dewy from sleep—she would say sweetly, "Dan, honey, go back to sleep. Of course not!"

Or she might not say anything. She might just hang up.

He lay still another minute and then reached for the phone book, found her number and dialed. It rang once, twice, three times.

On the fourth ring her voice came through just as he had imagined it, soft from sleep.

"'Morning, ma'am. This is your wake-up call."

A momentary silence, then a fuzzy giggle came across the wire.

"Dan! You clown! You're not supposed to be calling me."

"Just calling to remind you of our rendezvous at the meadow coming up."

Her voice came to him in a breathy whisper. "As if I could forget!" And then it changed to the voice of the judge. "Dan Sullivan, this is against all the rules, and you know it. I'll see you in court. Goodbye!"

The sharp click of the receiver sounded at the other end. Sullivan put the phone back in its cradle and sighed. If she only weren't so damned scrupulous about rules. All he'd really wanted to do was tell her he loved her. He'd try again tonight when he went to bed.

THE MORNING IN COURT was more of the same from the defense. When court reconvened after the mid-morning recess, the knot in the pit of Sullivan's stomach was back. The possibility he'd brought Resty Kerns all the way from Alaska for nothing was beginning to take on the look of certainty.

He finished a brief cross-examination of Corwin's current witness and went back to his seat. The defense attorney called Ashton, the owner of Ag Dusters, to the stand. Sullivan listened glumly as, under Corwin's questioning, Ashton gave an account of his experience in the field of crop dusting and described the company's flight patterns and protective procedures used in spraying a field.

And then, almost as if it were an afterthought, Corwin asked, "Mr. Ashton, how do you determine whether or not the spraying equipment on one of your planes is in proper operating condition?"

"Well, as a matter of fact," said Ashton, "I do a lot of the checking myself, and if I see something's wrong I turn it over to one of my mechanics before it ever goes off the ground. When the mechanic is finished with it, I check it again myself."

"And do you follow this same procedure with the spraying equipment before it goes out?"

"Yes, sir."

Sullivan's pulse quickened, but he continued to sit loose in his seat. He listened with bated breath.

"And on the particular day in question, did you check the plane that was going out to spray the safflower field according to your custom?"

"Yes sir."

"And in what condition did you find it?"

"Flight ready, sir."

"And did you also check the spray boom?"

"Yes sir."

"And what was the condition of the spray boom?"

"In good shape."

"Did you find anything about the spray boom that could lead you to expect it might leak?"

"No sir. There was no way that spray boom could have leaked."

"I have no further questions. Your witness, Mr. Sullivan."

Sullivan had what he wanted. Corwin and Ashton had just given Resty Kerns a ticket to the witness stand tomorrow. He cross-examined the Ag Dusters owner briefly and let him go. Corwin rested his defense, and after the noon recess Sullivan began putting his rebuttal witnesses on the stand. By the time the court was ready to adjourn, the jury had heard testimony to answer a number of the questions Corwin had shrewdly put in their minds. But the big one was yet to come, thought Sullivan with wicked satisfaction as he headed back to his motel to await the arrival of the travelers.

IT WAS CLOSE TO EIGHT when there finally came a knock at the door of his room. He opened it to find the rounded figure of Ollie Fox, red-faced and some-what rumpled, and beside him a neat, unwrinkled Jill, whose effort to appear her usual businesslike self was severely handicapped by a glowing face and sparkling eyes.

Sullivan looked behind them, his eyes hunting for Ollie's Camaro, which he saw to be empty.

"Where is he?" he demanded.

"Maybe you better let us come inside," Fox said a bit uneasily. Sullivan stepped aside and motioned them in.

"Sorry," he said, offering Jill and the detective the chairs and sitting himself down on the bed. "You *did* bring him, didn't you?"

"Yes, Mr. Sullivan," Jill replied reassuringly. "He came with us, and he's going to testify just like you want him to. But the only way I could talk him into it was to promise he could go and see Mr. Ashton first, and tell him what he's going to do. He took my car, and that's where he is."

"Oh, hell!" groaned Sullivan. He could see it all falling apart around him. Kerns would talk to Ash-ton, and then Corwin would get into it. Next thing, his witness would be coming down with a bad case of memory loss.

"What did you let him do that for?" he asked dully.

"I told you," said Jill. "He wouldn't come other-wise. And besides, it's the right thing for him to do. Mr. Ashton was good to him. He taught Resty to fly. Resty couldn't get up there on the witness stand and testify against Mr. Ashton without seeing him first and saying how sorry he is he has to do it."

"That's mighty pretty, Jill," Sullivan observed bitingly, "but you might as well have left him in Juneau. By tomorrow he'll be gone again. Ollie, you get out there and slap a subpoena on him."

"Don't do it, Mr. Sullivan," Jill said, her voice dead serious. "You can trust Resty, I promise. He came back because it was something he had to do, and he knew it. He's not going to run away again. He gave me his word."

Sullivan ran his hand through his hair in a gesture of helplessness. He had to trust them. What else could he do?

"Now, if one of you gentlemen will give me a ride home, I need some sleep," Jill said. "I spent the whole night working on Resty, and besides, who could sleep in all that daylight?"

"I'll take you home on my way out of town," offered Fox, whose headquarters were in Sacramento.

When they were gone, Sullivan walked downtown to the only restaurant that served dinners and had a bar. There he ordered a double martini and a steak, medium rare. He had no appetite for either but finished them both. He walked back to his motel room, undressed and took a shower, then lay down on the bed. He felt as if he'd been steamrollered.

After a while he reached for the phone and dialed Susannah's number, still fixed in his mind from the morning.

"Susannah," he said when he heard her voice, "I just wanted to say it's been a long day. And I love you."

There was a moment of silence on the line, and he waited, half expecting a reproach. What he finally heard was a soft sound, like the coo of a dove.

"Oh, Dan, darling, I love you, too," she said. "I love you, too."

CHAPTER THIRTEEN

HER MIND FULL to overflowing with Dan that Thursday morning, Susannah unlocked the private door to her chambers and stepped inside. His voice reminding her that he loved her was the last thing she had heard before she fell asleep the night before and the first she had heard this morning, telling her one more time.

"And I love you," she'd said, because it was true, and because it was beginning to seem hypocritical and a little silly to scold him for a harmless breaking of rules. And because, even if that were not the case, those were the words he needed to hear—and the words she needed to say.

As she unloaded her briefcase on her desk, a rap at the door from the reception room reminded her that today was Jill's day to return. She glanced up eagerly.

"Is that you, Jill? Come in."

The door opened and Jill was there, body erect, shoulders squared, wearing her dignity like a badge of office. Yet Susannah saw an inner glow beneath the mask of efficiency. The pure blue eyes were alive with a scarcely contained excitement.

"Welcome back," she greeted as Jill came to meet her. Susannah gave her a hug. "From the look of you, whatever your mission was, it was accomplished."

Jill hesitated. Not meeting her eyes, she said, "I...I guess you might say that."

"Come on, Jill! You look like a kitten in a puddle of cream."

"It's not *that* good," Jill replied, dropping her business-as-usual front to give Susannah a satisfied grin. "But it's not bad. At least I got him back to Cacheton. I think maybe he might even stay."

"That's wonderful, Jill!"

"Well, it is, and it isn't. He's been acting... uh...really funny with me. Cautious. Like I'm someone he's just met and hasn't decided how to treat. One thing, he's not acting like I'm his kid sister, but I don't know whether that's better or worse."

"Hmm...it sounds like headway to me," said Susannah encouragingly. "Tell me all about it, Jill. Where did you go? How did you find him? Come to think of it, I don't even know his name."

Suddenly Jill wasn't there. She had walked around Susannah to the closet, picking up her usual routine as if there had never been a break. Opening the closet door, she took out the judicial robe. Susannah sensed a withdrawal she was at a loss to understand.

"How's the campaign going?" Jill asked, overlooking Susannah's words as if they were never spoken. Her voice was warm and cheerful, but Susannah felt as if a door had been closed in her face. For a moment she couldn't speak.

"Better than I ever expected, thanks to the Kramers," she said when she had recovered from the jolt. "They have me booked to meet with every organization in the county from the Farm Bureau to the Harmony Ladies Club."

"Well, what about the trial? Any excitement while I was away?" Jill asked over her shoulder as she removed the robe from its hanger and put the hanger back on the rod. It was becoming clear to Susannah that Jill intended to leave no gaps in the conversation for a question to slip through.

"Corwin for the defense has managed to blame the tomato damage on everything but Congress and Harvest Helper," Susannah told her dispiritedly. "He finished yesterday, and the plaintiff's attorney started putting on his rebuttal witnesses right after lunch."

"How's he doing . . . Mr. Sullivan?"

"A masterful job, so far, of destroying the testimony of the defense."

In the act of opening up the robe for Susannah to slip her arms into, Jill stopped and studied her closely.

"You don't sound overjoyed."

"As the bumper stickers say, I'd rather be fishing," Susannah admitted with a wry smile. "If I'd had any idea this trial was going to bother me so much, I would have disqualified myself at the beginning."

Jill eyed her quizzically. "Didn't you just say Mr. Sullivan's doing a masterful job?"

"That isn't going to win his case for him, unfortunately," said Susannah with a sigh. "The fact is, sometime within the next few days, yours truly is going to have the painful duty of informing the court and Dan Sullivan that the jury has found for the defense."

"What makes you say that?"

"Yesterday Corwin put the owner of Ag Dusters on the stand to testify that before the plane went out that day, he personally had checked the spray boom the

Minerva man, Martin, swore was leaking, and found it in excellent condition," Susannah explained.

"Still, isn't that just the owner's word against the field checker's? It seems to me the owner is the only one with enough at stake to lie under oath."

"The jury believed he was telling the truth."

"How can you be so sure?"

"Intuition...educated guess," Susannah said. "After a while you get so you know. Mr. Ashton, the owner, comes across as such a nice man the jury *wants* to believe him. It's too bad Dan wasn't able to come up with someone to verify his field checker's testimony."

To her surprise, Jill demurred. "There's still time. He hasn't finished with his rebuttal witnesses yet."

I didn't tell her that! thought Susannah. But how else would she know?

Aloud she said, "If he'd had someone, he would have used him when he presented the plaintiff's case. As it is, the jury would think Martin said what he did because that was the price he had to pay to keep his job. He's been an employee of Minerva Farms most of his working life."

"I never knew you to be a pessimist. What's that old sports saying: 'It's not over till it's over'?" Jill said cheerfully. Too cheerfully, thought Susannah as Jill stepped around her to slip the black robe over her shoulders and she caught a glimpse of a grin on her secretary's face.

What had come over Jill Fitzgerald? Susannah wondered with a small sense of betrayal. Even last week, before Jill took off to wherever she had gone, she had withdrawn into herself and shut Susannah out. Now here she was back and so full of some private knowledge she seemed ready to burst with it. Probably would, Susannah thought dourly, before she would take Susannah into her confidence.

She made no effort to continue the conversation but hooked the fastener at the neck of her robe and walked to the door of the courtroom in silence. As always, Jill was there first to open and hold it for her. Susannah passed through, eyes ahead, feeling strangely hurt.

As SULLIVAN RESUMED his rebuttal questioning, a feeling of gloom settled over Susannah. She could see that though the battery of knowledgeable experts Dan was bringing to the stand were doing a splendid job answering the questions raised by the defense, the jurors had lost interest and scarcely listened. After the testimony of the Ag Dusters owner, the temper of the trial had changed. As far as she could see, Dan Sullivan had lost his case.

During the morning recess Jill brought coffee to her in chambers but showed no inclination to linger, nor did Susannah invite her to join her for coffee, as she often did.

Back in the courtroom, the morning moved slowly on, witness by witness, to the luncheon break. Then it was afternoon, and as a new cast entered and left the witness box, Susannah inwardly willed Sullivan to put an end to the agony. He had once had a kind of sixth sense in the courtroom. Surely he'd caught the mood of the jury by now.

In spite of herself, as she again took her seat on the dais, her eyes sought Sullivan's but never found them. Dan was deep in conversation with a witness she had not seen before. She tapped her gavel to signal court was in session. Sullivan looked up and rose to his feet.

"Your honor, I would like to call to the witness stand Mr. Oreste Kerns," he said, indicating the wiry, red-haired young man with the bold mustache sitting beside him.

As the witness walked over to the clerk's station to be sworn in, Susannah was puzzled to see on the handsome young face a look of grim determination. He was not happy to be here, she thought, and was at once curious as to why.

"Do you swear to tell the truth, the whole truth and nothing but the truth?"

"I do."

Ten to one the redheaded Mr. Kerns was another plant pathologist to tell them why the damage was not caused by powdery mildew...or some other extraneous factor.

As Sullivan stepped forward to begin the questioning of the witness, Susannah saluted him in her heart, then forced herself to put all thought of Dan Sullivan, the person, out of her mind and see him solely as the plaintiff's attorney, whose job it was to question the witness he had just put on the stand.

Q. What is your occupation, Mr. Kerns?

A. I fly planes.

It took all of Susannah's control to mask the surprise she felt at his answer.

Q. Where are you currently employed?

A. Juneau Charter Service in Juneau, Alaska.

Q. And where were you last employed before that?

A. I worked for Mr. Ashton at Ag Dusters here in River County.

Q. In what capacity?

A. I started on the ground as a flagman and later flew the planes as a crop duster.

Q. How long did you fly for Mr. Ashton as a crop duster?

A. For six years.

She might have known Dan Sullivan had a joker up his sleeve, thought Susannah, suddenly excited. The witness had grabbed the jury's undivided attention, she saw. Corwin was listening to the proceedings stoically, his face expressionless. For the first time since the trial began, Mr. Ashton was not in court.

Further questioning established that Kerns had been flying for Ag Dusters during the period of time in question and was the pilot of the plane from which the chemical, Harvest Helper, was said to have leaked. Sullivan then beamed in swiftly to the heart of what the young man was there to tell them.

Q. Mr. Kerns, were the plane and the dusting equipment, which I will henceforth refer to as 'the boom,' in proper working condition when you started spraying on the day in question?

A. Yes, sir. At least I thought they were.

Q. What made you think they were, Mr. Kerns?

There was a moment of hesitation that went on so long Susannah thought she might have to interfere to get the witness to continue. She was beginning to understand his earlier reluctance to take the stand. Finally young Kerns cleared his throat and spoke.

A. Mr. Ashton told me they were, sir.

Q. During the time you were spraying the chemical on the adjoining safflower field, each time making your turn over the Minerva tomato field, did you continue to believe the boom was working properly?

A. No sir.

Q. Will you please explain to the jury, in your own words.

A. Well, at first I was so sure it was okay I didn't pay much attention. You have to make your return over the tomato field without hitting the telephone wires, so I wasn't thinking about the boom until after a while when I thought I saw something out of the corner of my eye. So the next time when I crossed onto the tomato field I took a good look, and there was spray coming out the full length of the boom.

Q. Do you know how long it had been leaking?

A. It could have been leaking the whole time. The spray tank had a lot less in it than it should have had when I got back to the hangar.

Q. I see. One more thing, Mr. Kerns. Why did you leave Cacheton and Mr. Ashton's employment?

A. Because word was going around that Ag Dusters was going to get sued, and I knew if I was called as a witness I would have to testify against Mr. Ashton.

Q. And how did you feel about that, Mr. Kerns?

A. I didn't want to do it. I owe him a lot. Mr. Ashton taught me to fly.

A few more questions from Sullivan were followed by a searching cross-examination by Corwin that failed to alter the thrust of the crop duster's testimony. Kerns was the last of the witnesses, and when he stepped down from the witness stand, Susannah called the afternoon recess.

The main body of the trial was over, and closing arguments by the attorneys would come next. She withdrew to her chambers, grateful for an excuse to bring everything to a halt for a few minutes. She was too bedazzled by Dan's turn of fortune to think clearly. Too much had happened too fast. Her mind needed a chance to catch up.

Not until she was out of the courtroom and could turn her thoughts away from the discipline of the trial did pieces start to fall in place. She walked to her desk and pressed the button that summoned Jill, who arrived still wearing her "efficient secretary" persona. Susannah eyed her coolly for a leisurely count of five and then relented.

"All right, Jill Fitzgerald, pull up a chair and tell me just where the devil you've been since Monday," she said, her voice less severe than her words.

There was a moment of silence. Then Jill said, "I don't think you really want to know... that is, for the time being."

"You mean right now it's not convenient to have me as a friend?"

"That's not true," Jill protested. "That's not *ever* true. I mean, right now you are... *the judge*."

This time it was Susannah who held the silence.

"Oh," she said at length. Silence again, and then, "Just one question. Did you go after him for *Sullivan*?"

Yet another silence. Then, "No. I went after him for me."

BACK IN THE COURTROOM a short time later, Sullivan's closing argument launched the final phase of the trial. As in the beginning, the jurors were all his. Like an old friend taking them through a familiar neighborhood, he led them back over the trial, pausing to call special attention to significant testimony, as to landmarks, along the way.

It was Dan at his best, thought Susannah. Relaxed and confident, he walked back and forth before the jury box, eyes moving over the faces of the jurors as he talked, sharing bits of appropriate humor with them as with friends. His arguments were articulate, pithy, to the point, presented in an easy order that made obscure bits understandable without giving his listeners any sense he talked down to them. Shortly before four o'clock he concluded his arguments, and Susannah adjourned the court for the day.

Since there was nothing scheduled for domestic court, first thing in the morning Corwin would make his closing arguments for the defense, followed by a final plaintiff argument by Sullivan. Susannah would then instruct the jury on the laws that must be considered in its deliberation.

The case should be in the hands of the jury before noon, thought Susannah as she left the courtroom for the last time that day and retired to her chambers. She felt as if an oppressive burden had been lifted away. If luck was with her, tomorrow would bring a verdict.

And then what?

And then she and Dan would come to the end of their road—or was it possible it could be the crossroads Dan kept telling her was there to be found if they looked for it? A crossroads, with one of the roads a road they could travel together...a road where she could continue the judicial work she loved and Dan could...

But there the daydream stopped. She could go on being a judge and Dan could...do what? Or she could give up the judgeship and move to Fresno, and the person who was Judge Susannah Ross would cease to exist.

Some crossroads! she thought, and knew just how a dog feels when it chases its tail. She welcomed Jill's knock at her door.

"Come in, Jill," she called out.

Jill came bearing a handful of letters and papers to be read and signed. The few minutes they had talked together during the afternoon recess had cleared the air between them, but there were still too many questions unanswered for them to find conversation easy now. They smiled at each other a bit self-consciously and discussed the matters of business in Jill's hands, then could find nothing more to say.

"Would it be all right if I left pretty soon?" Jill asked uncertainly as she turned to leave. "Lucille and Jack—the Kramers—asked me out to the ranch for dinner, and I thought if you didn't need me I'd go out early and..." She left the sentence hanging.

The Kramers? Susannah smiled to herself, not believing her for a minute, but not about to say so. She would bet anything Jill had a date with the handsome, red-headed Oreste Kerns in some discreet, out-of-the-way place where there would be no one to notice that the judge's secretary was involved with the plaintiff's star witness.

"Go, by all means," she said, smiling. "With my blessing." Jill darted her a quizzical look.

"And my fond regards to the Kramers," she added, beaming wisely.

"Hey, no! Really. I *am* having dinner at the Kramers."

"I know, I know," said Susannah.

How typically Jill, she thought, when her secretary had gone. She was keeping Susannah in the dark because she believed whatever had happened this past week was not something the judge's secretary should be a party to. Inasmuch as it appeared to involve the plaintiff's star witness, Jill was no doubt right. Susannah was the judge in the case, and the less she knew about how Oreste Kerns got here, the better.

Knowing Jill cared enough to want to protect her warmed her heart enormously. Jill . . . and Dan who, unless she guessed wrong, had arranged it all.

THAT NIGHT SHE WAITED for Dan's call. She was in bed, the light out, wide awake and waiting. When the phone rang she forgot she'd decided not to answer it on the first ring. The moment it jingled, she lifted the receiver from its cradle, which rested on top of her stomach.

"Hu-ll-o," she said, her voice sultry.

"I must have dialed the wrong number. This sounds more like Marilyn Monroe than Judge Susannah Ross." Dan's voice came teasingly across the wire, and Susannah found herself suddenly tongue-tied with frustration. She wanted to tell him what a great job he had done in court today, but any mention of the trial was taboo. She wanted to ask about Oreste Kerns and if Kerns was indeed the missing man in Jill's life and if he was, what had Sullivan to do with Jill's absence. But she couldn't. It all had to do with the trial.

"D-a-a-n!" She rolled his name out over her tongue in a helpless sigh. "I've a million things to say to you, and every one of them is against the rules."

"How about, 'I love you'?" he asked.

THE FIRST HOUR of court time Friday morning belonged to Corwin, whose argument for the defense was strong on hypothesis and rhetoric and weak on facts. Susannah instructed the jury on points of law and sent them to the jury room to begin deliberations, then retired to her chambers to catch up on some paper work.

Four hours later court reconvened to hear the verdict the jury had rendered. When everyone was in proper place the court clerk handed Susannah the paper on which it was written. For a moment she couldn't believe what she read. Her first thought was that the foreman had made a mistake. It was wrong. A miscarriage of justice.

Her eyes went to the jury and then to the attorneys' table, where everyone sat as if frozen in place, waiting to hear the words she was about to read. In a second she found her voice.

"The jury finds for the plaintiff in the amount of..." She hesitated, finding it almost impossible to read aloud a figure that was one hundred thousand dollars greater than the amount of damages Sullivan had actually proved.

She read the number aloud. There was a moment of silence. Corwin and Sullivan looked equally stunned. In the spectators' section of the courtroom a buzz of voices arose.

Corwin, his manner dazed, glanced around as if to consult with his absent client, Ashton, then got to his feet.

Susannah tapped her gavel for quiet.

"Your honor, I'd like to have the jury polled," said Corwin in a choked voice.

"Will the clerk please poll the jury," Susannah ordered, still half believing the foreman had made a mistake.

Oh God, how she hoped he had! The award was so far out of line, Corwin was almost certain to make a motion for a new trial in spite of the weakness of his case. If that indeed was the verdict, she could see *Mi-*

nerva v. *Ag Dusters* stretching far beyond the limits of her patience.

There was no mistake. The poll showed the verdict to be the unanimous decision of the jurors, leaving Susannah no alternative but to thank the jury for its services, dismiss them and adjourn the court. That done, she left the dais to return to her chambers as Sullivan and Bancroft walked out to join a handful of people from Minerva Farms who had come to hear the verdict. As her eye caught them surrounding Sullivan, congratulating him excitedly, clapping him on the back, she reminded herself they had a right to their mood of celebration. They couldn't be blamed for being joyful about such an unexpectedly big win.

In her chambers Susannah peeled out of the bulky robe, feeling cheated. Moreover, she felt trapped. She sat down at her desk, staring blankly into space, a kind of sickness inside her at the thought of what now lay ahead. After a moment she buzzed Jill and asked her to hold her calls and see that she was not disturbed.

How could she make Dan understand that she couldn't in good conscience go with him to Patch Creek until she knew for certain that Corwin would not file a motion she would have to rule on? If the verdict had been reasonable, she would have had a right to assume Corwin would not fight it. She would have felt she had fulfilled her judicial responsibilities and was free to go where she liked.

But under the conditions that now prevailed, the matter was left unfinished. Corwin might at that very moment be preparing a motion for a new trial she would be obliged to act upon.

Her first thought after the clerk polled the jury had been to wonder how the jurors had arrived at such an unrealistic figure. The award obviously wasn't taken from the estimates by the Minerva Farms tomato superintendent and the two agricultural experts from the University, on which Sullivan had based his demand. All three had said that in their opinion the field would have yielded from fifty to fifty-two tons per acre if it had gone on to harvest undamaged—far less than the amount of the award.

Looking at it now that the shock had worn off, she saw at once where the numbers had come from. It was based on the figure of sixty tons tossed out mindlessly by Bancroft and reinforced by the swaggering cannery field man who had made much of his own expertise, which was questionable at best. The figure that had caught Sullivan by surprise, though he had disguised his anger well.

After the field man's credibility and his testimony had been destroyed by the defense attorney in cross-examination, she had assumed the jury would disregard him. The only explanation was that Corwin's efforts had done nothing but fix the sixty-tons figure so solidly in their minds that the lower figure given later by less pretentious but more knowledgeable witnesses had gone unheard.

Could it be, too, that the mood of the jury had been a bit vindictive? After all, Ashton had been caught in a lie and no jury likes to be lied to, no matter how personable the liar may be.

The light on her desk phone flashed, interrupting her train of thought, and when her efforts to ignore it were unsuccessful she reached impatiently for the receiver.

"I hate to interrupt, Susannah, but Mr. Sullivan's been wanting to talk to you for the last half hour," Jill said from the other end. "I'm sorry. I just can't say no to him again."

Susannah groaned inwardly. "You wouldn't believe how many times Dan Sullivan gets what he wants for that very reason," she said wryly.

He'd finally broken down Jill's resistance. She might as well face him, she thought. He wasn't going to take this well. Not well at all.

"It's all right, Jill. You can put him through." She listened for the connection. "You wanted me, Dan?" she asked when she knew he was there.

"*Always*, my dove." His voice was playful. Knowing Dan, he hadn't been drinking, but there was a sound of intoxication in his voice. That old "victory high" that comes over a lawyer when he's won a case by trial.

"How long before you can be ready to take off for the high Sierra?" he asked on the same exuberant note.

She caught her breath, dreading what she had to say. She forced the words out.

"I can't, Dan. Not tonight. Not . . . I don't know when."

"Susannah! The *hell* you say! You made a solemn promise. I kept *my* word. You can't back out now the case is over!" Disbelief, anger, refusal—they were all there in his voice.

"I *wish* it were over, Dan, but I don't think it is. You don't really think Corwin will let that verdict go by unchallenged, do you?"

"What's wrong with the verdict?" Dan asked, his voice bristling defensively. "Are you saying I didn't deserve to win that case?"

"Dan Sullivan! Of course you deserved to win. I'm talking about the horrendous award."

"The jury obviously didn't think it was 'horrendous.'"

"A hundred thousand dollars more than you actually proved, Dan? It's not fair. That's why I don't think the case is over." She broke off with a helpless sigh. "I shouldn't even be talking to you about this."

"Don't go high principled on me, Susannah! Not in the same breath you use to break a promise!" Sullivan said bitterly at the other end of the line.

"I'm not breaking any promise, damnit!" Her own voice was rising in anger. She was determined to keep it under control. If Dan would only be *reasonable*! She went on more quietly. "I said I'd go to the mountains with you when the case was over, and I will, but it's got to *really be over*, Dan. Suppose Corwin files a motion for a new trial? Where does that put me?"

Sullivan's groan came over the line. "My God, Susannah, the law gives him ten days before he has to file the motion! You don't expect me to hang around here ten days cooling my heels, waiting for him to file?

Susannah felt her control slipping. Damn it! Did he have to make it so hard?

"Nobody expects you to hang around and cool your heels," she said in a level voice. "The clerk will see that you are notified."

"Damn it, Susannah...oh...*hell*!" His words were born of pure frustration. There was a long pause on the line, broken at last by a sigh. "Okay. The clerk can let me know about the motion. I can be reached through my office in Fresno. Right now I've had about all I can take."

"Dan, honey. Oh, Dan, I'm sorry."

"I am too. I love you, Susannah. But God, how I wish sometimes you would unbend."

CHAPTER FOURTEEN

"Dan..." Susannah cried out softly, her voice choked, not knowing what she was going to say—wanting simply to keep him on the phone long enough to cool his anger. But she realized even as her lips shaped his name that she was too late. A click sounded at the other end of the line, followed immediately by a dial tone.

She couldn't let him go like this. If she could not make him understand why she refused to go to the mountains with him now, at least she could tell him she loved him and hated the situation as much as he did—maybe even more. He was the innocent bystander, after all. The trap they were caught in bore her label. It was her judgeship that was keeping them apart.

Quickly she thumbed through the phone book for the number of Dan's motel and dialed, only to find that he hadn't phoned from there. She left a message for him to call her when he came in, but something told her he wouldn't.

Suppose she was wrong. Suppose Corwin *didn't* go for a new trial, or fooled around the full ten days before he actually filed a motion, she thought sickly.

It was a relief to hear Jill's familiar tap on her chambers door.

"What in the world's the matter, Judge?" the secretary asked in alarm when she saw the distraught look on the other woman's face.

"It's this blasted trial!" Susannah said unhappily.

"I thought you'd be overjoyed. The courthouse grapevine says it's a verdict made in heaven for the plaintiff."

"Well, it was made in hell for me!"

Jill's eyes were bright with curiosity. She said cautiously, "If you'll pardon my asking, does this have anything to do with Mr. Sullivan?"

"It has to do with a highly inflated damage award that locks me into the case—at least until Corwin has had time to appeal it," Susannah said testily. "Dan's gone home to Fresno, furious at the situation. What's worse, he's convinced himself it's me he's really mad at."

"Oh?"

More than anything at the moment Susannah needed a sympathetic ear. Treading lightly around the intimacies involved, she gave her friend and secretary the background and events that had brought her to her present state of malaise.

"And when I told Dan just now that I couldn't go to the Sierra with him until after the deadline for filing the motion had passed, he acted as if I'd done him wrong," she finished, some of her earlier heat coming back to her voice.

"Wow!" said Jill, when she had finished. There was something in the very quietness with which she said the word that brought Susannah's head up to give her a closer look.

"But that's not the point," Susannah went on touchily. "The point is, I'm doing what's right."

When Jill made no response, she said, "Well, you *do* think I'm right, don't you?" When there was still no sound from Jill, she asked a bit truculently, "Was there something you wanted to see me about?"

"Not if you're still wedded to the *Minerva-Dusters* case."

"We-ell . . . at least give me a clue."

"I was going to tell you about where I was the first of the week and why, but it can wait."

In spite of herself, Susannah's curiosity overcame her.

"Surely it wouldn't hurt for you to tell me, now that the real trial is over."

But Jill shook her head. "If you feel so strongly about going to Patch Creek with Mr. Sullivan, I don't think you'd want to hear about this."

"If I didn't know you to be Ms Secretary Perfecto herself, Jill Fitzgerald, I'd swear you were trying to bug me," Susannah said tightly.

Halfway to the door, Jill turned back. "I almost forgot to tell you. Lucille says the campaign flyers are back from the printers—bushels of them. She's having trouble finding people to stuff envelopes. She's got everybody too busy doing other things. Oh," she added before leaving, "she also said to remind you to go to the Farm Bureau potluck supper tonight at the Grange Hall."

AS SHE UNLOCKED her front door on her return from the Farm Bureau's supper shortly before ten o'clock that night, Susannah could hear the phone ringing.

Could it be Dan? she wondered. Fearing the caller would give up, she tore into the house and snatched up the phone, her normal heart pounding fiercely. She tried to keep her voice normal when she answered, but it came out breathy.

"Susie? It sounds like I got you from a block away." Her father's familiar voice came to her over the line, but there was a sound in it that disturbed her.

"Dad, is anything wrong?" He almost never called. She sometimes wondered if she would ever know what was going on with her father if she didn't make it a practice to call him every couple of weeks.

"No. No, nothing's wrong. I was just sitting here wondering how your campaign is going."

"Don't worry about my campaign—it's in good hands," she assured him. "Tell me about yours. You haven't told me yet which of the city's candidates you're working for this time."

She didn't like the artificial sound of his laughter.

"I''m sitting this one out, Susie," he said, but his breeziness rang false. "That new crowd down at headquarters . . . not dry behind the ears. We decided to stay out of it this time. Let 'em find out what it's like to run a campaign without any experienced heads to advise them."

"We?" she asked gently, wondering how many of her father's cronies had been shunted aside.

"Oh, Benning and Guido and Urquhart and O'Toole and the rest," her father said dispiritedly.

She could have named "the rest" herself. They had played sports and politics together for better than half a century. When they got too old to play sports they bought season tickets together and watched from the sidelines, and played at politics even harder than before. Now they were being benched from politics!

"Good for you! They don't deserve you," she said with a catch in her throat, remembering that she had

turned him away herself. "I *said* my campaign was
nothing to worry about, but actually we do have a
problem, Dad. Our first batch of 'Ross for Judge'
brochures is ready for mailing, and we've got two
more coming up before election and no one to stuff
envelopes. Any suggestions?"

"Raise the ante."

"Raise the ante?"

"Offer enough money and you'll get all the stuf-
fers you need."

"Dad! We're not paying anybody. This is a small,
rural campaign. Remember? Our campaign money
goes to printing and signs and that sort of thing. The
rest is all volunteer."

There was a moment's silence on the line. Was there
a certain repressed eagerness in her father's voice, or
did she imagine it, when he finally said, "Would it
offend the sensibilities of your constituents if your old
dad and his bunch of Big City 'pols' stuffed your envelopes?"

"Oh, Dad! Would you?" Susannah said, gratified
that her father had jumped at the bait she'd tossed out
on inspiration, saddened that he'd gone for it so eagerly.

Showering him with thanks, she promised to see
that the first batch of campaign material was shipped
to him first thing Monday morning with the rest to
follow when it came from the printers. By the time
they said goodbye, she was relieved to note that the
self-confident, almost cocky tone was back in her father's voice.

Her eyes filled with tears and her heart with affection for her aging father as she hung up, regretting she
had so little to offer. This would keep him and his

"team" busy through *this* election, but in the end it would merely postpone the day of her father's last campaign.

SHE COULD DETECT the Kramers' fine managerial hands behind another phone call the following morning, this one from Nathan Richards, whom she hadn't heard from since the historical mansion's fund-raiser.

Was she going to the May festival at Barnstown? he asked, and rather than admit to her self-appointed political mover-and-shaker that the thought had never occurred to her, she lied and said yes.

"Good! That's a part of the county you haven't touched yet, and it could bring you several hundred votes," Richards said, then went on to explain, "It's a small town, but everyone old enough turns out to vote on election day."

It developed that the River County property Richards owned—which Jack Kramer had mentioned to Susannah the night of the dance—was located near Barnstown, a foothill town about equidistant between Cacheton and Sacramento. Nathan had just lost his present tenants and had to be up there today, he said. If she would meet him at the festival, he would be glad to introduce her around.

Having fully intended to spend the day at home licking her wounds, Susannah had little enthusiasm for attending the hill country festival. Under the circumstances, it was clearly an offer she couldn't refuse, so she reluctantly agreed to meet him at noon in front of an old livery stable on the main street, which he assured her she couldn't miss.

Gone was any thought of spending the morning quietly reviewing the rightness of her refusal to go with

Dan the afternoon before. She had all she could do to hurry through her daily routine and reach Barnstown by noon to meet Nathan.

His first words after they had greeted each other set the tone for most of the day.

"I've been meaning to talk to you about local press coverage for the campaign," he told her. "Jack says you're not getting any. Do you know the owner-publisher of the *Cacheton Courier*, Lew Hadley?"

"Just barely," she said. "I had to call the reporter who covers the court on a fairly serious mistake once. He should have corrected it in print, but he never did. I have a feeling he wouldn't have much good to say about me to his boss."

"You should have gone to Hadley, himself," Richards told her. "He runs a good, honest paper that can't be bought by advertisers or special interests. The Hadley family has owned the paper for three generations."

"You're saying I should go over and try to sell myself to Mr. Hadley and ask for his endorsement in his paper?" she said. "Nathan, I'm just no good at that sort of thing."

"Then don't do it. Besides, Lew Hadley hates to be arm-twisted."

"So what am I supposed to do?"

"We'll think of something," said Richards. "You need that endorsement. Maybe a town hall meeting where all three candidates get up and speak. Any objections?"

"Not at all, but what makes you think he won't send that same reporter to cover it?"

"Because I'll take him to the meeting myself."

It was another day spent largely in meeting and talking with people, peppered with an abundance of political tips from the knowledgeable Richards. She found, for the first time, that she was beginning to enjoy these forays around the countryside. It was simply a matter of seeing the people as people, not just as so many votes to be harvested on election day.

Having been born and raised in San Francisco, where Victorian row houses abound, Susannah was pleased to find that Barnstown boasted a remarkable collection of still lived-in houses from that era. When she was told that Nathan owned one of the older ones a couple of miles from town and he asked if she'd like to see it, she was delighted to follow him there in her car at the end of the day.

The house proved to be a lovely one-story white wooden structure of a style Susannah recognized as "Eastlake." Nathan told her it had been built in 1880. While she admired the well-kept exterior with its porticos supported by cast-iron fluted columns and acanthus-leafed capitals, Richards told her he had bought the house as a wedding present to his wife, and they had lived there until her death.

"I haven't had any luck with renters, and I'm looking for a couple to live here as caretakers," he explained when a tour of the inside showed signs of careless usage. "If I could find the right buyer, I'd like to sell it before it gets any further rundown."

A house to dream about, Susannah thought as she drove back to Cacheton late that afternoon, never expecting it would become just that to her in the troubled times ahead. Time and again she would find her mind escaping to the haven of the house, envisioning the worn, misused materials of its walls and furnishings replaced with the warm colors that were her trademark.

ALL WEEKEND Susannah had kept her mind doggedly on her election campaign and avoided coming to grips with the many-pronged problems that lay directly ahead.

Late Monday morning the county clerk's office notified her that Corwin had filed his motion for a new trial with the clerk and was awaiting an answer from Sullivan. When the motion and answer reached Susannah's desk at last and a time for an in-chambers hearing was set, she felt an incredible sense of relief. It was as if she had been marking time forever and had suddenly gotten the signal to take off.

By the morning of the hearing, two weeks had passed since she had last seen Sullivan. Now, in the presence of Corwin and the court clerk and a court reporter, there was a moment before Susannah could bring herself to look directly at him. When she did, she felt a momentary relief to see no rancor in his eyes, but neither did she see any special warmth. Rather, they were . . . *noncommittal*, she decided with a feeling of disappointment. Noncommittal and waiting.

Oh God! How she wished she didn't love him the way she did, she thought with a kind of desperation. But she knew that wasn't really true. All the beauty and brightness in her life was a reflection of her love for Dan. Without it, life would be gray.

Burying personal considerations deep in her mind, she snapped herself to attention. She acknowledged the motion and answer with dispatch and in typical fashion tackled the subject of the motion head on.

"Gentlemen, it is my opinion that a verdict for the plaintiff in this case is correct," she began in the formal voice of the court. "Nevertheless, the damage award set by the jury is excessive and insupportable. Mr. Sullivan, either you must agree to a reduction of $100,000, which is the amount the award exceeds the actual damage proven, or I will have to grant the defendant a new trial."

For a moment their eyes locked in stubborn combat. A corner of Corwin's mouth turned up in the merest suggestion of a smile.

"How much time will you need, Mr. Sullivan, to discuss the matter with your client?" asked Susannah, steeling herself against the frustration she saw in his eyes.

"A couple of hours, your honor," Sullivan said, his voice grim.

"Then I will see you gentlemen back here in chambers at three this afternoon."

A FEW MINUTES LATER Sullivan called Minerva Farms headquarters from the public phone in the courthouse basement. Finding Bancroft in his office, he headed out at once, anger seething in him; anger that was the sum of several angers—at himself, at Bancroft, at the jury that had rendered the flawed verdict, at the whole untenable situation.

A certain banked heat still remained from the resentment that had flared in him on the Friday afternoon Susannah had refused to go to the meadow with him, but there was no anger in him against the ruling she had just made in chambers. It was honest and correct.

It was her nit-picky ethics that galled him. Couldn't she see they must have time together if they were ever going to work things out? Wasn't their love important enough to her for that? Suppose she *had* given in to him and gone to the Sierra that Friday. What possible harm could it have done her court? She would have come back to Cacheton and made the same tough ruling she'd made in her chambers just now. Nothing that could have happened between them up there would have changed what she had to do.

It hadn't always been like this, he thought plaintively. In the good days in San Francisco he'd been able to appeal to her common sense. Had she changed since she became a judge? What would it be like, he wondered uneasily, to live in the shadow of a conscience like that the rest of his life?

It was something to think about, but not now. What he had to deal with now was something else, and none of it Susannah's fault. He and Bancroft and the jury had set up this situation. Susannah had simply done what was right. Now he had the unenviable job of telling Bancroft to give up the $100,000 gratuity the jury had given him or face the expense of a new trial.

Skidding to a stop in the loose gravel of the Minerva headquarters driveway, he slammed out of the Jeep and up the walkway to Bancroft's office door, his jaw set. He wasn't sure how he was going to handle the situation, but he knew he wasn't about to admit the truth. He didn't have to tell Bancroft that early in the trial he had been bemused by the presence of Susannah on the bench. If he'd been in proper control, Sullivan realized now, he would never have put the cannery field man on the stand at all.

No matter what, he didn't intend to leave without Bancroft's consent to the reduced amount. He would lean heavily on the fallacy of that sixty tons per acre and the fact it would never wash in another trial. And on the equally sure fact that a second time around could make everybody a loser.

An hour later he left Minerva Farms with what he had come for, but with the disturbing certainty that a vindictive Bancroft would do anything he could to get back at Judge Susannah Ross.

AT THREE O'CLOCK that afternoon, Sullivan and Corwin and the court clerk and reporter were in the judge's chambers again for the final act in the *Minerva* v. *Ag Dusters* case. By three-thirty it was over, and Susannah was left alone at her desk wondering how long it would be before Dan got in touch with her, never doubting he would. The fact he'd been out of sorts with her meant nothing now, she thought. He'd cooled off and seen how right she'd been. When she went with him back to the Patch Creek Meadow in the morning—could they possibly get away tonight?—it would all be forgotten.

The phone rang and her heart spilled over with the eagerness of her love as she reached to answer it. She was ready to tell Dan that maybe he was right. If they really cared enough, maybe they *could* find a way to go on together. Dear God, if they only could!

But it was Jill, asking if Susannah could spare her a moment. She swallowed her disappointment, and when her secretary stuck her head in the door, Susannah greeted her with a euphoric smile.

"I can tell by your face, it's all over," Jill said, grinning back.

Susannah laughed. "It's all over. Now you can tell me how you brought Oreste Kerns back from Alaska and saved the day for Dan Sullivan."

"Oh, Susannah, I've never been so scared in my whole life," admitted Jill. With typical Jill Fitzgerald efficiency, she proceeded to give a candid and orderly account of everything that had gone on without Susannah's knowledge from the time Dan Sullivan questioned Jill about Resty to the moment she and Ollie Fox delivered him back to Cacheton and Dan.

"It wasn't easy, getting him to come back," Jill said ruefully. "He wouldn't even see Mr. Sullivan until he'd gone out to Ag Dusters and told Mr. Ashton what he was going to do."

"I admire the young man's courage. That must not have set very well with his former boss."

"Actually, I think Mr. Ashton was glad to get it over with, but is it really over for him?" asked Jill. "He didn't tell the truth in court. Isn't he in trouble for perjury?"

"Who can say he perjured himself?" said Susannah. "He testified that when he checked out the spray boom it functioned properly. Who can say he lied? It could have started leaking after the plane left the ground."

"Whatever he did, he's not proud of it. Resty says he wants to get out of the flying business and is looking for someone to buy him out."

"By the way, I was quite impressed with your young man on the witness stand," Susannah said, and was rewarded with a pleased smile. "How are things going?"

Jill's whole face twinkled, but she raised a hand with fingers crossed.

"He's still trying to decide what I am since I'm no longer his little sister," she said. "If he only doesn't turn around and take off for Alaska again, I think I can help him figure it out."

"And if he does, you can always go up there and drag him back," suggested Susannah, smiling.

Her remark brought a giggle from Jill, which in turn drew a laugh from Susannah. Then, typically, Jill was all secretary again.

"I shouldn't be goofing off like this," she said primly. "I've got work to do."

The afternoon grew late, and still Susannah waited for Dan's call.

Four-thirty came and went, and her uneasiness grew. She read a code section over three times, her mind not registering a word as she thought, *Dan . . . Dan, beloved. What's the matter with you? Don't you know you're supposed to call?*

At a few minutes after five, Jill stuck her head in to say good-night.

"Shall I tell Resty to stay away from Patch Creek this weekend?" she asked with a grin that vanished at the look on Susannah's face. "Mr. Sullivan *is* coming back?"

"He . . . left?"

"I heard him tell Mr. Corwin as they walked out of the reception room this afternoon that he was leaving in a few minutes for Fresno," Jill said, her voice reluctant.

For a moment Susannah felt as if she were plunging into a bottomless pit. *Ordering the reduction of that award was something she had to do. It was a matter of justice. How dare he act as if she had betrayed him?*

"Never mind telling Resty," she said dully. "Patch Creek is all his."

A LETTER FROM DAN, dated the day before, was in Susannah's mail box the following morning.

> Susannah, my dearest:
>
> First, you must know I love you, always have, looks like I always will. You also must know that what I'm about to say has nothing to do with the hearing in chambers this afternoon. We both know what you did what was fair and right. I couldn't love you so much if you had blinked.
>
> I've got to have time to think things through before I see you again. The truth is, I have to make sure in my own mind that I can live comfortably in the shadow of a conscience I suspect surpasses my own. Until I can answer that to my own satisfaction, I can't help feeling shaky about a future relationship between us.
>
> Still you have all my love, Dan

CHAPTER FIFTEEN

ON HIS WAY BACK to Fresno, Sullivan had stopped over in Sacramento for the better part of two days. He wanted to follow through on something he and his partner, Jerry Curtis, had discussed at length during the interim he'd spent at home base between the trial and the hearing.

The phone call he'd made to Susannah that Friday afternoon after the trial had put an end to what he had looked forward to as a new beginning—or so he had felt in the immediate wake of what seemed to him a rejection. He had reached Fresno in a sour mood, expecting to find the office of Curtis & Sullivan in a state of minor chaos, with Jerry out of commission and himself gone for a full three weeks. To his surprise, the two young associates were running the law practice like seasoned attorneys, with some supervisory advice from Jerry, who was in a traction derrick and an orthopedic bed the hospital had rigged up for him at home.

Jerry had spent the three weeks Dan was gone working out a detailed plan for a second Curtis & Sullivan office in Sacramento, to be run by Dan while Jerry continued to head the Fresno office. Jerry had only to show Dan a record of business mileage one or the other had traveled in the past three years—thanks to a rapidly growing law practice in farm country upstate from the capital—for Dan to see the second of-fice made sense and to fall in with the plan.

It was not until several days later, when a deep yearning for Susannah had gradually replaced resent-ment, that Dan saw the move as a way to reconcile his and Susannah's careers. Cacheton was a mere fifty miles from Sacramento. Half the people who worked in the city commuted farther than that every day.

But still . . .

Easy does it, Sullivan, he chided himself. Once he was settled in Sacramento he would have time to search for the truth in the question that weighed heavily on his mind: Could Susannah still permit her-self an occasional impiety now that she had become a judge?

He loved her as he could never love another woman, but he'd be damned if he wanted to live with her hair shirt.

After agreeing to the reduction in verdict for his client, Sullivan had stopped off in Sacramento to sign the lease for office space before returning to Fresno. He'd been of half a mind to go back to Cacheton and have it out with Susannah then and there, but in the end, he hadn't. He wrote her a letter instead.

STRANGELY, before the full import of Dan's letter closed in upon her that Saturday morning, Susannah felt only relief. Thank God, he was the same Dan Sul-livan. Where hard principle was at stake, Dan was still with her all the way. She felt a sudden sorrow that she had assumed he had gone off in a rage because of the reduced award when it was so unlike him. She was ashamed she had given up hope.

But *was* there hope? she wondered dreamily, as she read his letter for a second time. In those young days in the city they'd stood solidly together on what was important. The trivial he'd taught her to shrug off. Had she changed so much in the years they'd been apart? Had she become so inflexible in her role as judge that she could no longer distinguish one from the other?

Deep in the doldrums, she sat at her breakfast room table with a mug of coffee and stared out across the small backyard, too wrapped in thought to see the full blooming hawthorne tree whose crimson warmth normally gave a light to her spirit.

The door chime failed to rouse her from her lethargy. She let it chime a second time before she forced herself reluctantly up from the table to answer it.

"Jill!" she said, her mood brightening at the sight of her secretary carrying a bulging manilla envelope under her arm. "I hope you're not bringing me work. It's Saturday. Don't you ever take a day off?"

"Relax, Judge. I've got the pictures I've been taking of you for the campaign. If I do say so, they came out very well." It was obvious Jill was pleased with her accomplishment. "You'll have to decide which ones you want to use on your posters."

"Come in and have a cup of coffee while you show them to me," Susannah said, trying to match the enthusiasm in the other's voice. She didn't especially want to see these pictures the Kramers and Jill had insisted she must have for the campaign. She hated to have her picture taken and hadn't seen anything wrong with her résumé photos. They were old, true enough, and her face looked like something left in a mold too long, but she felt uncomfortable when she got in front of a camera. That's the way pictures of her always came out.

She poured a cup of coffee for Jill and watched her open the flap of the envelope and spill a dozen or more prints of all sizes and shapes out on the table. The pictures were of Susannah, taken mostly in her chambers at court, some in black robe, others in mufti. In most cases she had been so hard at work she'd been scarcely aware Jill had a camera pointed at her.

She riffled through the pictures quickly then looked up at Jill with surprise and an added respect.

"Why, Jill, you are very good at this," she said wonderingly. "I had no idea you were such an expert. They're not just mug shots. They *look* like me. They look like there's a real person under that black robe."

"You think so?" Jill's face glowed at the compliment. "Well, pick the ones you want to use."

"They're all fine. I couldn't begin to pick one over another. You and the Kramers do that." She glanced over them again then handed them back to Jill.

"Don't go," she said as Jill started to get up. "I need to talk to you." Jill settled back in her chair, eyeing her curiously.

Susannah went on almost accusingly. "You thought it was wrong for me not to go up to the mountains with Dan while that motion was pending, didn't you?"

Obviously taken aback, Jill instantly reverted to the starch-faced secretary.

"I . . . I don't really know what you mean, Susannah," she said stiffly.

"Cut it out, Jill. This is not Judge Ross speaking. This is me . . . Susannah, who doesn't need a secretary at the moment but is in very great need of a friend."

Still Jill appeared hesitant. "Well...all right," she said at last. "Look at it from Mr. Sullivan's standpoint a minute. There he was on a high over the trial he'd just won, glad to have it over so he could get back to the *really* important business of *you*. And what do you do? You rain on his parade. You can't blame him for seeing red!"

"But look, Jill, the way I see it, if I'm going to play the game, shouldn't I be willing to play by the rules?"

"Even when you know you're the only one who can get hurt if you break one? One that doesn't matter at all, if you play fair otherwise?"

There was a thoughtful silence from Susannah. "What would the old judge say?" she finally asked.

Jill gave a wicked grin. "I can't really see Judge Randall in this particular situation."

"I'm *serious*, Jill," Susannah said, her voice touchy.

"I'm sorry," Jill apologized, then considered the question a moment. "He had his own way of dealing with ethical issues. The rules of judicial procedure were designed to serve two purposes, he always said. To ensure justice and to protect the judge. A judge's first duty was not to do anything that would endanger what he called 'the cause of justice.' After that, if you bent a rule to suit your convenience, it was up to you to decide if the particular temptation was worth whatever embarrassment it might cause you if someone found out."

Again Susannah lapsed into silence. *It would have been worth it,* she thought wistfully.

Aloud she said, "Your Judge Randall must have been a remarkable man."

"Oh, he was that!" agreed Jill.

"I'm sorry I missed him."

WITHOUT KNOWING exactly when it happened, the entire focus of Susannah's life outside her actual work as judge was on the coming election. Every night there was a meeting or people to meet or a community event her advisers suggested she shouldn't miss.

She found herself doing and saying the same things over and over until she couldn't distinguish one event from another. Only the people were different and the surroundings. Each day became a repetition of the day before, except on those rare occasions when something good or bad or unusual would fix a particular day in her mind.

Most of the good occasions had nothing to do with politics. Like the evening at the Kramers when she met Oreste Kerns, who was there with Jill, and decided her friend had nothing to worry about. Resty at last was getting the idea about where Jill fit into his life. Whenever he looked at her it was there in his eyes to see.

And the day Jill threw away all decorum and flew into her chambers, happier than Susannah had ever seen her, to announce that Resty was not going to return to Alaska. He was going to buy Ag Dusters.

It seemed that from the time he started the dangerous but well-paid work of crop dusting, Resty had been saving for some kind of flying service of his own. Now Mr. Ashton was willing to take what money Resty had to offer as down payment on the business with the balance to be paid in installments. All that was left was to have the papers drawn up.

"And, oh, Susannah, have you noticed how he *looks* at me now?" Jill burst out in a final bubbling over of joy. Smiling, Susannah assured her friend that she had indeed noticed, whereupon Jill sobered and straightened herself sedately.

"Okay, Judge. It's time to get back to work."

It had been one of the good days Susannah wouldn't forget.

WITH THE ELECTION little more than two weeks away, Susannah dutifully spent a sunny Saturday afternoon at a quilt fair and bake sale in Appleton, a small town to the west of Cacheton where many of the people were retired. Because she couldn't resist it, she bought a quilt designed and quilted by a woman as old as her father, whose arthritic fingers had put many thousands of tiny stitches into sun-bright circles of California poppies appliquéd on a field of white. It belonged on a four-poster bed she'd seen in one of the rooms at Nathan Richards' Eastlake house in Barnstown, she thought, and wondered for the first time where she could find a place for it in her own small house.

By the time Susannah finally tore herself from the altogether pleasant gathering it was late. She had barely time to go home and change into something fresh before driving out to the Kramers', where she'd been invited for supper. In a hurry, she turned into her driveway sharply, and the strawberry-rhubarb pie she had bought to take to the Kramers slid across the seat beside her to the very edge. Braking, she made a dive for it and rescued the pie. The car came to a jarring halt, and her ear caught a hissing sound that told her all was not well. Settling the pie box back on the seat, she realized she had run the front wheel off the driveway. She gave a moan of dismay as she stepped out and saw that her tire was impaled on a sharp metal stake left upright in the ground by the gardener. The tire was completely flat.

"I just wrecked a tire," she told Lucille Kramer worriedly over the phone a few minutes later. "By the time I get the Triple-A out here to fix it, I'm going to be all kinds of late."

"No problem. I'll send someone in to get you," Lucille said, interrupting cheerfully when Susannah started to demur. "Don't worry about it. It's no trouble. Can you be ready in twenty minutes? You can get the tire fixed tomorrow."

Showered and changed to a cool terra-cotta paisley print voile dress with short bell sleeves, Susannah opened the door at the first ring to find Nathan Richards on her doorstep.

"Why, Judge," she said, her voice making no secret of her pleasure at seeing him. "Lucille didn't tell me you were coming."

"She was going to send Jack, but I insisted," he told her.

Dinner was a typical overly bountiful Kramer meal. Conversation was almost exclusively political. For the first time Susannah fully understood why Nathan Richards had thrown himself into her campaign with almost as much enthusiasm as if it were his own. Like Jack Kramer, he was a political being, and to that extent like her father. She suspected she would see little of him for the next six years, once the election was over.

At the end of the evening, as they were about to leave, Jack remarked that he had two tickets to the harness races at Sacramento Expo the following day.

"Susannah, you need a break. How about you two..."

Susannah and Nathan interrupted in unison, "Sorry, but I can't—" then broke off in bursts of laughter.

"Thanks, Jack, but I've got to stay home and get caught up on dozens of urgent matters that have been swept under the rug for the past two weeks," Susannah finished for herself.

"Thanks, just the same," Nathan said without elaborating.

In the car, he said thoughtfully, "Do you get the feeling Jack was playing some game other than politics tonight?"

"Matchmaking?"

"Well?" When Susannah laughed in assent, he said, "I thought about setting them straight, but it sounded a little blunt to say I've already got a date with another woman."

Susannah laughed appreciatively. It felt good to have this man for a friend.

"Glad to hear a real laugh from you," Nathan told her. "I thought maybe the election was getting to you, but I get a feeling it's something bigger than that."

"I don't know how *big* it is. I'm beginning to wonder if some of it is something rather small that I've turned into something big."

"Mind telling me about it?"

As she looked at him, she realized that she desperately needed the opinion of this kind, dispassionate man who was governed by the same rules of judicial ethics that she was.

"I'd like very much to, but I should warn you, it's a long story."

"I have the time."

Going back ten years to San Francisco, Susannah told Richards with complete candor of her relationship with Dan and his reappearance in her court weeks earlier. By the time the car pulled up in front of her house, she had told him about their meeting in the Sierra meadow. When he turned off the motor, neither made a move to leave the car as she described her pact with Dan to go to the meadow again when the trial was over.

And finally she told him about the flawed verdict and Sullivan leaving in bitterness for Fresno when she refused to go with him to the mountains because of the probability of a motion she would have to act upon.

"What bothers me now, Nathan, is the possibility that I'm letting my scruples blind me. Was I really taking a strong moral stand or was I just chickening out? I'm not sure anymore."

The man beside her was quiet. "I wish I had an easy answer," he said at last. "These things work differently for everybody. Most of the rules are there to protect the interests of justice, so it's a matter of principle for a judge to obey them. The rest each judge has to decide for himself, I suppose."

"That sounds like it might have come right out of the mouth of the late Judge Randall," said Susannah in surprise.

"In a way, I suppose it did," Richards said. "I worked in his office every summer when I came home from law school. Some of it had to rub off. He used to say that if your conscience tells you that what you're about to do will interfere with the meting out of justice in your court, don't do it. On the other hand, when you're sure in your mind it won't, it's more a matter of how much you're afraid of being found out. And one more thing . . .'' He paused and gave a remembering laugh.

"What's that?" she asked, suddenly curious.

As Jill did when she quoted her beloved judge, Nathan Richards imitated the voice of Judge Randall.

"Just take care you don't get too dang-blasted pious."

Susannah smiled. "Thanks. I guess it's up to me to take it from there," she said musingly and reached for her seat belt buckle, which she'd forgotten to release.

Richards got out and came around to open the door.

"I think Jack's right. You need a holiday. How about taking tomorrow off and going to the wine country with us for the day?" he asked as she stepped out of the car. "You'll get along famously with Caroline. She's an old friend. Teaches veterinary medicine at the University at Davis . . . a person you'd like to know."

"I'm sure I would, Nathan, but with this darned election coming up fast, I don't dare stop until it's over."

It had been one of those *good* days.

But there were bad days. They began when Jack Kramer came to the courthouse to break the news that Hubert Bancroft was putting all the money and power of Minerva Farms into her defeat. He brought her the first of a series of vicious flyers, all on the theme she would hear again and again until election day.

Judge Ross, if elected, will trash the jury system in River County as she did in the Minerva case.

"Worse than that," Jack told her gloomily, "the

word's going around that Bancroft's backing Mel Parker against you."

"Won't that split the vote against me between Parker and Elmer Fairchild? I thought that would be good," said Susannah.

But Jack took a dark view of it. "Fairchild'll get the votes of some of the old families that loved his father, but Parker will get most of the rest."

"You really sound grim about it, Jack."

"Listen, Susannah. Parker is interested in just two things. Money and Mel Parker. He'll screw the people of River County any time it's to his advantage."

The next week Susannah felt the full impact of the Bancroft flyers at the town meeting where she and Parker and Fairchild were given equal time to make their election pitches. Susannah thought she'd come off rather well against the other two, when the question-and-answer period came and she realized all the questions were being fired at her and they were all variations on the Bancroft theme. In every way, shape and form it was repeated by people well placed throughout the large audience.

It seemed a vicious and well-planned attack that left her wrung out and exhausted by the time the inquisition was over. When Nathan brought Lew Hadley, the publisher of the *Cacheton Courier*, to meet her she felt sick.

In the heat of the questioning she'd forgotten all about the man. She would never have let Nathan make such a point of getting him there if she'd known she was going to be chopped up in little pieces the way she was.

The evening had been a nightmare. Even Nathan's assurance later that she should thank the Bancroft forces for giving her such a golden opportunity to lay herself open to her constituents made her feel no better.

"What did Mr. Hadley say?" she'd asked.

"He didn't say," said Richards. "Sorry, Susannah. Lew Hadley's not a talker."

By Wednesday of the week before the election Susannah had resigned herself to a silent belief that the election was lost. In the face of all the bright hope poured on her by her supporters, she kept her feelings hidden, but in the end, she was sure, she and all her hard-working campaigners like Jack and Lucille Kramer would be buried under a snowstorm of Bancroft's insidious flyers.

Beneath the pain was the buried, ever-present hurt of Sullivan and a nagging feeling she should be doing something about him, if she only knew what.

Sometimes, in one of those rare solitary moments that became fewer and fewer as election time drew near, she would think about how to reshape her life when she was no longer judge, and the full force of her loss would crash in upon her. She had lost Dan and she was about to lose the judgeship.

She found a certain sardonic humor in remembering what her stern-visaged mother used to say.

"I won't have it, Susannah! I didn't raise my daughter to be a loser."

Up until now the words had always worked.

CHAPTER SIXTEEN

ON MONDAY of the last week in May, Sullivan sat down at his desk and called Curtis & Sullivan in Fresno to say that the firm's new Sacramento office now had a telephone. Otherwise, except for wall-to-wall carpet and the desk and chair, it was completely empty.

"A call came for you a few minutes ago, Mr. Sullivan, from Cacheton," the receptionist told him. "Now that you have a phone, maybe you'll want to make the return from there."

Sullivan's pulse leaped.

"Cacheton?" he asked, wondering if the excitement he felt could be heard in his voice.

"A Mr. Oreste Kerns. I told him you'd call him back as soon as I could get the message to you." She gave him a number to call.

When he had recovered from a moment of acute disappointment followed by one of curiosity and surprise, Sullivan got Resty Kerns on the phone in Cacheton.

"What can I do for you, Mr. Kerns?" he asked.

"I need some legal advice about buying a business, and I've got some papers I'd like you to look over," the young man told him. "I could be in Fresno tomorrow morning, if you could see me then."

"If you can come to Sacramento and don't mind getting legal advice out of a packing case, I can see you sooner than that," Sullivan said, and went on to explain where he was calling from and why. Resty voiced his satisfaction and agreed to be in his office in the next hour.

About to hang up, Sullivan said, "I'd appreciate it if you didn't mention to Jill right now that I'm setting up a branch office here."

There was a short pause. "Oh, sure. Sure. That's okay with me. I won't mention it to anyone."

Sullivan hung up moodily. He hadn't liked asking Kerns not to tell Jill, but to tell Jill was to tell Susannah. No matter what Susannah had read into his letter, if she knew he was less than an hour away and hadn't tried to see her, she would translate it as a permanent sign-off on his part.

His whole being ached to hold her in his arms, to remind her again that he loved her, yet remembering the San Francisco scramble, which had taken all these years to straighten out, he knew the way he was handling the situation was right. Between her election and his relocation there were too many outside tensions pulling at them to risk taking up anything as touchy and personal as what he had expressed to Susannah in his letter. He only hoped he had the sense and the strength to stay away from her until the time was right.

Young Kerns arrived within the hour. Sitting on a packing box provided by Sullivan, he gave a detailed account of the crop-dusting venture he wanted to go into, asking intelligent questions as he listened to the lawyer's suggestions and advice. Sullivan asked him to return the following day, after he had a chance to go over the agreement papers Resty had brought.

As he reached to shake hands with his new client, who was about to leave, Sullivan said, "I was a little surprised to hear from you today, Mr. Kerns. After all, you met me more or less under duress. I suppose I have the persuasive Ms Fitzgerald to thank for your coming to me. Please give her my best when you see her."

Kerns gave Sullivan an uneasy grin. "Look, if it's all right with you, just call me Resty. That Mr. Kerns stuff makes me feel like someone I'm not. Oh, and about Jill...no. She says you're a good lawyer, but I'd already decided. I liked the way you went out and got what you wanted in that trial."

Out of this first meeting an easy client-attorney relationship developed between the two. On his next visit, Resty's manner was breezy and comfortable. Sullivan, correctly assuming Jill kept him well informed on the election, ventured to ask the young man a few cautious questions.

"What do you know about the judge's race over there, Resty?"

"Jill won't even talk about anyone winning but Judge Ross, but it looks to me like it's anybody's race," Resty said with a frown. "Jill says the Judge puts up a good front but is really feeling low, like she's already sure she's lost, Jill thinks."

"She must be wrong. That doesn't sound like—" Sullivan stopped short.

"Judge Ross?" Resty eyed him curiously. "Maybe all the dirty stuff has gotten to her."

"*Dirty* stuff?"

"Yeah. Flyers. That guy, Bancroft's behind it. He's papered the whole county with them."

Sullivan's face was ominously grim. "I'd like to see one of those flyers."

"There's probably a bunch of them in Jill's trunk. I'm still driving her car," Resty explained. "Whenever she sees one floating around it makes her so mad she picks it up and sticks it in her trunk. Let me go take a look."

He was back in a minute with an assortment of the offending papers, which he spread out on Sullivan's desk. Sullivan studied them a while. When he finally looked up, his eyes reflected an icy rage.

"Who's in charge of Judge Ross's campaign?" he asked tightly.

"The Kramers, but Judge Nathan Richards here in Sacramento is an old hand at this kind of election, and he's been doing a lot, too."

A few minutes later, Resty was on his way back to Cacheton, and Dan Sullivan was on the phone to Judge Nathan Richards.

ON THURSDAY, two days later, Sullivan and Judge Richards were waiting at the *Cacheton Courier* reception desk for the editor-publisher when he came back from lunch.

"Lew, I want you to meet Dan Sullivan, the Minerva Farms attorney in the recent tomato trial," Richards said when he and Hadley had greeted each other. Hadley turned curious eyes on Dan.

"Mr. Hadley, I want to put an ad in Saturday or Monday's paper, in the form of a letter," Dan explained. "Here's what I want to say."

It had taken Sullivan two days and many rejected drafts of angry letters before he finally came up with a version that pleased Nathan Richards's critical political sensibilities.

"Keep at it, Dan, until you get the sound of your *mad* out of it," Richards had advised with each rejection. "You sound mad, and the readers think you've got some kind of a personal vendetta against Bancroft and are just venting your spleen. They don't listen to what you say. All they can hear is your rage." The letter Richards finally approved read as follows:

An Open Letter to the Voters of River County:
During past weeks the judicial integrity of River County Superior Court Judge Susannah Ross has been subjected to a tireless attack based solely upon inferences mistakenly drawn from a single case: *Minerva Farms* v. *Ag Dusters*, heard by Judge Ross last month in River County Superior Court.

Because of a clear danger you may be influenced by this widespread misinformation when you cast your vote on Tuesday, I feel it is my responsibility as plaintiff's attorney in that case to set the record straight so that you may make your judgment at the polls on the facts.

Briefly, the verdict in the case gave my client, Minerva Farms, an award considerably in excess of the damages asked for by plaintiff's attorney or proven by testimony from the witness stand. When, understandably, the defense motioned for a new trial, Judge Ross quite properly said that unless Minerva Farms would agree to a verdict fairly reduced by the amount of the excess, she would grant the motion. My client agreed to the reduction and a new trial was denied.

The change in the verdict is correct under the law and *not* an arbitrary whim on the part of Judge Ross or an attack on the jury powers, as implied in the material being circulated against the judge. A California code section provides for just such a contingency and may be found clearly stated in California Civil Procedures, CCP %662.5(b).

Respectfully,
Daniel L. Sullivan, attorney at law

The editor read the letter through slowly then looked up at Sullivan and Richards.

"How about running this in Saturday's editorial columns next to the *Courier*'s endorsement of Judge Ross for reelection?" Sullivan and Richards stared at him in astonishment.

Sullivan spoke first. "Well, I should say *so!*"

Richards turned to Sullivan with a broad grin of approval. "Congratulations, Dan. Susannah picked a winner!"

Dan scarcely heard him. He had other things on his mind.

"Could you print enough of those papers to cover every household in the county?" he asked Hadley.

"Sure, I can print them, but there's no way you can get them distributed," Hadley told him.

"You print 'em," said Sullivan. "I'll pay for the extra press runs, and I'll find a way to get them all delivered between press time and late Monday afternoon, before the election."

"GUESS WHO Judge Ross holds in contempt? The
jury. Vote Mel Parker for judge. You know he never
will."

In a gesture of frustration Susannah turned the
knob on her kitchen radio from the local station and
a moment later flicked the Off switch. It was a paid
advertisement, she knew, but every time she heard
herself maligned over the air she felt as if it were a
personal attack on her by the man who was mouthing
the words.

May, which had always been her favorite month,
had dealt her one low blow after another this year. For
the first time in her life she had harbored a continu-
ing sense of depression and had hidden it rather badly,
she feared. She felt sometimes as if her face had been
permanently reshaped into a forced smile. Jill, she was
sure, suspected how unhappy she was...about Dan,
about the election she was about to lose. Most of all
about herself. She should have done better on the
other two.

As she stood staring, unseeing, out the window into
the full-blooming backyard, the door chimes rang, but
she made no move to answer. She didn't want to see
anybody now. Not even Jill, who had taken to dropping by sometimes when she knew Susannah was
home. Pretty soon, she thought, she would go into her
bedroom and change out of the kimono she still wore
into something appropriate for the last-ditch pro-
gram Lucille and Jack had laid out for her on this final Saturday before the election. Right now all she
wanted was to be left alone.

The chimes sounded again, but still she stood, back
turned away from the door, yet seeing nothing of the

yard. *Damn. Oh damn!* Why wouldn't they go away? She *needed* this time to herself.

But it was not in Susannah to let a door go unanswered. On the third ring she turned from the window and walked across the living room, through the entry hall, pausing to recompose herself before she opened the door.

"Paper boy!" a voice sang out.

For a moment Susannah imagined her heart had really stopped beating. She had no voice. She stood fixed to the spot as if hypnotized by the sight of the man who meant more to her than any other person in the world.

"Madam, may I come in?" he asked, and his words set her free.

"Dan...Dan. Yes, please do come in," she said foolishly, her throat suddenly dry and her voice ending in a squeak.

Dan followed her as she turned first toward the kitchen and breakfast room, and then, in response to an unexpected feeling of formality, even shyness, into the living room. She motioned him to a chair and took another nearby herself.

"I brought you a paper," he said, handing it to her before he sat down. "I thought you might like to look at it."

"Why, thanks. That's nice," she said inanely. "I'll look at it later."

"No, Susannah," he said firmly. "I brought it to you to look at now."

"If you could only imagine how much I've been missing you, Dan Sullivan," she said, as if his words had snapped her out of a trance. "Don't you realize it's been *forever* that you've been gone? It was sweet of you to pick up my paper, but if you think I'm going to read it now you're crazy. All I want to do is just sit here and *look* at you and digest the fact you are here."

"Susannah . . . !"

But she was out of her chair and on her knees beside him, reaching to caress his face.

"Dan, *darling*. Wait! Let's get out of here and go to Patch Meadow for the weekend. I can be ready in . . . oh . . . say ten minutes?"

Dan laughed with genuine amusement. "Nice try, loved one, but you know you can't do that. You've got an election coming up in four days, and this is the last weekend you have to go after the voters."

"Really, Dan, I'm dead serious," Susannah said earnestly. "While you've been gone I've done a lot of thinking. I've come to the conclusion that there are some things that just aren't important enough to let stand between us."

"Sweetheart, wait . . ."

Susannah's mouth pressed over his quickly to silence his words, and just as quickly pulled away as he reached out to hold her there.

"This election is one of them," she went on. "Whether I stay here and ring doorbells all weekend or go to the meadow with you isn't going to make any real difference in the vote count, but I can tell you this—it makes a difference to me you wouldn't believe." She started to rise to her feet, but Dan placed his hands on her shoulders and held her down.

"Please, Dan, let me go," she protested. "I want to get dressed and be on our way before I get caught in a trap. I promise you my undivided attention once we're headed out of town for the Sierra."

Dan groaned. "I never expected to see the day when one of us wanted to play, and I'd be the one to hold back," he said wryly. "The truth is, I shouldn't even be taking time off to talk to you now. Judge Richards and I have papers to be delivered between now and Monday night—thousands of them, and we've got to get our crews set up."

"Nathan...? I didn't know you knew—" She sat bolt upright. "Dan Sullivan, would you please tell me what you're talking about?"

Dan stood up and reached for the paper she had abandoned on the coffee table as she came in.

"This!" he said, opening it to the editorial page and folding it back so her eyes fell at once on his letter, printed two columns wide, side by side with Lew Hadley's editorial endorsement of Judge Susannah Ross for reelection.

Susannah finished reading Dan's letter and looked at him with tear-filled eyes.

"Thanks," she whispered, her voice too choked to say more. After a moment she fumbled in her kimono pocket for a fresh tissue, gave her nose a blow and said, "Darn!"

Dan watched her, puzzled.

"And I was going to show you the new, insouciant Susannah Ross," she said wistfully. "Now you'll never believe I really intended to walk out on the election campaign and follow my heart."

Sullivan sat down on the carpet beside her and scooped her into his arms.

"I believe," he said, and tipped her face to bestow on her a tender kiss. "I believe so much, I'm about to suggest we get married."

"Mmm, that would be lovely," she said. "Suggest it again after next Tuesday, darling. I haven't told this to another soul, but I honestly think I'm going to lose this election."

"You're not going to lose it, but either way, it doesn't have anything to do with our getting married. How about if I move in here with you until we can find a house of our own?"

She pulled away to look directly into his face. "Tell me," she said seriously, and Dan told her about the new Curtis & Sullivan office in Sacramento that would put him within commuting distance of Cacheton.

When everything had been said and all the questions answered, Dan got to his feet, pulling her up beside him. He nuzzled her neck gently for a moment until her arms slipped around his waist and her hands eased under his belt, her fingers touching his bare back. He drew a deep breath and detached himself from her.

"Oh God, Susannah, none of that! It makes me forget all about what we both have to do," he said mournfully. "Right now the judge is waiting with the papers, ready to chew me out. Let's get you elected first. The good things will have to wait."

"Since you won't go with me up to the meadow, I might as well ring doorbells, I suppose," she said with a goodbye peck to his cheek at the door. "But I'm warning you, I've already arranged for two days off after the election, and I won't take any excuses then."

For the first time in the whole campaign, Susannah really began to think she might get reelected.

IT WAS JUDGE SUSANNAH ROSS by a landslide on Tuesday night when the votes were in, both opponents conceding defeat less than two hours after the polls closed. Whether the victory came from Sullivan's letter in the county-wide edition of the *Cacheton Courier* or Lew Hadley's endorsement or the campaign work of the Kramers and their battalion of volunteers or her father's team of old pros in the city or the fact that Bancroft's campaign tactics brought most of the undecided voters into Susannah's camp—all were moot points. Dan and Jill and the Kramers had their own opinions. They all said the victory came from Susannah herself.

The party the Kramers threw in their barn to listen to the election returns turned swiftly into a victory party during which Susannah managed to slip away from Dan long enough to spend a few moments alone in conversation with Nathan Richards.

Later, feigning innocent concern, she said to Dan, "Darling, maybe we should think twice about your moving to Cacheton." At his look of resistance, she hurried on. "Commuting doesn't sound bad when you say Sacramento's only forty-five minutes away, but twice a day it adds up to ninety. An hour and a half every day on the road."

"Don't knock it," said Sullivan. "Consider that the alternative is Fresno. This way at least we're together."

"Could I interest you in a house in Barnstown—about halfway between Cacheton and Sacramento and less than twenty-five miles from them both? We could split the commute. Think of how much more time that would give us together."

"Hmm. It wouldn't hurt to look." From the absent sound in his voice, she knew he was barely listening.

"Dan!" she said, begging his attention, her voice singing with happiness. "Nathan Richards owns one that I've fallen in love with and so will you, I promise. He just told me he'd like us to have it and is sure we can come to terms."

Looking into her eyes, his own warm with consent, Sullivan clasped her shoulders with both hands and pressed gently, signaling his love.

"You can tell the judge we'll buy his house if he'll marry us, but it'll have to wait till next week." His voice was unexpectedly husky. "Right now we've got miles to go and promises to keep."

They slipped away from the crowded barn unnoticed. Rounding a dark corner on their way to the Jeep, they ran head-on into Jill and Resty.

"Where do you two think you're going?" asked Jill saucily.

Susannah looked up at Sullivan, and for a long, dreamlike moment they were lost in each other's eyes before turning together to smile absently at Jill. It was Susannah who answered her question.

"To catch a mermaid," she said.

THREE TOP NOVELS –
A GREAT READING SELECTION

DILEMMA – Megan Alexander   £2.50

With her future all mapped out, Shannon Gallagher hadn't counted on the dilemma she now faced – the return of her ex-husband, which threatened to change the tender memories of the past into a living nightmare.

WHISPER IN THE WIND – Ann Hulme   £2.95

In the sequel to her bestselling novel *The Flying Man*, Ann Hulme poignantly depicts the contrasts of World War II – the tragedy, the danger, the sadness and the snatched moments of lovers destined to wait for what the future holds.

THE WHOLE TRUTH – Jenny Loring   £2.75

The compelling novel of a woman at the top of the career ladder. As a respected judge, Susannah Ross faces a case which could compromise her entire career.

These three new titles will be out in bookshops from June 1989.

W❤RLDWIDE

Available from Boots, Martins, John Menzies, W. H. Smith, Woolworths and other paperback stockists.

UNPREDICTABLE, COMPELLING
AND TOTALLY READABLE

MIDNIGHT JEWELS – *Jayne Ann Krentz*   £2.95

Jayne Ann Krentz, bestselling author of *Crystal Flame*, blends romance and tension in her latest fast-moving novel. An advert for a rare collector's item sparked not only Mercy Pennington's meeting with the formidable Croft Falconer, but also a whole sequence of unpredictable events.

SOMETHING SO RIGHT – *Emilie Richards*   £2.75

The high-flying lifestyle of top recording artist Joelle Lindsay clashed with her attempts to return to her simple roots. This compelling novel of how love conquers disillusionment will captivate you to the last page.

GATHERING PLACE – *Marisa Carroll*   £2.50

Sarah Austin could not confront the future before she had settled her past trauma of having had her child adopted. Her love for Tyler Danielson helped, but she could not understand how his orphaned son seemed so uncannily familiar.

These three new titles will be out in bookshops from July 1989.

W☾RLDWIDE